liquid damage 3/21

Out of This World

Out of This World

JILL SHALVIS

KENSINGTON PUBLISHING CORP.
http://www.kensingtonbooks.com

BRAVA BOOKS are published by

Kensington Publishing Corp.
850 Third Avenue
New York, NY 10022

All Kensington titles, imprints, and distributed lines are available at special quantity discounts for bulk purchases for sales promotion, premiums, fund-raising, educational or institutional use.

Special book excerpts or customized printings can also be created to fit specific needs. For details, write or phone the office of the Kensington Special Sales Manager: Kensington Publishing Corp., 850 Third Avenue, New York, NY 10022, Attn: Special Sales Department, Phone: 1-800-221-2647.

Brava and the B logo Reg. U.S. Pat. & TM Off.

ISBN 0-7582-1444-8

First Kensington Trade Paperback Printing: September 2006
10 9 8 7 6 5 4 3 2 1

Printed in the United States of America

Out of This World

Chapter 1

It was one of those should-have-stayed-in-bed days. I should have given my alarm clock a one-way flight out my window courtesy of my old high-school softball arm, and just stayed home watching soap operas and stuffing my face with ice cream.

And I might have, if there'd been a nice, warm, hard male body next to mine. But nope, just as my mother has been woefully predicting since puberty, I'm still single. Not for lack of putting myself out there, mind you. But trust me, no matter what you read, the men in Los Angeles are slim pickings.

Oh, there are lots of them available. But they're attached to their mirrors, or to their cell phones, where they have their shrinks and personal trainers on speed dial.

I could move away, of course, but where else could I go and have people pay me to paint murals on the sides of buildings? Where else could I wear flip-flops all year long, and have my biggest decision be whether to paint a night sky or a city panorama?

Yeah, despite myself, I am perfectly suited to L.A. living, to the come-what-may, no-plan-ahead lifestyle.

Most mornings I get up, toast half of a sesame-seed bagel and drink a large iced tea with lemon, heavy on the sugar. I shower, pull on a T-shirt and shorts (the upside of three hundred sixty-five days of sun a year), grab my paints and go to work, where, like my father before me, I paint on-spec murals to my heart's content, while wishing it could be to my checkbook's content as well.

But at least I love my job, right?

At night I go out to dinner with friends and bemoan the fact that we're living the best years of our lives single. We have dessert—even though in my case, my shorts are getting a little snug around the waist—and then I go home, feed the fish, get into bed and dream of the cute FedEx guy, who still hasn't noticed I'm alive.

Then I get up and do the whole thing all over again.

Or that's what I always did, with some variation—until my great-great-aunt Gertrude died and changed my life.

She didn't leave me a forgotten fortune or even a diamond necklace, though either would have been nice. No, what dear old Great-Great-Aunt Gertrude willed to me was a B&B in the wilds of Alaska—specifically, just outside the Katmai National Park and Preserve.

I, Rachel Wood, owner of an inn just outside a preserve—it boggled the mind, or at least my city-grown one.

Why had she owned such a thing in the middle of nowhere? Probably because she was mean as sin and liked being far from her entire family. But that's another story entirely. In this story, here I am: a twenty-seven-year-old L.A. muralist with a B&B in Alaska. What's a girl to do but go look?

Which means that this morning, instead of grabbing my paints, I packed a bag (okay, two bags), and I was now on a plane heading north.

And I mean waaay north. Nosebleed north.

With some trepidation, I faced my fear of heights and peeked out the plane window, then promptly got dizzy and clutched the armrests.

Wow, Alaska sure was big. And green.

And big.

As far as my eyes could focus lay jagged peaks, some still white-tipped, and it was August. *August.* It was almost beyond my Southern California imagination.

Lining those rugged mountains were ribbons and ribbons of trees. No buildings to paint murals on—not a single one. No coffeehouses in sight either.

Or movie theaters.

My stomach dropped some more, because in fact there were no signs of life at all—at least, not human life.

Gulp.

And more than just my stomach hurt now, because a world without concrete, without drive-throughs and drive-bys, seemed . . . alien. I knew this was a bit wussy of me, but fact was fact. If I ever had to go on the TV show *Survivor*, I wouldn't make it past the first day. I need food on a regular basis. I need a bed every night.

And I need a bathroom, complete with electrical outlets, thank you very much.

"This is insane," I whispered.

"Tell me about it."

That voice belonged to Kellan, brother of my best friend, Dot McInty. Kellan was squished into the seat next to mine, his long legs banging up against the seat in front of him, his equally long arms hugging his beat-up leather saddlebag.

Dot is a physical therapist and therefore has a regular job and regular hours, complete with a boss who frowns on his people taking unplanned long weekends simply because their "best friend inherited a B&B in Alaska and needs hand-holding."

So Dot sent Kellan in her place. Kellan is an actual, true-to-life dolphin trainer at Sea World. What this means is that he's a tall, lanky brainiac who communicates with animals better than with humans and smells like the sea.

I have no idea what help Dot thought Kel would be to me here in the middle of Nowhere, USA, but he got the long weekend off, and I do have to admit, he's funny and smart, even if sometimes he is so easygoing and laid-back that I have to check him for a pulse.

The plane dipped, and I gasped.

"Hey, it's okay," Kellan said. "Just turbulence."

"I don't mean to sound like Chicken Little, but we're falling out of the sky."

"No, we're just coming into Anchorage for our landing. No worries."

Right. No worries. No worries at all.

I bravely looked down, ignoring my stomach, now somewhere near my toes. The entire horizon was nothing but that disconcerting blanket of rugged peaks and wild growth for as far as I could see. "*Where* are we going to land?"

Kellan pushed his glasses up his nose and pulled a file from his saddlebag. He flipped through some papers and located a map. With his disheveled brown hair falling into his eyes, the strands at least six weeks past the need for a trim, and the glasses already slipping again, he looked a little like an absent-minded professor as he unfolded the map and studied it. "Here." He pointed to a circle in red ink. "Here's Anchorage. See it? We're going to land there, then take a float plane up King Solomon River to . . . here." He tapped his long, work-roughened finger on another spot on the map. "There we're going to be dropped off at a spot where we can rent a Jeep and ride up a short road to Hideaway."

Apt name for a B&B in the wilds of Alaska, I decided.

He looked up, his eyes meeting mine. "You know all this already."

Yes, and I knew that in this current leg of the trip, we were heading nearly three hundred air miles to the Alaska Peninsula, directly into unspoiled, unpopulated wilderness.

No highway system touched the area. Access was by small plane only.

Unimaginable.

And yet here we were. Willingly heading into isolation, into unstable weather, into an area where even the winds could be life threatening, where time seemed to be measured in terms of pre- and postvolcanic eruption, judging by all the articles I'd read.

Good God. Volcanic eruption . . .

"Somehow it all seemed far less threatening from inside my apartment," I said, "surrounded by four walls and electricity, with the comforting sounds of traffic coming in my window."

"No traffic here." Kellan leaned over me and glanced out the window, his bony shoulder poking me. "Unless you count the four-legged variety."

"Oh God." This was a whole new horror I hadn't considered. I looked down at my pink ruffled top and Capri jeans. Not much protection against wild animals. "You think there'll be wolves?"

"I was thinking even bigger."

"Moose," I said. Were moose friends or foes?

"No, not moose." His face gave little away, which was exactly the problem with Kellan, because I could never quite tell when he was kidding. "Bears."

"*Bears?*"

"Yep, bears. And maybe mountain cats, too." He had these intense baby blue eyes, which always seemed slightly magnified behind his glasses, eyes that were amused now, at my expense.

"Well, that settles it," I said, only half-kidding. "We have to turn around."

He smiled, pushing up his glasses again. "You wanted to come out here, Lucy."

As if I'd forgotten that this was completely of my own doing. Or that my nickname was I-Love-Lucy, due to my uncanny ability to land myself in outrageous situations without even trying.

Welcome to my most outrageous situation yet.

"In fact," he went on, still amusing himself, "I think your exact words were 'I want to broaden my horizons, Kel. I want to take my adventures to a whole new level.'"

"I did *not* say that."

"Yes, you did. You said Alaska was going to be a good start on the rest of your life. A change from the dull and mundane."

Okay, I'd actually said that, but it hadn't sounded so cheesy at the time. "Thanks for throwing my own words back in my face."

His knowing smile said "any time," and I rolled my eyes and stared out the window again, at the sharp, craggy precipices and dizzying valleys coming up to greet us at stomach-shrinking speed as we came in for a landing.

Nerves hit me like a one-two punch, knocking the air out of my lungs. I didn't need a restart, I thought hastily. My life was just fine! But unfortunately, they weren't kidding when they said "starving artists." And though I wasn't exactly starving (in fact, I was stuffed into my Capris with some overflow), I wasn't exactly flush with cash either.

Truth was, I barely scraped by each month.

Being broke wasn't anything new to me, but this B&B hadn't come with a college fund. So really, I had no choice but to come here and check it out, to decide what to do with it before—I don't know—someone got stepped on by a moose and sued me.

"Hard to believe that just yesterday I was hanging off the CFS building," I said, "painting a forty-five-foot mural of a seascape, while ten thousand cars passed by on the 405 during rush hour."

"Nice dolphin on the far right, by the way," Kellan said. "I caught it yesterday while stuck behind that two-car pileup."

I managed a smile, sidetracked by the praise. "It was harder to do than I thought."

"No, you got the dorsal fin just right."

If I'd gotten it right, it was because he'd hounded me about it night and day since he'd learned I'd be painting it, sending me e-mails, faxes, pictures. "Thanks."

"You're really good."

"He said, sounding so amazed."

A grin split his face, and he went back to his notes, his too-long hair falling over his forehead and into his eyes. He wore his usual faded Levi's, athletic shoes that looked as if they'd been on their last legs for a while now and a T-shirt that invited the general public to KEEP THE OCEAN BLUE.

He was, undoubtedly, a complete geek, but he was my geek, and I was very fond of him.

The plane dipped again. Just beneath us, I could see treetops, dense undergrowth and narrow canyons, which challenged the contents of my stomach, and I clutched Kellan's big, warm hand. "Should we say our last rites? Admit our sins?"

"Oh, you don't have time for that," he said. "We're going down."

I think I squeaked.

"Down as in *landing*. It's going to be fine, Rach. An adventure, remember?"

Right. An adventure to the land of snow and moose and mountain men.

Sounded good.

Really.

And it wasn't as if I had something else to do. Long-term planning was not a strong suit of mine, much to my perpetually exasperated mother's frustration. She'd long ago given up trying to coax me into a "real" career, or a marriage, for that matter.

I love painting, and I don't intend to give it up. A man, however, that might be nice. But I've been through quite a few, and I've learned a few lessons.

Such as that a good thing never lasts.

The nose of the plane took a sharp dip. Oh God, oh God.

Just descending, I told myself. As if I couldn't tell by the way my eyeballs pressed back into my head.

Finally the wheels touched down. Actually "slammed down" would be more accurate, so hard I nearly ate my own teeth, and I reminded myself I'd done this out of curiosity, which was a good thing, a healthy thing, and I'd make the best of it.

Then I remembered something else: Curiosity was all well and fine, but it'd also killed the cat.

We switched planes in Anchorage, and now we sat in a tiny tin can, a butt-squeaker of a float plane.

"Oh. My. *God.*" I gripped Kellan's hand, and stared at the lake below, racing past us at a dizzying speed. We'd been on the float plane for only five minutes.

A *lifetime.*

The wind made tears stream out of my eyes, and I think I had a bug in my teeth. "Kellan!"

"You're going to break my fingers." He tried to free his hand from mine, but that wasn't going to happen. I had a death grip on him, and the only way he was getting free was to chew free.

Supposedly this "air taxi" could handle both water and air, though as near as I could tell, we hadn't left the water more than a foot or two below us. The top was open, like that of a biplane, the noise incredible.

The landscape whipped by so fast, I couldn't catch more than a brown-green-blue blur, the only constant being Jack, the pilot. He sat behind the controls yelling "Woo hoo!" at the top of his lungs as he dodged trees like we were playing some sort of Xbox game with our lives.

Jack looked the mountain-man part: long hair held back by a leather string, the mass flying out behind him. He wore aviator sunglasses, beige cargo pants whose every pocket was filled with God-knew-what and a long-sleeved shirt open over a T-shirt that said FLY MY FRIENDLY SKIES—PLEASE.

The light in his eyes as he flew the plane said he was either very good at what he did or he was thoroughly, one-hundred-percent insane. I was betting on the former, while praying it wasn't the latter. In spite of the way I had led my life—that is, without much precaution or a single thought-out plan—I was not reckless.

And yet, here I was, on a plane I could have parked in my bathroom, with a man who might have smoked a crack pipe for lunch, flying over the wilds of Alaska.

I'm telling you, the crazy streets of Los Angeles were tame compared to this. Here, there were peaks on peaks, each bigger than the last, layers upon layers, stabbing up into the sky to heights I'd never imagined.

"Seriously, Rach"—this from Kellan, at my side—"I need my fingers back."

We made another heart-stopping turn at the speed of light, following the river below. Ignoring Kellan, I closed my eyes, then felt my stomach leap into my eyeballs. Whoops. Definitely not a good way to fight vertigo, so I opened them again. "Are we almost there yet?"

Jack craned his neck. "Why, what's up? You need a pit stop?"

I looked at him hopefully. "You have a bathroom on board?"

He laughed. "Nope. But I can find you a tree."

Even Kellan laughed at that—the jerk—and I squeezed his fingers harder, until he paled.

There. That made me feel marginally better, but the only thing that could fix this situation entirely was to have Dot at my side. She wouldn't have found any humor in my need to pee. She'd have been right there with me, demanding a bathroom complete with blow-dryer and scented hand soap.

"Serious," Kellan gasped, "my fingers—"

I squeezed harder. Suck it up, I thought. And then I couldn't think, because right in front of us—right in the middle of the river whipping by me so fast that the landscape looked like one of my paintings, still wet and also blurred, as if I had swiped my fingers over it—was a fallen log the likes of which Paul Bunyan had never seen. The thing was massive, with branches still reaching into the sky, like the arms of a downed giant ghost.

And we were going to hit it.

So I did the only sensible thing: I closed my eyes, opened my mouth and screamed.

And screamed.

My stomach bounced, down to my pink toenails, then back up into my freshly touched-up roots and finally to somewhere near the region where it was supposed to be, so I knew Jack was doing some fancy flying—not that I looked. No sirree, my looking days were over.

Then I realized Kellan was saying "It's okay" over and over in my ear, his breath tickling my skin. Maybe it was the fact he'd grown up with only his mother and three sisters, smothered in feminine woes and Barbie dolls. Or maybe it was from all that practice with the dolphins. However he'd gotten the gift of knowing the right thing to do and to say to a woman, I was grateful. Especially since comfort was an almost foreign concept, given that the men I dated tended to be, well, badasses, and badasses typically don't do comfort.

Kellan was not a badass by any stretch of the imagination, which for once was a good thing. He was nice to have in an emergency, and this felt like as big an emergency as I could imagine.

"We're going to be okay," he was saying. "So you can let go. Any time now, Rach . . ."

He sounded a bit strangled, and as I took stock, I saw why. At some point, I'd climbed out of my seat and into his, which meant I was in his lap, my arms shrink-wrapped around his neck, which probably accounted for his sounding like he couldn't breathe. Chances were, with the death grip I had on him, he couldn't.

My face was pressed into his throat. Since he hadn't shaved today, and maybe not yesterday either, his skin was roughing up mine, but that felt like the least of my worries, so I just kept holding on as tightly as I could. Our bodies were sandwiched together, like peanut butter and jelly, and though he was definitely trying to put some space between us, I wasn't allowing it.

"That was hella fun," Jack said from the cockpit.

I looked up. The crazy bastard was grinning.

"It was a little close," Kellan pointed out, still holding me. He didn't really have a choice, since I hadn't loosened my grip.

"Nah," Jack said. "Should have seen last time. Lost the tip of the right wing. Anyhoo, we're here now." He hoisted himself out of his seat.

I could still feel Kel's heart beating against my breasts. I could feel a lot of him: his chest, his belly and . . . "Kel? Something in your pocket is digging into me."

He sighed, still sounding a bit strangled. "If you'd just let go—"

I looked up into his face in time to see a flush ride up his cheeks. Oh. *Oh.* I could feel every inch of him. Apparently there were just more inches than I'd realized.

"Here you go." Jack tossed our bags from the upper storage down to our feet, and put his hands on his hips.

I unwrapped myself from Kellan, who looked very happy to have me do so, then I stood up on legs that were still quivering.

"Tips are welcome," Jack said, "so don't be shy."

"I have a tip," I said. "*Take flying lessons.*"

His grin broadened.

Free of my weight, Kellan sat there gasping for breath.

I scowled down at him. "I wasn't that heavy."

"Of course not."

"You're just too scrawny." Only he hadn't felt so scrawny a moment ago . . .

He rubbed his chest as he stood, gesturing to me to leave the plane ahead of him.

I hopped down. In Los Angeles, we'd have felt a wave of heat, but here there was no wave. Fresh, late-afternoon air brushed over us, cool and clear and crisp, and utterly devoid of the burn of smog.

It did feel good to have solid ground beneath my feet. We stood on the shore of some wildly raging river, surrounded by forest and mountains so tall, I had to tip my head back to see them all. In spite of the noise of the rushing water, we were enveloped in silence, the kind that comes from the utter lack of civilization. At least, the human kind. I looked around for bears, but thankfully, I didn't see any.

No mountain cats either.

Jack dropped four boxes out of the plane next to our bags. "The weekly drop of supplies for Hideaway," he said, then began to shut the door.

"Wait," I said, a bad feeling gathering in my belly along with the remnants of terror from the flight. "Where are you going?"

"Back."

"*Back?*" We were going to be alone here? I wrapped my arms around myself and moved slightly closer to Kellan, which was silly. He was more city than me. "You can't go back!"

"Sure I can." Jack turned away, then slapped his forehead. "Oh, wait. I forgot to list the warnings."

"Warnings?"

He ticked them off on his fingers. "Watch out for sudden rainstorms—they come with flash floods. The mosquitoes are a bitch—real killers. You should spray the hell out of yourselves so you don't get any diseases. Oh, and don't feed the bears." He flashed his grin. "Okay then. Have fun. See you on Monday."

Flash floods. Killer mosquitoes. Bears for real. Oh God.

"Hold on." Kellan looked around. "I don't see the car rental place." In fact, there was nothing but trees and sky, and our bags at our feet. "We have a Jeep waiting."

Jack laughed hard and long. "Car rental place." Still grinning, he shook his head. "They get you tourists good with that one, don't they? Look, just take the path there"—he pointed vaguely behind us—"up about a quarter of a mile. You'll find the bed and breakfast, no problem. There's a Jeep there, available to guests. But there's no roads, just four-wheeling. You're not going to actually get anywhere except by my plane."

"But—" I was having a hard time wrapping my brain around the quarter-mile hike, much less the no-road thing. "You're leaving?" I repeated weakly.

"Back on Monday," he said again, as if deserting us was no big deal.

For *days*.

In the wilds.

"Um . . ."

But I could "um" all I wanted. He'd started his plane and was taxiing down his runway—the river.

"We're in the wilds," I said. "Alone. With neither of us knowing a pine tree from an oak."

"I know a pine from an oak."

"Really?" I shot Kel a sideways look. "Do you know what all this is?" I waved a hand at the growth nearly swallowing us whole.

"Sure." He looked around. Pointed. "There. Those are spruce. And there? Birch."

"Are you kidding me? You know the types of trees these are?"

"Yeah." He craned his neck the other way, and studied the landscape some more. "And those"—he pointed to the bushes lining the path, or rather, practically taking over and suffocating the path—"that dense stuff right over there is a bunch of alder thickets, see?"

"Huh." I couldn't believe he knew what he was talking about. This in itself was disturbing enough, but then, right next to me, a thick, overgrown so-called alder thicket began to shimmy and shake, as if someone had turned the thing on vibrate.

Accompanying this was a series of undomesticated, ear-piercing whistles in different tones, reminiscent of C-3PO from *Star Wars* having a bad day.

I didn't think; I simply reacted, and threw myself at Kellan.

He caught me—barely—against his chest with an "oomph," staggering back a few feet.

"Do you hear that?" I whispered, pointing with a shaking finger at the bush, which yep, was still rocking and rolling. "What is it?"

Kellan was still struggling to hold us both upright, but he let me burrow close, and after a moment, he cupped my head in a sweet gesture belied by his next words. "You're not going to like it."

"No?"

"It's something terrifying."

"My God." I couldn't handle anything else, I was sure of it. "What? What is it?"

"Big Foot."

"What?"

"Okay, it's not. It's just two squirrels fighting."

Lifting my head, I stared at him.

"They're out-of-control squirrels, too. Wild. *Vicious.*" His voice had laughter in it. "Better run, Rach."

I shoved free, and closed my eyes. "This is not nearly as funny as you seem to think."

"A little bit, it is."

I opened my eyes now, and glared at him. "Seriously? You

have no idea how good running sounds. *Running.* I never run, Kel."

He just kept grinning.

"Kel?"

"Yeah?"

I'd planned on saying something not very nice, but the truth was, I had no temper available because I was working on pure nerves. *"What have I gotten us into?"*

He managed to stop grinning and reach for my hand, and unlike me, he squeezed only very gently. "I don't know. Why don't we go find out?"

"Yeah." I looked down at the boxes at our feet. "There'd better be cookies in there. Lots of cookies."

Chapter 2

At least there really was a trail. We trudged along it, a sheer rock cliff on our right, a sharp drop-off on our left, at the bottom of which the river rolled and charged along its path. Some really loud birds squawked, as if scolding us for the interruption. Then a cute little squirrel ran out on a branch of a huge, towering tree and chattered at us.

"Oh, look how sweet," I said.

He chirped again, and then chucked a pinecone at my head.

I ducked and screamed, and Kellan rolled with laughter.

"You wouldn't be laughing if he'd hit me," I said, pouting a little. "You'd be carrying my limp body!"

Kellan tried to stop laughing but couldn't.

I huffed onward, and did my best to regain some dignity. But I'd like to point out, a quarter of a mile is a helluva lot farther than I could have imagined. Probably if I exercised, I wouldn't be huffing and puffing and wishing for a box of cookies. But I didn't. And I was.

But there *was* a trail. I grasped onto that fact, clinging to it like it was my fondest memory. It meant Jack had been telling the truth and, at the end of a quarter mile, we'd find the B&B.

And food.

And, God willing, a telephone, and even better, an Internet connection, which I'd use to find us a way out of here.

"How fast do you think we can get back home?"

"Not fast."

"I bet I could call someone to come for us."

"You're not really going to chicken out that fast." Kellan was right behind me on the trail, taking up the rear, which worried me.

What if we were being stalked by wolves or bears this very minute?

Or worse, the dreaded mountain cats?

Kel would get eaten first, and then I'd be all alone. On second thought, maybe being in front was a good thing. Still, I sped up as much as I could carrying my two large duffle bags and a box, which was filled with frozen meats. Yes, I'd peeked. This left Kellan with his single duffle bag and *three* boxes, all loaded with fruits, veggies, pastas and many more supplies, but no cookies.

I'd checked those boxes, too.

I really hated that Kellan knew me well enough to know I wouldn't chicken out, that I would want to see this through. But that want was more abstract than actual. Because now that I was here, I was discovering a whole host of things about myself. Such as that it's one thing to *think* of yourself as adventurous, another ballgame entirely to really *be* adventurous.

"I'm hungry," I said.

"What, you missed that first-class meal on our last flight?"

Okay, in spite of myself, I laughed. My last boyfriend had been a leather-wearing biker guy from Santa Barbara. Mouth-wateringly gorgeous. He'd been a doctor, too. Perfect, right?

Except for his utter lack of a sense of humor. In fact, he'd been something of an egotistical asshole, and in the end, I'd discovered I wanted more than hard pecs and a nice bank account.

Go figure.

Good things never last.

Dot claimed that was just an excuse to hold back, that I dated the wrong men on purpose, in effect sabotaging my own happiness to prove my own point.

Whatever. All I knew was that Kellan never went for the wrong women. No, he dated sweet, kind, peace-loving, tree-hugging, sensitive women who were his perfect complement.

But I couldn't help noticing, none of his relationships lasted either. "Huh," I said over the crack of various pine needles and twigs beneath my feet.

"Huh what?" Kel asked.

"I'm just wondering why you aren't taken."

"You mean because I'm such a catch with my high-powered job and buff bod?"

I didn't look back, because I was still keeping an eye out for kamikaze squirrels, but I could hear the humor in his voice. I knew he didn't make big bucks at Sea World, but he had a job that he was extremely passionate about and that had a certain sex appeal to it. And no, he wasn't exactly a buff guy, not with his tall, lanky frame, but he had a great face and an easy smile that was contagious, and that a woman might pass him up made me mad. "You're a catch, Kel."

He let out a low laugh. "Okay."

"You are."

"Such a catch that you're dying to nab me yourself, right?"

I was pretty sure that was a rhetorical question because one, he'd never made a move on me in all these years, and two, I'd never thought of him that way. I was spared from thinking that way now by the sound of my stomach growling so loudly, it startled a bird into flight.

"Feel free to tuck into that meat you're carrying," Kellan said, shifting the weight of all he carried. Not that he'd complained once.

Nope, not Kellan. At one point, he'd calmly opened his backpack, pulled out twine and rigged himself some sort of arm strap for the three boxes he carried. He'd offered to do the same for me, but I'd said I was fine.

If "fine" was hot, tired and increasingly grumpy.

"Believe me," I said, "if anything in here was cooked, I'd have dived in by now." I already had my sights set on a New York strip steak, as well as on one of the potatoes from box number three in Kellan's arms. Loaded with butter and sour cream . . . Oh yeah . . .

"You okay?" Kel asked.

"No, but why?"

"Because you just sort of moaned."

"It was nothing." Only the thought of melted butter . . .

"Why are you huffing and puffing?"

"Um, because I'm out of shape, thanks for asking."

Kellan, the jerk, wasn't huffing and puffing at all. Probably because for his job swimming with dolphins, he actually used physical exertion.

I ought to try that sometime.

Or not.

"This stuff is heavy," I said, adjusting the straps of both my duffle bags.

"You packed too much."

"Did not."

"Really? Then why do you need two gigantic duffle bags for three days in the wilderness?"

"Because things might come up."

"Like what?"

"I don't know. *Things*."

"Tell me what you brought," he said.

"Oh, you know. Just the essentials."

"Bet you brought makeup and fingernail polish."

"Neither of which is heavy," I pointed out.

Laughing, he shook his head.

Actually, the whole makeup thing had been a quandary. I'd

had no idea what I'd need for the great outdoors, so I'd packed it all.

And truthfully? It was a tad bit heavier than I'd imagined.

"And what about shoes?" he asked.

Now *there* was a discussion I most definitely didn't want to have. "What about them?"

"How many pairs?"

"Six."

"Jesus."

"Okay, four."

"Haven't you ever roughed it, Rach. Ever?"

Hey, I rough it every day of my life in the mean, tough streets of Los Angeles. I didn't see a need to rough it on vacation as well.

"How many pairs of shoes did you really bring?"

"I don't know why it matters to you," I said, sniffing. "I'm not asking you to carry my bag."

"Bags. Plural."

Damn it. I hated that he was right. "See, this is why I don't have a boyfriend. I don't want to have to disclose certain matters."

"You don't have a boyfriend because you date guys who are allergic to commitment."

Okay, maybe that was true, too.

"I'm sweating," I said, looking for just a little sympathy.

"Sweat is good for you."

I couldn't have heard him right, because I sure hadn't received an ounce of sympathy anywhere. "Excuse me?"

"It's good for you," he repeated patiently.

My eyes narrowed, and I stopped and faced him. "Are you saying I could stand to lose a few pounds?"

"What?" He shook his head. "Of course not. What I said was—"

"I'll have you know, I'm only a few pounds over my goal weight."

"I do know—Look, you're fine—"

"And most of those five pounds are water weight."

"Rach, I *am* speaking English, right?" He asked this in the baffled tone of men everywhere who'd stepped into uncharted territory: a woman's psyche. "I said you look *fine,*" he said. "You heard that part?"

"*Fine?*" I made a snort that sounded like my head had just gotten a flat tire. "The word 'fine' should be erased from the English language!"

He blinked, and eyed me like an unstable rock wall. "What's wrong with the word 'fine'?"

"If you don't know, I can't help you."

"Okay, clearly the excursion has gone to your head. Take a lighter box," he said, sounding a bit desperate to change the subject.

Typical guy.

"Here, take the fruits-and-veggies box," he said.

Great. Fruits and veggies. I hate fruits and veggies. "*Fine.*"

This made him frown. "Why do you get to use that word, and I don't?"

I didn't answer. I was still obsessing over my weight. I really did plan on losing those extra five pounds. Okay, ten. Honest. Just not right now. Not when I was wishing for some cookies.

Or the end of the quarter mile.

I was *really* wishing for that, but the woods had swallowed us up. I had a blister on my left heel and my stomach was still growling, but I couldn't complain because I was with a guy whose arms could fall off and he wouldn't say so, and I didn't want to look bad.

I really hated to look bad.

"What do you suppose are the chances there's a day spa at Hideaway?"

He let out a laugh between pants. "Only you, Rach."

"Hey, it's possible."

Something buzzed. It was either my brain matter beginning

to boil or the biggest fly on the planet. Wait. Not a fly, but—

"Ack, *bee*!"

And it was after me. Like really after me. This was no simple flyby either, but a serious I'm-going-sting-your-ass attack by a dive-bombing, maniac bee. I lifted my box higher, trying to protect my face, while screaming like . . . like the girly girl I was.

"Stand still," Kellan advised.

Stand still? This was a bee, the mother of all bees, out for my blood.

"Rach, your box." Kel was trying to balance his own three boxes while watching me dance around like an idiot. "I'm telling you, you're going to spill—"

Just as he said it, my box toppled right out of my hands and crashed to the ground.

Good news: The bee got the hint that I was crazy, and took off.

Bad news: The box imploded upon impact. Frozen ribs, steaks and ground meat all scattered across the ground, their plastic wrap loosened, becoming marinated in pine needles, dirt, ants and who-knew-what-else.

I dropped to my knees, looked at that New York strip steak I'd wanted and let out a pathetic sound. I think my eyes welled up, but I pretended it was from the dust.

Beside me, two battered tennis shoes appeared. One was untied. I have no idea why I noticed such a thing at a time of crisis like this.

With a sigh, Kellan lowered his knees to the dirt beside me.

"A little dirt never hurt anyone," he said in way-too-kind voice.

And how pathetic was it that I actually wanted to believe him? I tried not to fall apart. "You think we can apply the thirty-second rule?" I asked in a weak voice. "You know, if we pick it up within thirty seconds, it's like no-harm-no-foul?"

"I do," he said solemnly.

"Good. Because we can't just leave it all here, right? I mean, we might attract those bears Jack mentioned, and he did say don't feed them. *Right?*"

"Right," he said dryly as we reached for the fallen meats, dirt and all. "*That's* what you're most concerned about: the bears eating your steak."

See, this was the problem with good friends. They knew you too well.

We shuffled the contents of the boxes around—meaning Kellan gave me an easier load.

"You know what I don't get?" I asked, again breathless after only one minute, and also boggled by my thought. "Guests pay to come here. As in, they pull out their checkbooks and *pay.*"

"Maybe they like the great outdoors."

"And kamikaze squirrels?"

"And kamikaze squirrels."

I still didn't get it. "Are you telling me they all walk this same trail?"

Kellan lifted a shoulder. "Maybe besides a love for the outdoors and kamikaze squirrels, they also get a thrill out of killer bees."

I laughed. I always laughed with him, I realized, even when things sucked. "You'd think they'd have put that on their Web site. Warning: Alaska is not for sissies."

"I'm pretty sure most people know that already," he pointed out. "Besides, you saw the Web site. It's . . . lacking."

Yet another concern on my mind. Hideaway B&B was mine now—assets and liabilities and all. I had no idea how good or bad things were financially, but one thing I *did* know: Whatever state the place was in, I was responsible for it, for the people who worked for it, for the bills, for still making a living back in L.A.

Yikes, I was going to have to be a real grownup here, not just the farce of a grownup I'd been up until now.

Scary stuff.

And funny, considering I'd never so much as bothered with the responsibility of anything more troublesome than fish, and yet now I owned a business.

A business I knew too little about. From the outdated Web site, it'd been difficult, if not impossible, to get a sense of what I was up against. There'd been only two pictures of the tall, mysterious inn: one in summer, one in winter.

The summer pic had been taken at dusk and had been too dark to be effective, not showing any of the inn's distinguishing features, nor anything of its surroundings. The winter shot revealed snow up to the windows, and had been taken at night.

Snow.

Up to the windows.

During a night so dark, it gave a whole new meaning to the color black.

Boggling.

The site did boast that Hideaway was a hundred years old, and as we turned a corner and suddenly came to the clearing in which the inn sat, I could believe it. It looked just like the pictures, though I don't know why that surprised me. The place was bigger than I'd expected, and it looked a bit like an old Victorian, but without the warmth and charm. Four stories high, it had a sharply slanted roof, myriad dark windows and eaves that made it look . . . foreboding. No, that had to be my imagination, because not only was the sun out but, despite it being early afternoon, smoke was coming from the chimney. Those should both be calming, right? So why did I suddenly have goose bumps?

My mom had warned me many times that Great-Great-Aunt Gertrude had been somewhat of a loony toons, and that no doubt her staff would be just as crazy. But coming from my mother, that had been, like, Hello, Mrs. Pot, I'm Black . . .

"At least someone's here," Kellan murmured, and nudged

me up the walk with the big load in his arms, reminding me of the weight we were carrying. Or that he mostly carried. "Hopefully they're expecting us. You did call ahead, right?"

"I called," I said, the front porch creaking ominously beneath our feet. I looked at the hanging sign that read HIDEAWAY B&B. "But no one answered, not even an answering machine."

"Is that code for 'I didn't really call because I forgot to think ahead'?"

"No," I said a bit defensively. "My inability to organize or make plans and keep them has nothing to do with this. I really did try."

It'd been frustrating and a little unnerving. This was a business, right? *My* business. "I e-mailed the contact from the Web site, too. Nothing." We set down our boxes and bags on the front porch, and knocked.

No one answered.

I stepped off the porch, and looked up.

And up.

Wow, the place was tall. The chimney still had smoke coming out, so someone had to be here. Then I blinked because I thought I saw something. There, on the top floor, one of the windows . . . *glowed*, as if someone had walked past it with a flashlight or candle. But it was gone so quickly, I couldn't be sure. "That's odd," I said in a normal voice that belied the way my heart had skipped a beat.

It got odder, when, in that same high-up window, I suddenly saw two faces, a young blond woman and a guy who looked like a twenty-something Harry Potter, their foreheads pressed to the glass as they stared down at me the same way I stared up at them.

And yet, in the very next blink, they were gone.

Vanished.

"Did you see them?" I asked Kellan hoarsely, because my voice had nearly gone, along with all the air in my lungs. I tugged on his sleeve. "There, in the window."

"What did I miss?" He craned his neck and looked up in pretend horror. "Another squirrel tea party?"

"Ha ha, you're a laugh a minute."

But I couldn't take my gaze off the window. Real or Memorex? Hard to tell. *"Kellan."*

At the serious tone in my voice, he looked at me, amusement fading. "So what did you see?"

I shook my head. It sounded kind of crazy. "Never mind. It was nothing."

Kellan knocked again, but we still got no answer.

Which meant I'd definitely imagined the couple. Oh boy. And they said losing touch with reality was the first symptom . . .

Kellan tried the doorknob. We stared at each other, both jumping a little when the door creaked as he pushed it open.

From inside came nothing but a big yawning silence.

"Hello?" I called out.

Nothing. Not a single sound. It was like the entire inn was holding its breath, and something cold and creepily foreboding danced down the back of my neck.

And then, from somewhere far upstairs, a door shut with a definitive click.

Kellan glanced at me, face unreadable. "Was that nothing, too?"

Thank God, I thought. He'd heard it. I wasn't losing my mind.

At least, not completely.

Strange how much comfort I found in that one small fact. Still, I was feeling sorry—extremely sorry—that I'd so hastily jumped on a plane and hightailed it up here without more details. Honest to God, one of these days I was going to get it together and think things through.

"Hello?" Kellan called out, his voice louder and surer than mine. "Anyone home?"

"Yo, dude. In the kitchen."

Kellan raised a brow so that it vanished beneath the hair

falling into his eyes. That voice had come from an entirely different direction than the door closing upstairs. The voice was also Los Angeles, specifically San Fernando Valley, spoken in the slow, purposeful voice of a career slacker.

Kellan took my hand, a gesture for which I felt very grateful as we entered the house of horror. We stepped over the threshold into a large reception room with scarred wooden floors and scattered throw rugs, none of which matched. A giant moose head hung over the stone fireplace, its glassy-eyed stare seeming to pierce right through me. The windows were covered with lace slightly yellowed with time. The huge, L-shaped, chocolate leather couch and two beat-up leather recliners looked extremely well lived-in.

Spartan, but actually quite homey, even cozy, and somehow not nearly as bad as I'd imagined standing on the porch looking up at those two ghosts . . .

"You coming, or what?" asked the slacker voice.

Kel and I looked at each other, then moved through the large room and into a kitchen that smelled like wood smoke and spicy tea. This room was painted a bright, sunny yellow and white, also far more cheerful than the outside had let on. The ceiling was light pine siding, with copper pots hanging from the slats. There were also a few huge plants, green and thriving in a way that made me want to grab a paintbrush and a canvas.

But best yet, there was a large woodstove, lit and sending off a wave of warmth, which drew me like moth to flame.

There was a humongous oak table in the center of the room, and on it sat a large vase filled with fresh wildflowers, which gave off a scent that I imagined I would have smelled in the woods if I hadn't been too busy whining all the way up here to notice.

The counters held various appliances and, most interestingly, a guy sitting Indian-style, facing away from us.

He grabbed our attention immediately. He wore a pair of

army green cargo pants, a white thermal top and a wool hat with tassels that hung down and swung beneath each ear like earrings. His hands were in front of him, out of sight, but I feared he was cradling a bong as he stared out the window. "Ohhhmmm," he sang.

Kellan craned his neck, and glanced at me. *Nutso,* his eyes said. I shot him a pacifying look.

"Um, hello?" I said.

Nutso—er, the man—slowly turned, and looked at us with eyes the color of light milk chocolate dotted with gold specks of mischief.

He was maybe thirty, with shaggy brown hair and a silly, crooked smile that was somehow contagious. And he wasn't holding a bong, as I'd feared, but had his hands out in front of him with the palms together, in a yoga position.

"You're Rachel Wood," he said, hopping down off the counter, revealing a tall, athletic form. "The new boss here at Hideaway."

I'd never been called a boss before—I was barely my own boss—so the greeting threw me for a loop.

"And you are?" Kellan asked him.

"Oh!" He shot us an amused grin. "Sorry. I'm Axel."

When we both looked at him blankly, he said, "Expedition leader here at Hideaway."

Kellan introduced himself while I chewed on the fact that I was "the boss."

"Did you know Rachel was coming up here today?" Kellan asked Axel.

He shook his head. "Nah. When Gertrude's attorney sent us the money she left us, he told us about her, that's all. Said she was L.A. all the way, an artist, who'd be showing up eventually to see what's what and then heading back to her murals in the city."

I didn't catch much of what he said after "the money she left us," and I shook my head. "Wait. So you got something in the will?" I hadn't even *seen* the will; I'd only spoken to the attorney on the phone.

"Well, of course," Axel said. "I'm going to take a nice vacation. Somewhere warm, of course. I'm thinking Virgin Islands. Maybe the Caymans, depending on the surf reports, you know?"

Did I know? No, I didn't know. I knew nothing. In fact, I knew less than nothing.

"Oh, and dudette, now that you're here," Axel went on, "you've got some back wages to pay."

"But, what if I'd never shown up?" I asked, overwhelmed.

"Well, of course you were going to show up." He smiled that smile that normally I'd consider contagious and return full force, but I couldn't smile back right now because anxiety was gripping me.

"You're Gert's niece, aren't you?" He chuckled, and the long tassels on his beanie swayed back and forth. "Probably just as organized and anal as she was, right?"

I smiled weakly. If he only knew . . . "I've been calling"—I tried to sound as if I was in control, when I was so not—"but I couldn't get through."

"Yeah. We lost the phone a while back."

"We?"

"Marilee's here somewhere, too. She's the cook and housekeeper. You owe her some back wages as well."

This just got better and better, didn't it?

"We just heard her shut a door upstairs," I said.

"Nope. She's out back watering her flowers. As for getting a hold of us, you can text me on my cell, though I mostly don't have any reception up here." He patted his pocket, found it empty, frowned, then patted another pocket.

And yet another.

Still came up empty, not that he looked too troubled. "I had the thing earlier," he murmured. His tassels hit him in the face as he bent, slapping at his pants.

"I also sent an e-mail," I said.

"Yeah, not so good with the computer, dudette. Sorry." Giving up on finding his cell, he turned away to grab a steaming mug off the counter.

"If there's no phone, and no one is manning the Web site, how do potential guests make reservations?" I asked.

He blinked, then scratched his head, as he sipped at his drink. "Dunno. Gertrude used to do that."

The woman had been buried for three weeks. A really bad feeling began to work its way through my system. "So no one's been handling the business since she—"

"Well, I keep meaning to find that phone . . ."

Three weeks with no income, and yet the staff had been working. That seemed like unnecessary out-of-pocket expenses to me.

My pocket.

"Well," Axel said, heading for the door, "time for my nooner."

I had no idea what he meant, and I wasn't sure I wanted to know. "But it's past noon," I said, looking at the small cuckoo clock on the counter. "It's nearly four o'clock."

Not seeming too concerned—and I had my doubts that he could get concerned about anything, even if his life depended on it—he shrugged. "You know what they say," he said in that slow voice. "Better late than never."

"Yeah. So who's upstairs?"

"No one."

"But—"

"Relax, Rachel Wood." He accompanied this with a pat on my shoulder. "You're here now, in God's country. Just take it easy."

Easier said than done.

"Time stands still here, dudette." His smile widened. "Everything's good."

And with that, he was gone.

"Probably misplaced his crack pipe," I said into the silence.

"I think it's more a bong-type love affair," Kellan said, and looked around. "Truth is, this place isn't as bad as you imagined, Rach."

"In what realm of reality?"

He shrugged. "If it wasn't so completely inaccessible, it'd be worth something pretty decent on the real estate market. Might still be worth something."

Yeah. I was thinking the same thing.

Hoping the same thing.

Chapter 3

As Kel and I stood there in the kitchen looking at each other, still a bit shell-shocked, the back door opened, and in walked a woman.

She appeared to be in her mid-twenties, like me, and she was of average height and weight, but that was where her averageness ended.

She looked Native Alaskan and gorgeous; shiny black hair to the middle of her back, matching eyes and flawless, exotic features combined to leave *me* speechless, so I could only imagine what it would to do a red-blooded man.

I took a quick look at Kellan.

Yep, his mouth was agape, as if maybe he was planning on catching some flies. Any second he was going to start drooling.

Men. Poor, stupid, helpless creatures, completely led around by their penises.

"Um . . . hi," the woman said, clearly surprised at the sight of us, but holding it together with a grace and elegance I could only admire, because I hadn't been given either grace or elegance at birth.

She held a small flowerpot in her hands, and she set it in the sink. "Who are you?"

"Rachel Wood," I said. "I—"

"Inherited. I heard." She dismissed me fairly quickly, then eyeballed Kellan with those midnight-black eyes.

Kellan stood up a little straighter, while I rolled my eyes, because I figured his chances of scoring with this woman lay somewhere between zero and fat chance.

Marilee moved with that beautiful ease of someone who had no doubt about how good she looked at all times, grabbing a glass and heading to the refrigerator. Meanwhile, I tried to see Kel as she did. He still had that perpetually messed-up caramel hair, a good part of it stabbing into his eyes, hiding their gorgeous color from the general public. Not "artfully" mussed, but neglectfully mussed. Tall and gangly, he carried himself with no grace or ease.

Right now, for example, his shirt was wrinkled from traveling, and also a little on the shabby side, as if maybe he'd had it since the nineties. Knowing Kellan, he had. Not that he was frugal. He was the opposite, actually. He happened to be one of the most generous people I knew, giving time and money he didn't always have to his causes, but fashion was not one of them.

Which meant he didn't always put his best foot forward when it came to first impressions.

Still, in the manner of clueless men everywhere, he smiled at the woman, one of those inherently goofy smiles men got when they were pathetically hopeful about getting sex in the current millennium, but of course didn't really have a chance in hell of actually getting it.

It wasn't that he wasn't a catch. Truthfully, I'd secretly always thought he'd make a hell of a boyfriend because he'd been raised by women and knew them inside and out in a way most guys did not. Kel would never, for instance, send a mother screaming into the night, fearful for her daughter.

The thought of Kellan being an asshole in any way made me want to smile. Nope, he didn't have a bad bone in his mellow, easygoing body. Not a single one.

A damn shame, let me tell you.

Apparently the stunning woman in front of us didn't go for the absentminded-professor thing any more than I ever had, because she dismissed Kel as fast as she had me, filling her glass with ice cubes, while my gaze locked on something in the still-open freezer.

Two boxes of Girl Scout Cookies. Specifically, Thin Mints.

Oh. My. God.

My absolute favorite thing on the entire planet. I'd run over my own mother for a box. Hell, I'd do unspeakable things for two boxes, and just looking at them, my mouth began to water.

Oblivious as usual, Kellan held out his hand to the woman, who shut the freezer, damn it. "Kellan McInty," he said, adding his most charming smile.

Nada. No return smile, no sexual energy aimed at him, nothing. She did thrust her hand out, though. "Marilee. Cook and housekeeper."

"Both? That's a tough job," Kellan said in sympathy, still hopeful, because he was a man, and hope sprang eternal for men.

At least, between their legs.

Poor guy. He was heading directly toward Shot Down Alley, and we all knew it. At least, the two females in the room did.

A part of me knew that I should be wishing for him to get lucky. He was currently in the middle of a long dry spell sexwise, which had left him feeling a little down and a lot restless.

Yep, the friend in me should want him to get laid.

But oddly enough, my belly twitched at the thought. I had no idea what that meant, because I *did* want the best for Kellan. I really did. He deserved it. Knowing that, I even forced myself to picture it—Kellan and this woman, arms and legs entwined . . . mouths doing the tango . . . bodies writhing . . .

They'd look good, this exotic woman and the man who

would be a most amazing lover because he was passionate, tender and eager to please—

Something in my stomach pinched now. Odd, but the thought of Kellan having wild, up-against-the-wall animal sex physically hurt.

What the hell was that about?

But I couldn't dispel the picture of him having gotta-have-you-or-die sex, don't-hold-back-until-you-scream sex. Only suddenly, the woman I was picturing with her head back, mouth open, panting Kel's name was . . .

Me.

My face heated. Other parts of me did as well, and I had to let out a low, careful breath and remind myself that traveling made me light-headed. I really should eat something.

Like cookies.

Marilee moved to the stove, giving Kellan a quick second look-see, and I had to fight the ridiculous urge to step between the two of them to block her view.

Kellan smiled at Marilee, and I knew that smile. It held a unique combination of careful caution and checked desire, giving out the message that he'd expect little because it would be a fantasy come true if anyone actually wanted to sleep with him.

Damn it, Kel, have some pride!

"My new creation," Marilee said, lifting the lid off a simmering pot on the stove. With a smile that seemed to dazzle and daze Kel, she offered him a taste from a wooden spoon.

Of course he leaned in, tongue practically wagging.

"It's sauce for tonight," Marilee murmured in a musical voice. "Assuming you brought the pasta I need from Jack."

"That we most definitely did." Kellan opened his mouth for Marilee to slip the spoon between his lips. Her own lips were curved in a confident little smile that said, *Yeah, I know how beautiful I am, but try to concentrate on my food.*

Kel's eyes roamed over her gorgeous features, practically

soaking her up, and I shook my head. Note to self: Men are easy.

Kellan swallowed the sauce. It took a second, but his eyes bugged out and he lost all the color in his skin, going from a pleasant tan to a sort of pasty white-green. A sound escaped him, the noise a half-choke, half-gag.

Marilee lifted her gaze to his, and he quickly sucked it up, even managing a smile, though definitely a weak one.

"Well?" she demanded, hand on her hip. "Good? Great? What?"

"Um," Kellan said, more green than white now. "Delicious?" he said with a straight face that was pretty admirable, considering that the moment Marilee turned her back, he gagged again.

Men. Jeez, you wouldn't catch a woman faking a damn thing—

Okay, so you wouldn't catch a woman faking *this*, though maybe sometimes we did fake other things.

"Glad you like it," Marilee said with a composed smile. "I'll make sure you get extra tonight at dinner."

"Oh. Great." Behind her back, Kel looked at me in horror.

Like I said, *men*.

"Would you like to see the rest of the house?" Marilee asked.

"Please," Kellan answered quickly, clearly terrified that if we stayed, she'd want him to taste something else. He practically shoved her out of the kitchen, following her like the puppy he really was.

I pretended to follow, but instead executed an about-face and headed straight for the freezer.

I wanted a cookie.

Ah, who was I kidding? I wanted an entire box, all to myself, right now, now, now. I opened the freezer.

Damn.

Neither box had been opened yet. *Now what, Sherlock*?

For a moment I stood there, wrestling with my conscience. What was the likelihood that the owner of said cookies would remember he or she hadn't opened a box?

You are not that desperate, I told myself.

But I was. I *so* was.

I reached for the box, ripped it open and shoved not one, but two cookies in my mouth. Frozen. Chocolate. Mint. "Oh my God," I moaned, and added another, just as the kitchen door opened again.

I whirled around, mouth closed tightly over the remains of the two cookies.

Kellan raised a brow. "What are you doing?"

I shook my head. Nothing. See me doing nothing?

His eyes narrowed. "What are you eating?"

I sighed. "Cookies," I admitted around the mouthful.

He laughed. "You stole cookies? That's pretty desperate, Rach."

"Oh really? You want to talk about desperate, lover boy? *Delicious*," I said, imitating him. "*Please have sex with me, Marilee.*"

He frowned. "I didn't say that."

"You might as well have." I shoved one more cookie in.

"Stop," he said.

"Easy for you to say. You're a damn geeky bastard who doesn't understand stress in the slightest."

"Damn geeky bastard?"

"Hey, if the shoe fits."

He shook his head. "You can finish insulting me later. She's waiting to show us around."

I gave one last, fond look at the freezer.

"Rach."

"Fine." I followed him out of the kitchen.

Marilee was waiting to give us a tour of Hideaway, standing in the foyer rearranging wildflowers in a vase there.

On the other side of the reception room was a great room, with an air hockey table and darts and a jukebox. "Keeps people from going stir-crazy in the winter," Marilee explained, and showed us a small library and a laundry room.

From there we went upstairs, where we viewed four guest bedrooms on the second floor, then four more bedrooms on the third floor, which was reserved for staff. Each of the rooms had been decorated rustically, in a sort of country style, with pine furniture and four-poster beds. The floors were scarred hardwood, covered with a variety of throw rugs in different shapes and sizes. The place was in decent shape, each room sporting thick bedding, which Marilee assured us we'd need in extreme weather, and pictures on the walls that provided proof of said extreme weather. I looked at one photo of the inn, with snow up past the first floor, and gulped. "Yikes."

Marilee just smiled grimly. "It isn't the Bahamas," she said.

All the rooms were empty. No sign of the two faces I'd seen earlier. I looked out the window and saw a small guesthouse.

"It's Gert's place," Marilee said, and took us out there. She stood on the tiny porch, long hair shiny, eyes fathomless, as she peered in. "Here you go."

I gestured her in ahead of me, but she shook her head.

"Oh, no thanks."

I walked in. Gert had the place stuffed to the gills with Victorian furniture and lace, lace, lace everywhere. Looking at it all, I gulped at a new thought.

Who was going to clean all this out?

Kellan followed me, and sneezed, his allergies coming to life from the weeks of dust.

Marilee still stood just outside. She hadn't moved or said a word, and yet her anxiety was palpable.

This, in turn, brought back my goose bumps. "What?" I whispered.

"You're going to have to deal with her things," Marilee whispered back, and entwined her fingers until the knuckles turned white.

"Why are we whispering?" Kellan asked both of us.

Marilee just tightened her lips and looked around uneasily, as if the ghost of Great-Great-Aunt Gertrude was watching us from above.

Or from wherever she'd landed.

"Seriously, this is silly," I said, gesturing for Marilee to come inside. "Come in."

"Oh no. I . . . couldn't."

"Why not?"

"I'm . . . busy." Marilee stayed firmly put on the threshold, and given the stubborn set to her jaw, nothing short of an apocalypse was going to budge her. If that. "Besides, Gert never invited us in."

"Never?" I asked.

"*Never.*"

Wow. That seemed pretty harsh. It wasn't as if the staff had a lot of places to go, which brought me to another question.

What did people do out here when they weren't working?

"She's gone," I pointed out, purposely speaking in a regular voice, though I had to admit, I felt a little spooked. "Surely now that's she's gone—"

Marilee vehemently shook her head, her long, gorgeous hair flying around her face. "You're on your own."

"Okay." I looked around, uneasy myself. "No problem."

Yeah right, no problem.

Kellan ran a finger over the huge wooden snowshoes on the wall. "How did she get all this stuff up here?"

"Gertrude had a thing going with Jack's grandfather."

"A thing?" Kellan asked. "As in . . ."

"They were doing it," Marilee said. "Right up until he kicked the bucket last year. Gertrude would order stuff from catalogs, but no one would deliver way out here. So she got Jack to bring her a piece every time he came up here. It took a while."

Looking at the room, which was so stuffed that pieces were

literally on top of each other, I could well imagine it'd taken a while. *Years.*

Now I had to decide what to do with it all.

Suddenly it felt so overwhelming. All of it. I had no guests, bills that had to be paid, probably a mortgage of some kind . . . and no revenue.

"Do you know a good Realtor?" I asked Marilee, thinking, *Who am I kidding? I'd be lucky if she knew* any *Realtor, much less a good one. Who'd be crazy enough to come all the way out here?*

More importantly, who would be crazy enough to buy Hideaway?

Marilee turned to me, her eyes no longer unreadable but now filled with shock. "You're selling?"

"I'm just going over my options—"

"But Gertrude told us you'd never sell. That you loved her so much, you'd keep everything status quo. That's why she left the place to you. You weren't supposed to even think about selling."

Um, okay. Except I hadn't "loved" Gertrude, as Marilee thought. I hadn't even known her. She'd never shown the slightest bit of interest at all in me or my life.

There was a six-pack of water on the coffee table, and since my throat had suddenly become parched, I grabbed one. Only I was still shaking a bit, and the bottle hadn't been perforated correctly, so with a frustrated sound I handed it to Kellan, who had no luck opening it either.

"Look," I said as gently as I could. "I don't know how I can possibly afford to keep up with everything this place requires."

"It's not hard."

Seriously, she had no idea. This place was so far out of my realm, not to mention that it probably required organization and planning skills, neither of which was part of my repertoire.

Plus, Gertrude and I had spoken exactly twice in my lifetime. Once had been at my high school graduation, where she'd handed me a card with five bucks in it, then demanded to know what I was going to do with my loot. The second time had been at my father's funeral, after he'd died from a fall off a building he'd been painting.

Great-Great-Aunt Gertrude had stood by his casket at his funeral and tutted, then looked over at me. "You an artist, too?"

Unable to speak for the grief, I'd nodded.

"Well, that's a damn waste," she'd said.

Yeah, family closeness at its finest. Needless to say, that she'd left me the inn still had me speechless.

But now Marilee was looking at me, waiting for reassurances that I didn't have. I dug up a small smile. "Looks like I have a lot to think about."

Marilee seemed as if she might argue with that, but in the end, she only nodded. "Yes."

"I'm sorry," I said. "I'm just . . . tired after this whole day. I need a few minutes to freshen up, rest a little bit. Do you mind?"

"No." Ever the hostess, Marilee bowed her head briefly, expertly masking any emotions, as if she'd never had them. "Of course I don't mind. This is your home while you're here. You do as you please."

Kellan looked at me. "You okay?"

"Yeah, I'm fine."

Nodding, he turned to Marilee. "I'll help you get all the supplies inside." He sent me a look over his shoulder. "I'll be right back."

Yep, with your tail dragging, I thought. Ah hell, Kel, don't get hurt.

But of course he would, poor bastard.

"Oh." Marilee hesitated. "It's Friday afternoon."

"Yeah." I waited for more, but she just looked at me expectantly. "What about it?"

Marilee blinked. "You . . . don't know?"

"I don't know what?"

Another long, assessing gaze, but she didn't answer.

Earth to Marilee . . .

"Nothing," she finally said. "Just . . . be careful."

Okaaay.

"And, uh, you should stay close," she added.

As opposed to what—walking back to civilization? "I can do close."

After she left, with Kellan following her—exuding that eternal hope only a man can summon—I stood there, in the doorway of Gertrude's place, not belonging inside and definitely not belonging outside.

Belonging nowhere.

With the late-afternoon air came a cool breeze that felt crisp and refreshing against my heated skin. I could see a path that wound its way into the woods.

Stay close.

The words echoed in my head. I'd stay really close, and right on the trail, but the scenery drew me. I wanted—needed—to soak it in for a minute. Then tonight, maybe I'd spend some time drawing, to soothe my nerves.

I'd gone about twenty yards when four deer appeared, silent and watchful. They looked shaggier and darker than I'd imagined they would be. But then again, my deer experience was pretty much limited to the movie *Bambi*. Still, they were beautiful in an awesome sort of way, and I stood still.

So did they.

After a moment, at some invisible sign I didn't catch, they all bounded back into the woods, vanishing as quickly as they'd appeared.

I let out a long breath, feeling . . . changed somehow, and kept going. It was gorgeous out here, I had to admit. Gorgeous but foreign, in another-world kind of way. There were so many trees and bushes and growth that I couldn't see farther than a few yards in any one direction. Yet when I lifted my eyes, I was surrounded by a three hundred sixty–degree vista of jagged, granite mountain peaks that looked like something right out of a book. My artist's soul ached, it was all so beautiful, and my fingers itched for paints.

Maybe my next mural would be of these mountains. You know, when I was back safe and sound in the city.

In less than three minutes, I was completely swallowed by the forest, and I stopped, a little unnerved by how quickly that had happened, and by how isolated I was. I couldn't be more than a football field's length away from the B&B.

Right?

And then I realized something: The temp had dropped. I looked up, and gasped.

The sky had changed from a stunning blue to a dark, swirling mass of black and gray. A storm was brewing, and I hadn't even seen it coming. This storm wasn't like anything L.A. ever saw either. I was talking a big, badass storm.

Adding to the sense of urgency was the utter and astonishing silence. It was as if even the insects had stopped breathing. And then . . .

Plop. A single raindrop landed on my head, making the only sound in the entire world.

And then another.

Plop.

The sudden and overwhelming urge to turn back and run like hell to the inn nearly overcame me, but one, I never run, and two, my mother always warned me about running in a storm.

"Rachel!"

I nearly collapsed in relief at the sound of Kellan's voice. He was coming . . . down the path? I couldn't see him. Why couldn't I see him?

"Rach!"

I whipped around in a circle, but I still couldn't see him. "I'm here!" I yelled.

"Rach?"

He'd sounded so close a moment ago, but now—now he could have been calling to me from another country. Hell, another planet.

"Rachel, where are you?"

I circled again, panic racing up my spine, blocking my throat.

Why couldn't I see him?

"Right here! Kel? Kel, I'm right here!"

"Rachel!"

It was like he couldn't hear me, and the hair rose on the back of my neck, the way it did every time he forced me to go see whatever the latest horror flick was at the movies.

There I'd spend the entire two hours with my face pressed into his neck, listening to him occasionally laugh softly at me, but he was still always there to comfort me.

Damn it, I wanted his neck right now!

And then I thought, *to hell with the moratorium on running. It's okay to be terrified bone-deep and to act on that terror.* So I took off like a bat out of hell.

Only I didn't get very far before I was abruptly and rudely stopped cold by the loudest, most resounding, most terrifying *CRACK* I'd ever heard—

And then nothing, as my world faded to black.

Chapter 4

I love good dreams, and I was in the middle of a doozy. I was hanging off the HOLLYWOOD sign painting a mural. It was a typical gorgeous Southern California day, not a cloud in the slightly pink, smog-tinged sky. The temp was in the upper eighties, of course. *Perfect.* And not a worry sat on my mind.

Because in my pocket was a check for a cool mil, payment for said mural.

A million dollars, all mine.

Since I'd never had a savings account with more than even five hundred dollars in it, this fact kept blowing my mind. I wanted to help the poor; I wanted to stop world hunger; but a girl could do only so much on her own. So I kept thinking about the car I was going to buy, one that would run *all* the time and *not* stall in the rain or fail to hop to it when I stomped on the gas to try to get on the 405 in the mornings.

Yeah, this was a good day.

Below, holding and belaying my ropes, stood the gorgeous actor Josh Duhamel, and he kept smiling up at me.

God, he was hot, and I smiled back.

That's when the dream shifted.

Josh wasn't smiling at *me* per se, but at the view up my dress. Odd, since I never wore dresses, but there I was, in a little gauzy number that revealed much more than I'd intended to reveal.

Oh no. No, no, no . . .

Yeah. I was wearing granny panties.

Shit. Just my luck.

Surreptitiously I looked down the bodice of my dress to make sure, and groaned. Yep, plain white grannies, the ones with the hole over the hip. I'd have thrown them away, but I had a tendency to forget to do laundry, so I'd always saved them for the day when I woke up to no panties in the drawer.

Natch, today had been that day.

Stupid. Hadn't my mother drilled this one thing into me: *Never ever wear underwear with holes because you never know when you'll be in an accident and some cute ER doctor will see your holey panties and refuse to marry you.*

I should have just gone commando—

Wait. This was a dream, which meant that, theoretically, I could be wearing anything I wanted. Anything at all.

So I went shopping mentally and picked out a thong. A black lace thong . . .

"Rachel?"

Hmm. That didn't sound like Josh's voice. And his face was doing something funny now. Sort of smearing, changing . . .

"Rachel!"

Damn it, that wasn't Josh's voice at all, and I was no longer hanging off the HOLLYWOOD sign. I wasn't sure where I was, to tell the truth, because everything was dark.

Waaay too dark. My heart kicked into gear, because suddenly it was all coming back to me.

Hellacious flight from L.A. Dropping the steak. B&B with the oddest staff members. And the coup de grâce: Girl Scout Cookies in the freezer.

"Rachel! Jesus, where are you?"

Yeah, there it was—everything I'd been through in the past

twenty-four hours, including my most stupid move of walking into the woods by myself, then the sudden storm and—

Another boom of thunder made me shudder. Had I really been hit by lightning?

Since I could smell something burning—possibly me—I had to come to the conclusion that this was a definite possibility.

Not good.

Just in case it was gruesome, I kept my eyes tightly closed. I'd never been good with blood or guts, always being the one to faint in biology class when we'd had to dissect the poor little froggies.

I could feel rain plopping down on my face—or, at least, I hoped it was rain and not someone slobbering over me.

More smoke . . .

Maybe it was my own blood I could feel on my face, and with some sort of morbid curiosity, I lifted my hand and touched my jaw, then cracked an eye to peek.

Nope, not blood. Just rain. I closed my eye again, because somehow, ignorant bliss felt good for now.

Guess my mom had been correct about that whole running-in-a-storm thing. And damn, you know I hated to admit that.

"Rachel!"

At the extreme worry in Kel's voice, I forced myself to open my eyes again. I looked up at the individual raindrops falling through the sky in such a mesmerizing pattern, landing on my face. I could feel water from the wet ground soak into my clothes, and probably more than a few bugs along with it, and I *knew*.

Somehow, in some way, I was different.

I peered at the tree next to me. The trunk looked weird, and it took me a moment, but finally I understood why. I could see through it, past the layers and layers of natural wood to the myriad ants crawling inside, winding their way up—

My heart kicked into gear really well on that, right up to heart-attack level, because it turned out I didn't understand at all . . .

Breath hitching in my chest, I shook my head, and looked up into the sky again. Oh good. Everything there looked normal. But then I focused and . . . no, not normal.

Not even close.

Already the odd and violent storm was moving on, those horrendous black and gray clouds vanishing before my very eyes. Now I could see the moon, and it looked funny. This was because I could see each and every crater on it—which, by the way, seemed like they might be fun to explore.

One step for mankind and all that.

"Christ, there you are." Kellan dropped to his knees at my side and leaned over me. He had a smudge of dirt on his jaw, and his glasses hung from only one ear. His hair was plastered against his skull, his shirt saturated. In his hands he held what looked like a pen, but a beam of light came from it.

The guy actually carried a flashlight on him.

"What the hell happened?" he demanded. A few drops of water fell off the tip of his nose onto my face. "Why are you lying on the ground? *Are you okay?*"

Was I okay? Hmm, wasn't that the question of the hour? Trying to figure out that very thing, I looked back up into the sky, watching the raindrops coming down, one by one. Wow, it was really beautiful.

Every part of everything around me seemed deeper, more colorful, richer . . .

More intense.

"Rach?" Kellan tossed aside his glasses and leaned over me, protecting me with his body, stroking my hair from my face. "You're silent. You're never silent."

A bird flew overhead, and when I concentrated on its body, its wings flapping, I found I could see its heart pumping, beating . . .

Oh.

My.

God.

"Rach."

"I think I broke a nail," I whispered.

He stared at me. "Tell me you're kidding."

"I'm kidding." I lifted my hand and studied my plain, trimmed-by-my-own-teeth nails.

"You're scaring me, Rach. Here, can you sit up?" He took my hand to pull me upright, then steadied me, his hands firm on my upper arms. "Are you all right?"

Without his lenses, his eyes were so clear and blue, I could have just looked at him all day long.

Wow. Gorgeous.

I wobbled, then set my head against his chest. Beneath the drenched shirt, his heart beat a bit fast but steadily, and he was warm, deliriously warm. Sturdy and solid and always-there Kel.

He extended his arms, pushing me back, so he could peer into my face. Man, he was cute. I smiled up at him dreamily, thinking I'd no idea just how cute . . . and while thinking it, a shiver wracked me. Probably it was the cold, but it might have been the totally and completely inappropriate surge of lust I was experiencing.

Kel kept his hands on me, drawing me back against his warm body, making me all the more aware of him, of his sweet but firm touch, of the strength that allowed him to easily take on my weight. I sighed in pleasure.

"You're scaring the shit out of me, Rach."

"Did you know you have the most amazing eyes?"

They narrowed on me. "Huh?"

"Seriously," I said, reaching up, touching his face, which was wet from the rain. "I could drown in 'em. Anyone ever told you that?"

"Uh, no. You're the first. Hold on there, champ," he said

when I tried to get up, holding me down with a hand to the middle of my chest. "Don't move."

Good idea, since everything had begun to swim. I put my hands to my head. "What happened to me?"

"That's what I was going to ask you."

He was so cute with all his worry that it made me smile. "Kel? How come we've never gone out?"

"Out?"

"Hooked up."

He went still, then lifted two fingers. "Okay, how many?" he demanded.

"I'm fine," I insisted.

"I thought we were erasing that word from the English language."

I tried to stand up on my own. "Whoa." I reached for him, because maybe I wasn't so okay after all. "Hey, stop the world, would ya? I want to get off."

"You're dizzy?" He gripped my shoulders. "What the hell happened? Did you fall?"

I closed my eyes. But just like on the plane, that only made it worse, so I opened them again. I focused on a tree. Again, I saw right through the tree, as if I had X-ray vision, meaning I could still see the long line of carpenter ants making their way through the trunk. I followed their line down to the ground, where they emerged from a hole only a few inches from me.

One crawled out near my foot, and I would have sworn on my own grave that it craned its neck and glared at me for being in its way. I stared at it, stunned. "Uh . . . Kellan?"

"Jesus," he breathed, and for a minute my heart surged, thinking he could see through stuff, too, but he shook his head and pointed at my clothes.

They were smoking.

"You were hit by lightning," he said, and looked into my face. "My God. Are you okay?"

His eyes still seemed luminous, and filled with far more

worry than before. I dropped my gaze from his, and then gasped.

Like with the moon, like with the tree, I could see through him. As in *beneath his clothes.*

Um, yeah, I was definitely different.

"I can't believe it," he said. "I mean, what are the chances?" Leaning in again, he began to run his hands over my limbs. Up my legs, over my hips, over my ribs—

"What are you doing?"

"Checking for broken bones," he said tightly, mouth grim.

"I didn't have an accident."

"You were hit." Beneath his shirt, his muscles rippled with every movement, and this mesmerized me. Muscles rippling? *Kel?*

When had that happened?

"Kel, I'm okay." Okay enough to enjoy his hands on me . . .

"If you're okay, then why are you looking at me funny?"

Because I just realized you have this hard chest and nicely chiseled abs, and you're totally, completely *ripped.*

Only two weeks ago, he'd come over to help me wash my car. This had, of course, involved a spirited water fight, and I'd been the victor, nailing him good with the hose from head to toe and back again. We'd laughed, and before going inside my apartment, he'd stripped off his shirt.

I hadn't nearly swallowed my tongue then. Not once.

And yet now, staring at him, *through* his clothes, at his hard pecs, sinewy biceps and that yummy belly, I just wanted to lap him up, or swallow my own tongue.

And then this.

"I think," I said slowly, "that I must've hit my head after all."

"Jesus, really?" He pulled me into his lap right there on the wet ground, slipping his hands beneath my hair, cupping my head, gently probing. "I don't feel a lump. I think that's bad. Look at me."

I didn't want to, but I did. I looked back into those drown-in-me eyes. Then, because I couldn't help myself, because they were such a gorgeous color, I sighed.

"Hurting?" he asked.

"Um . . . a little. But I'm okay. Really." My clothes were indeed smoking, a disconcerting fact, let me tell you. "So how much electricity is in a lightning bolt anyway?"

"Enough to fry a few brain cells."

I laughed, sounding a bit hysterical even to my own ears. So I'd fried a few brain cells. I had spares.

I think.

But how to explain that I could see right through everything? "Kel, can you—Now, I know this sounds weird, but just stick with me here . . . Can you see through me or anything?"

"Okay, that's it. Stay seated." He took a good look at my pupils, pretty darn cute in his concern. "You do know who you are, right?"

"Yep." I noticed a scar low on his belly, and remembered his emergency appendectomy in high school. Then I struggled not to look lower . . .

"And you know me," he demanded. "Right? You know who I am?"

"Double yep."

"What year is it?"

"It's 1605," I quipped.

"Not funny."

"Sorry." I was trying really hard to control myself, and fight the overwhelming urge to peek below his scar. You know, south of the border.

"Quick," he said, obviously oblivious of my inner struggle. "What's twelve times eight?"

"Um . . ." Ah, hell. "You know I suck at math."

He sighed. "Two plus two, Rach. Try that one."

I batted my eyes. "I'm too cute to have to do math."

He just looked at me blandly.

And I sighed. "Honestly, I'm okay." Well, maybe not quite honestly, but how could I explain what I didn't understand myself? To prove I was good, however, I had to stand up, which took more effort that I'd imagined, and I promptly staggered around like a drunk.

"Damn it." Kellan grabbed me, pulling me against the nice, warm, hard body I'd just discovered he had.

I mean, *who knew*?

"Kellan?"

"Yeah?"

My legs really were rubbery, so I wasn't faking it when they gave way. Kellan's arms tightened around me.

"Mmm," I murmured.

He went still. "What was that?" he asked.

Crap. Had I just moaned out loud? *What was wrong with me?* "Nothing."

"It was something."

"No, you must be hearing things."

"No, I—"

"I didn't say anything!" I said a bit too defensively, but the cold had seeped into my wet clothes, and I shivered. "Nothing at all."

"Fine."

"Fine."

I was trying to maintain here, but it wasn't easy. In fact, wasn't this why women were reputed to be from Pluto and men from Uranus? Or something like that? Not only did we speak different languages, we were different species all together.

Then I realized he was still holding me, and my body was acting without my brain's permission, doing as I'd wanted earlier, pressing my face into his neck.

Oh, yeah, he smelled good and he knew how to give a good hug. I nestled in even closer.

Now a groan escaped *him,* and a little shiver ran through my body at the sound. He pulled me in tighter, against his warm chest, his fingers moving through my hair, massaging my scalp in a melting, mesmerizing way.

The guy had the gift of touch, there was no doubt. I just kept on burrowing, like the heat-seeking missile I'd become.

"Rach?"

"Yeah?"

"What are you doing?" His voice was sort of husky and tight at the same time. Sexy.

"Just . . ." Yeah, Rach, what are you doing? "Holding on." I discovered I liked the feel of his skin against my lips when I talked, and as I thought this, that cute, erotic little sound escaped from him again. I don't know why, but for some reason, it made me open my mouth and . . . okay, I bit him.

"Ouch!" He pushed me back, gripping my arms as he stared down into my face. *"What the hell was that?"*

"I don't know." I bit my lip. "I'm sorry. I don't know why I did that."

He continued to hold me away from his body now, which was a shame, but it made me realize something. "Um, Kellan?" I stared at his shirt, at the smoke rising from it. "Don't look now, but you're smoking, too."

He looked at himself. A line furrowed between his eyes as he took it in. "Not smoke. Steam. I'm just drying is all."

"But—"

"I'm fine." He shook his head. "It's you who's a little off."

Yeah, go figure. I guess being struck by lightning did that to a person. I slapped at the smoke rising in little curls from his chest, his arms, his back, enjoying the contact a little too much. "Are you sure—"

"Stop," he said, catching my hands in his. "You're wet, and starting to shake."

True enough. In fact, even my teeth had begun to rattle, hard enough that I worried the fillings would fall out.

"Let's just get you back and warm you up."

Actually, I had a much better thought about how to get warm, but if he'd gotten all prudish after just a bite to the neck, I could imagine what he'd say to my other, much more fun-sounding idea.

So I kept it to myself.

Darn it.

Besides, I did feel . . . off. And cold, so very damn cold, all the way to my bones.

And then there was that other little issue, of being able to see through things . . .

Kellan had turned away from me to look for the trail, and I couldn't help myself.

I looked at his butt.

Bad eyes.

Great butt.

I had no idea what was up with me, but it was starting to get a little annoying.

I honestly felt as if my every nerve had been sensitized. I felt like I needed to be touched.

Right now, right here.

Kel looked over his shoulder and caught me staring.

Uh-oh. I tried to look away quickly, but there was no denying it. I'd been checking him out.

He frowned, as if trying to figure this out, as if the idea of me staring at his ass was so foreign, it couldn't possibly be.

"Come on," he said.

"Right." I smiled as if everything was normal. As if I got hit by lightning every single day and then could see through people's clothing, people whom I'd had no idea were hiding such an incredible body . . . "Coming."

I just wished that were really true.

Chapter 5

Kellan's view of things

Here's the crazy thing: I've wanted to hold Rachel Wood in my arms for, oh, only my entire life.

No kidding.

Well, that's not quite true. Half the time, I've wanted to strangle her.

But the other half of the time . . .

She entered kindergarten the same year as my sister. I'd sit outside during my second-grade recess and watch Rachel dance around on her tiptoes, like a little ballerina in high-top tennis shoes, and even way back then, something within me had fallen head over heels. Of course, that changed pretty quickly when she went on to torture me at every turn for the next two decades.

In fourth grade, she told her teacher that I called her a butthead (which I had) and got me sent home from school *and* my mouth washed out with soap. In seventh grade, right before my state championship baseball game, she sneaked into my locker and replaced my jock with her bra. Ever get stepped on by the catcher when you're in a home run slide without your jock? Not a good time. In ninth grade, she told

Cece Brodington that I kissed like a frog. (In all fairness, that one might have been true, too.)

In high school, she copied all my accounting and algebra work with regularity, but since she got me through the English and world history classes that were hell on Earth for me, I had no real recourse.

During those years, she began her lifelong lust-affair with badasses, and though I fantasized about being one of them, I couldn't have been a badass even if I'd learned to smoke without choking. I just didn't have it in me to be a jerk. But that was okay. I met a lot of girls who liked me just fine how I was.

Well, maybe not a lot.

Maybe not even many, but whatever.

We did kiss once, Rach and I, at my high school graduation. Dot made us do it so she could take a picture. Rachel rolled her eyes, but she leaned in and put her lips to mine for the briefest, most glorious second in history, and then she pulled away laughing.

I didn't laugh.

Hell, I didn't even breathe.

I went off to college after that, and I pretended to be relieved of her presence, but that was one big fat lie.

The entire time she was at UC Santa Barbara studying art and I was at San Diego State studying marine biology had been hell.

I still live in San Diego, but we get together for weekends now, and without the pressures of school, life is pretty damn good.

Of course, if Rachel would just realize that I'm her soul mate, then things might be great, but I figure I'm more likely to be the next man on the moon, so I don't put a lot of stock in hope.

Besides, one thing I do have is her eternal friendship, which I've long ago talked myself into believing is enough.

Now here we are, stomping through the middle of the

Alaska wilds, and she's been hit by lightning—God!—and I think, *I think,* I've just caught her checking out my ass . . .

No doubt I dreamed that last part, but I didn't dream her crawling up my body a few minutes ago as if she wanted to eat me alive. Nope, that had been real, because I pinched myself to make sure. I just tried to maintain after that. Not easy.

"Do you know where you're going?" she asked. Her Capri jeans were filthy, and her ruffled pink top was wet from the rain and newly sheer because of it, though I was desperately trying not to notice that as she squeegeed water out of her hair.

Did I know where we were going?

Not so much, actually. When I wasn't under water with the dolphins, I could get lost finding my way out of a paper bag, and we both knew it. Plus, I didn't feel so hot myself. I looked around me at the woods, which had all but swallowed us whole. The trail was gone.

"I'll figure it out."

"How can you see?" she asked, and picked up my glasses, which had fallen to the ground. "I thought you were as blind as a bat without them."

Yeah, I was. Always have been. I took them and stuck them in my pocket, because oddly enough, for the first time since kindergarten, I didn't have to squint to see. No blurry edges, no fuzzy lines. Nothing but perfect clarity. Must be the air. "Not so blind right now."

"Huh," she said, looking at me, "that's weird."

No, what was weird was the trail she'd come in on had vanished into thin air. It'd been right here before the sudden and shockingly vicious downpour, but hell if there was any sight of it now.

"So do you know where we're going or not?" she asked.

"Sure."

"Just admit it. You don't."

"I do."

She let out an unladylike snort. "What is it with men that they can't admit when they're lost?"

"What good would it do to admit it? It's not like I can stop and ask for directions."

"As if you would if you could."

"I would!"

"Okay, big guy. Whatever you say." She tossed her hair back, going to work squeezing water out of her pink, ruffled top. Her *sheer*, pink, ruffled top. Let's not forget that part. She fisted both hands in the thin material, molding it to her body, as she watched the water drip off her.

And damn, though irritating as hell, the girl was beautiful. She had this curvy body that I knew drove her insane because it wasn't model thin, and she had no idea how her curves could make a grown man beg for mercy. Coupled with her wildly wavy brown hair and melting chocolate eyes, she always made *me* want to beg for mercy, especially now, because her shirt was giving me some serious wet T-shirt fantasies.

"Men don't ask for directions," she scoffed, hands on her hips. "You're just not programmed to admit when you need help."

Beautiful *and* obnoxious. Did I mention obnoxious?

"Let's just start walking, okay?" I said.

"Humph," she said, and stomped past me.

It was wrong, I knew, but when she got pissy, it turned me on. I snagged her arm, pulling her back around, doing my best not to notice that whole sheer-shirt thing she had going on and the fact that she was very cold. Very cold.

Or turned on.

The thought that she might be was a huge distraction. "What did that last 'humph' mean?"

"Nothing."

"Oh, it's something."

She looked away. "I just thought you were worried about me, that's all."

"I am."

She tossed back her wet hair, and sent me a mulish look. "If you're so worried, you'd have . . ."

"What?"

"Offered to carry me or something," she muttered.

I had visions of tossing her over my shoulder and stalking off with her to my cave like a caveman. Me Tarzan, you Jane. "Do you *want* me to carry you?"

"Of course not."

Yeah, definitely pissy, which made me a whole lot relieved. After all, how hurt could she be if she was already back to her usual disagreeable self?

"I'm worried," I promised. "Enough that I nearly had heart failure back there, all for you. Okay?"

"Okay."

I reached my hand out to her and wiggled my fingers.

She looked at them.

She was beautiful, but what made her so irresistible, at least to me, was that she couldn't hold a grudge. Not when we were kids and I did some stupid boy thing, or when we were teenagers and I did some even more stupid boy thing. And not now . . .

Truth was, at heart she was a happy-go-lucky soul, optimistic and hopeful. Staying mad just wasn't in her genes, and she wrapped her fingers around mine. We looked at the growth and trees all around us, dripping from the oddly violent but short-lived downpour, and at my side, Rach shivered.

"It's funny," she said, craning her neck, her eyes apprehensive, "but I can't even remember which way I came from. Everything looks so different."

Looked different and felt different, though I wasn't exactly sure how. It was hard to concentrate with her standing there, clothes wet and clinging to her every inch. And there were a lot of off-the-chart gorgeous inches on her. I was trying really hard not to notice, or at least, not to make it obvious, when a rustling sound came from the bushes just to our right.

Rachel latched onto me. "*Kel.*"

Pretending to be tough and secure, I held her against me—not exactly a hardship—and turned to face the alarming sound.

Axel crashed his way free of the bushes. "Hey, dudes. What's shaking?"

Rachel pulled free. "How did you find us?" She shook her head. "Never mind. Just get us back to Hideaway."

"Why, what happened?"

"Well, did you see that lightning?" she asked.

Axel scratched his head through his wool beanie. The tassels swung with his every movement. "Lightning? We don't get much lightning here in Alaska. Now wind—we get a lot of that. One-hundred-mile-an-hour gusts that can knock a man flat on his ass."

"You're sure you didn't see the lightning? Or hear the thunder?" she asked him incredulously. "It shook the earth like a huge quake."

"I heard the rain, that's it." Axel peered into Rach's eyes. "You been smoking or something?"

Rachel made a sound of annoyance and looked at me, the question in her eyes.

In answer, I shook my head. I had no idea how Axel could have missed the unmistakable thunder-and-lightning storm, brief as it'd been.

"*Whoa,*" Axel said, getting a good look at us.

"What?" I actually glanced behind us for the source of horror on his face, but to my great relief, I saw nothing.

"Dude, look," Axel insisted, pointing at my chest. "You're smoking."

Rachel looked at me as well, and gasped. "I told you!"

I glanced down at myself. It was a little disconcerting to find it was true. I was smoking.

"We had a little incident," I said.

"Sweet."

Sweet?

"Listen," Axel said, looking around us a little uneasily, "I think we should go back to the inn."

"I agree," Rachel said. "You lead the way."

"Oh." Axel eyeballed the landscape all around us. Then he stuck his hands into his pockets, and looked around some more. "Why, you lost or something?"

"Not technically," I muttered.

Rachel shot me a look. "Yes, technically. We're lost. L-O-S-T, *lost.*"

"No prob." Axel scratched his chest, looking around as if he had all the time in the world.

I looked at Rachel. She looked right back. Was this really happening to us? Because it was getting hard to tell if this was real or just some crazy-ass nightmare.

"Axel?" Rachel prompted after a full moment of silence.

"Yeah?"

"Get us out of here?"

"Oh. Right." He turned and began to walk, then stopped. "No, not this way," he muttered to himself, and did an about-face. "This way. Yeah."

Rachel reached for my hand as we went to follow him, and pulled me close so that she could whisper in my ear. "Maybe you should take off your shirt."

My stupid heart leaped. "What for?"

"So we can tear it into strips and tie pieces on branches to mark our way. Since our guide is as lost as we are."

"We're not lost."

She sent me a baleful look. "We are *so* lost."

Axel pointed to the bushes through which he'd come a moment ago. "There. Follow me." And he vanished into them.

Now that my erection was gone, I had enough blood to operate my brain again. And I was able to think that we hadn't ducked through a bush to get here.

"Yeah, not going in there," Rachel said, staring at the bushes as she backed herself into me. "No way."

"Why?"

"Axel?" she called out to the bush.

No response, and she wriggled closer to me, which wasn't so good for my thinking capabilities.

"He's gone already," she said. "He thinks we're right behind him." Grabbing my hand, she pulled me after her at a speed that was shocking given I'd had no idea she could even move that fast. "Rach—"

"We're going around the bushes," she said, still gripping my hand as if it were a lifeline. "There are . . . things in those bushes. Spiders, and creepy crawlies, and more spiders."

"Okaaay."

"Axel!" she called out as we rounded the bushes.

I thought I heard him call back to us, and we followed his voice, but after a few twists and turns through the heavy growth with no sign of him, we stopped again.

Rach sagged against the closest tree for one brief beat before letting out a soft cry and straightening away from the trunk as if it were possessed.

But she was the possessed one.

"Oh my God." Turning in a circle, she looked madly around the small clearing like a cornered animal, one hand over her mouth, her eyes wide and wild. "They're everywhere!"

"What's everywhere?"

"Creepy crawlies!"

"Rach?"

She shook her head violently, holding up a hand to hold me off.

Uh-oh. She'd cracked. She'd utterly lost it. I knew firsthand that she didn't fall apart easily. She had an inner strength that got her through any hardship that came her way. I'd seen her struggle through a tough college curriculum while working full time to support herself; I'd seen her work like crazy to make it on her own in the art world; and I'd seen her go through the death of her father. She'd lived through them as she experienced everything else: with her spirit and strength intact.

But she was at her limit here. That, or she'd hit her head harder than she'd let on. Fearing that, I stepped toward her, but she backed away. "Hey. Hey, are you okay?"

"No. No, I'm not okay. There's . . . *things* out here, Kel. Rabid raccoons and crazy squirrels and gigantic bugs and . . ." She clamped her mouth shut. Still wet, she shivered.

I took another step toward her, and she jerked.

"It's just me," I said in the voice I used with the dolphins when they were spooked. "Just me, Rach."

Her gaze ran over my face, my body, and then she went beet red, squeezing her eyes tightly shut. "Yeah. It's just that, well, it's a lot more of you than you think."

Huh? "Come on. We'll go back."

Her laugh sounded more than half-hysterical. "Yeah. How exactly?"

I reached out my hand for hers, tugging her close. "We'll get back."

"So you're not lost?"

"Well . . ." I looked around. "Maybe just a little."

"Oh God."

"But I can get us unlost. Okay?"

"How about to L.A.? Can you get us back to L.A.?" she joked weakly, then stopped my heart when she snuggled against me, pressing her face to my throat.

God, I loved when she did that.

Unable to help myself, I banded my arms tightly around her. I might have buried my face in her hair and inhaled deeply, too, but no one had to know that part, because it was the story of my life: lusting and yearning after this woman who usually thought of me as something she might absently pat on the head and feed a cookie.

So instead, I just held her for as long as she wanted.

"Something's really—" She broke off.

"Really what, Rach?"

"Wrong. Really, *really* wrong."

Pulling back, I looked her in the face, feeling an underlying sense of anxiety brought on by her tone.

"You mean something more than all this?"

She resisted looking into my eyes. Instead, she tried to burrow in again, tighter this time, nearly strangling me in the process.

But that was fine with me, because there were better things than breathing. Like holding her. Her lips brushed my neck, her hair stabbing into my eyes, but I didn't mind, because the silky strands smelled like honey and vanilla, and I could have smelled her all damn day long. Jeez, I was pretty far gone if I was noticing the scent of her hair over the thought of any injuries she might have sustained. . . .

"I want to go back," she whispered. "We can talk there."

"Okay." Besides, I wasn't any happier than she was, out here, in the middle of nowhere, with killer lightning bolts. "Let's go."

And holding her hand, I started to lead the way.

If only I knew exactly which way that was.

Chapter 6

Hi, my name is Rachel, and I'm officially freaked out, thank you very much. The clouds had all but vanished from the sky, which still seemed a very strange color, and when I looked at it for more than a second and focused, that odd sense of seeing right through everything hit me again. You'd think there'd be nothing up there in the wild blue yonder but clouds. Wrong. There was plenty: birds, satellites, planes filled with people watching movies, sleeping, talking.

God.

I couldn't look down either, because the ground was no better. It was filled with things like slugs and worms and other bugs the likes of which might make one go crazy if one thought about it for too long.

So I purposely drew a deep breath and didn't focus on anything but the intangible. Axel, still missing. Kel and I, still standing here all alone. And, at least in my case, frightened half to death.

Kel squeezed my fingers. "No worries, Rach. We'll be okay."

I was trying not to panic, but I wasn't having much luck. "No worries," I repeated like a mantra. "No worries . . ."

"This way," Kellan said, pointing. Then he pulled off his

T-shirt, and even though I'd already peeked, the sight of him left me utterly speechless.

"Um," I said ever so intelligently, my tongue hanging out at the sight of all his well-toned flesh and hard sinew, "what are you doing?"

"Just as you suggested." He ripped the hemline off the T-shirt with shocking ease, the muscles in his arms rippling, causing me to drool more. I swallowed hard and tried not to stare at his bared chest or abs, but as I've already established, I have no willpower at all.

He tied a strip of cloth around a branch, then touched my jaw, oblivious to my lusting. "No worries, right?"

Let's face it, the men in my life—both the bad boys I tend to collect and my brothers—spend little time coddling me, much less soothing or reassuring me.

Having Kellan do all three felt both foreign and utterly, shockingly . . . lovely.

Kel took a moment to look all around us carefully, as if memorizing landmarks.

Meanwhile, I couldn't tear my gaze off him. "Kel?"

"Yeah?"

"Why don't you need your glasses?"

He went still, then lifted his head, those piercing baby blues meeting mine. "I don't know."

There was a moment of silence, which I characteristically broke first. "That's a little freaky, don't you think?"

He actually went to push his glasses farther up his nose, and remembered they weren't there. "A little, yeah."

"Just so you know, the *Twilight Zone* theme song is running through my head."

"As long as it's not the sound track from *Psycho*." Taking charge and my hand at the same time, he pulled me onward.

I stared at his sleek, smooth back, damp from either the rain or sweat. Which one didn't matter, because both appealed. I was dizzy, wet and confused.

And desperately hungry for cookies.

Kel stopped to tear off a second strip of his shirt and tie it around yet a different branch. "Come on."

"Right." This take-charge Kellan was new. And incredibly appealing. "You think this is the right way?"

"Yep."

Confident, too. Double whammy. We made more stops, tying a handful of strips to branches. Kel did the tying, muscles tight, brow furrowed. His jaw was scruffy, his hair its usual riotous mess. His eyes were fierce with concentration, and just looking into them made me shiver. The good kind of shiver, the kind that started at the toes, made pit stops at every erogenous zone and ended at the roots.

He lifted his gaze to mine, catching me staring, and some of his intensity cleared, but none of the heat.

And just like that, I knew.

I wanted to kiss him.

Shocked by the unexpected need, I shifted closer. Since he was so damn tall, I had to tip my head back to see into his face, which I did just in time to catch him taking a hard swallow.

"Rach," he said, suddenly, endearingly, looking uncertain and off-balance again. "What are you—"

"Shh." I wanted to just look at him forever, but that was weird. In any case, I'd definitely been staring for a beat too long now, and we were verging on awkward.

He swallowed again, and I slid my hands up his bare chest, giving myself another shiver, because his skin was warm and tough. I could feel his heart leap.

I could see it, too, but I didn't want to accept that, not right now. Right now, I wanted oblivion, I wanted comfort, and I wanted his kiss more than I wanted my next breath. "Kellan?"

He gave one unsure shake of his head, and touched mine. "You're hurt."

"Not so much." I lifted my hand to cover his on my jaw.

He pulled free and took a step back. "You're off your axis, then."

But I'd seen it, the hint of something restless and hungry behind the mellowness.

He wanted me, too.

I closed the gap again, just one step, bringing us back within each other's breathing space. His was such a nice space, I thought.

How was it I'd never seen that?

He had that stubborn lock of wet hair falling into his eyes, dripping onto his nose, and unable to help myself, I pushed it over his forehead. And then there I was, my fingers in his hair, wanting more, so much more.

And given the way his hands went to my hips and squeezed, he felt the same way.

Unbelievably, everything around us seemed to sort of fade away, and I found myself lost in something new: his heated eyes.

"Rach, you're sending off a weird vibe here, and—"

I nudged my body up against his, and in response, he let out a rough, ragged breath.

Not so Zen-like now, was he?

The knowledge made me smile; the power made me feel drunk. One look at my face, and Kellan groaned. "I don't know what's up with you, but—"

"Shut up, Kel." And to make sure of it, I kissed him.

He went utterly still, like a wall of stone, like a man who'd just entered either heaven or hell but wasn't sure which.

Then I touched the corner of his mouth with my tongue, and with another ragged groan, he hauled me up off the ground and dove in like a man starved for a feast.

And in perhaps the best surprise of the day, I learned something new about Kellan McInty.

The guy could kiss.

I mean, seriously kiss. Unlike anyone in my past, which had

always been a little like the story of the Three Bears—either too much or not enough—Kel had it down: a hungry pressure, an uncivilized connection and just the *right* amount of tongue.

And then my mild-mannered, easygoing Kel did something a little shocking. He bumped it up to the next level, sinking his fingers into my hair, gripping my head so that the angle suited him better, and took it deeper, pressing me back against the closest tree. Now I had the hard tree trunk against my spine and Kellan's hard body against my front.

I'd been kissed plenty, but I had to admit, not as if nothing else mattered—not the lightning, not being lost in the woods, not a single thing . . .

Finally he lifted his head, his blue eyes so dark, they were nearly black. He stroked my lower lip with his thumb as he looked at me. "That was different for us."

Before I could say a word in response, he kissed me again. And when I say kiss, I mean more like *devour.* As in no-holds-barred, destroy-any-lingering-thoughts, melt-all-the-bones-in-my-body *devour*. Seriously, I couldn't have whispered my own name if my life had depended on it.

Then he upped the heat even more by pressing a thigh hard between mine, while still taking my mouth with a possessiveness I'd never ever have guessed he carried. He kissed me long and deep, and so thoroughly, I'd completely forgotten where we were by the time he lifted his head.

His mouth, wet from mine, curved wryly. "Yeah. Definitely different."

I couldn't tear my gaze from his lips, which I desperately wanted back on mine. "*Very.*"

From somewhere behind us came a thrashing sound, familiar now, so I didn't leap out of my skin this time. And then two seconds later, Axel appeared, sticking his head through a bush. "Dudes, you gotta keep up."

"Yeah," Kellan said, holding my gaze, not to mention still

having me pinned against the tree so that I could feel what the kiss had done to him. *Yowza.* "We'll try to keep up."

I might have spoken, but my body kept humming with an undeniable sexual tension. Plus there was that underlying headache from whatever had happened to me out here.

Oh, and let's not forget my new superpowers.

Yeah, lots on my mind today, and I was quiet on the walk back. With Axel's dubious tracking skills, it definitely took longer than it should have, but with my thoughts racing faster than the speed of light, it didn't matter.

Unfortunately, out here in the Twilight Zone, day faded faster than a blink of an eye. No twilight, no dusk, just a disconcerting blink, and *poof*, daylight to nightfall with no warning at all.

Eeriest thing ever.

Well, except maybe for waking up on the ground with the ability to see through everything.

Luckily we had been within easy reach of the B&B when everything had happened. Unlike earlier though, the house wasn't lit, but was dark as can be. Without meaning to, I focused, and saw right into the house, into the darkness, and saw nothing.

So why did the hairs rise on the back of my neck?

"Lost power," Axel declared with a shrug that said it was no big deal. "Shit happens, right?"

I gulped. I hated the dark, had ever since I had gotten hooked on reading Stephen King novels in eighth grade. "Does it happen a lot?"

"Enough. No biggee."

No biggee, the stoner said. Okay, then, I'd just relax.

Not.

Kellan pulled me aside and lifted my face, studying me for a long moment the best he could in the dark, letting me study him back, which wasn't such a good idea, as I drowned myself in his eyes. "It's going to be okay," he said.

Again, I felt that melting sensation, as if he really could make it so.

"I have the flashlight, remember." He flicked it on and handed it to me.

I silently blessed his mother and sisters for drilling the sweet, sensitive gene into him, because he knew I hated the dark.

"Thanks," I whispered, my throat unexpectedly thick.

"You're back to being very quiet," he said. "Making me a little nervous."

He should be more nervous about the fact that I now knew the answer to the age-old question, Shorts or briefs? But as he didn't yet know my secret, he might not appreciate the fact that I found his plaid boxers both sexy *and* amusing. I did manage a little smile, but he didn't catch it, his eyes holding mine captive.

"Everything's not okay, is it?" he murmured.

And much as I wanted to pretend it was, or at least to make fun of his plaid boxers, I slowly shook my head.

"Let's get inside," he said. Then, so briefly I might have imagined it, he stroked my jaw. "Get you dry, hopefully fed with something other than that pasta sauce Marilee's working on, because trust me, yeesh." He paused, waiting for another smile, but I couldn't muster one, not even for him.

"We'll figure it all out from there," he said very quietly, still holding onto me. "Okay?"

I'd always prided myself on my independence. Having him comfort me still felt foreign. So I have no idea why suddenly I wanted to put my head on his shoulder and cry.

Silly. I'd never lacked for much in my life—well, except money—but maybe, as I was discovering, having a bit more warm-and-fuzzy in my life wasn't a bad thing.

"A few cookies, and I'll be fine. Good as new," I said.

"Atta girl."

We entered the back door of the inn, clomping into the kitchen with our wet clothes. The room glowed from candles and the lit woodstove, each causing flickering shadows to dance in the dark corners.

I purposely didn't look in the corners.

Marilee stood at the woodstove in black leggings, sheepskin boots and a long white sweater. Beneath she wore some damn expensive-looking lingerie, which I tried like hell not to notice.

She was stirring her large pot, frowning into it so fiercely, I wondered if she'd just taken a taste and discovered how bad it was.

She glanced up when we came in, her eyes widening at the sight of us drenched, probably still looking a little wigged out and, in some of our cases, still smoking. But her gaze kept returning to Kel—specifically, to his bare chest. "My God," she murmured. "What happened?"

"Lightning," I said.

In the dimly lit room, she exchanged a long look with Axel. "We don't have lightning here," she said.

"Yeah, so I've heard." I'd just made up that incredible strobe of electricity. "*You* saw it, right?" I asked Kellan.

He nodded. "Saw it. Heard it."

Axel opened a long, narrow closet and pulled out two sweatshirts. He handed one to me and one to Kellan.

"They got lost," Axel told Marilee, and mimed the motion of smoking.

"We have not been smoking!" I said, exasperated, pulling on the borrowed gear, both relieved because Kel was now covered and Marilee could stop staring at him, and disappointed because that meant I had to stop staring, too. "And we did get lost."

"The woods around here are tricky," Marilee said. "They close in on you if you don't know where you're going. Next time, take a two-way radio with you. I can talk you in. I know this whole area like the back of my hand."

"It was no problem," Axel said. "Our faithful guide brought 'em back."

Marilee looked confused. "Who?"

Axel frowned. "Me, of course. *I'm* the guide around here, not you."

"Ah." Marilee's lips twitched. "Right."

Axel scowled. "I am."

Marilee swatted lightly at one of the tassels on his hat, sending it swaying. "Okay."

Still scowling, Axel leaned over her shoulder and peered into the pot. "What the hell is that?"

"Dinner."

Axel grabbed a spoon and took a tentative taste. With a shudder, he made a horrendous face. "Jesus, woman!" He tossed the spoon into the sink. "What did I ever do to you?"

I peeked at Kellan, who was struggling to bite back a sympathetic smile.

"It's fine," Marilee said defensively, hunching her shoulders as she stirred with much more aggression than necessary, making a few splatters, while Axel choked dramatically.

"Fine? Fine for what?" he asked, grabbing a towel and swiping his tongue on it. "Poison?"

Marilee huffed. "Kellan liked it just fine, didn't you, Kellan?"

Axel swiveled toward Kellan in disbelief. "*Dude?*"

Kellan winced, and Axel sighed. "Yeah, I know." He turned to Marilee again. "Look, you know you're off-the-charts hot, right?"

Marilee lifted a shoulder, looking slightly mollified at the compliment.

"Yeah, well, you should also know it makes men stupid," Axel said. "They say things they don't mean."

Marilee glanced speculatively at Kel, then back at Axel. "Do you?"

Axel scratched his head.

"Axel Leon Hanson, do you say things you don't mean?"

When he didn't answer, she pointed at him with her

wooden spoon, then poked him with it in the chest, leaving a red sauce stain right in the middle of his Grateful Dead T-shirt that even in the barely lit room we could all plainly see. "Talking to you, *dude.*"

Axel sighed again. "Now why did you have to go and ruin my shirt?" He pulled at the material, which came away from his chest with a wet suction sound. "And I *don't* say things I don't mean. You know that."

She stared at him. "So when you said I can't cook worth a damn . . ."

"Yeah, I meant it."

At her shocked, hurt expression, he grimaced, then put his hands on her arms. "But I think you're amazing outdoors. Does that count? I love the way you can name all the trees and flowers and shit. And then there's how you always know where you're going. You never get lost."

"You're just jealous."

"Maybe." Axel headed toward the, table and without a care, began to empty his pockets. Penknife, loose change, fish hook, nail, gum . . .

"Hey, what are you doing?"

"Unloading."

"Whoa. Stop right there, bud."

He arched a brow, smiling at her—that contagious smile—but Marilee resisted like a champ.

Instead, she pointed at him with the wooden spoon again, her expression fierce, like a den mother, like a housekeeper at the end of her rope. "When we have guests, you're not supposed to treat this place like it's your house."

"Oh. Yeah. Forgot, sorry." Reversing his progress with a bit of a sheepish smile, he scooped everything back into his pockets. "See? All cleaned up now."

"Yeah, I see. I see that you forgot to wipe your boots again."

He looked at the floor and winced.

So had I, because we'd all tracked in some mud.

"We have guests?" I asked.

"Oh." Marilee shot Axel one of her long looks, which made me very curious and very uneasy at the same time. "I meant you two, of course."

Axel moved to the refrigerator, and my gaze followed. I realized I could see right through it, to all the food on the inside, which made my mouth water.

No, I was not going to get distracted by food, no matter how much I was starving.

"Don't open that," Marilee said to Axel. "We don't know how long the power'll be out."

"They're hungry." Ignoring her command, he began filling his arms with bread, butter, apples, oranges, cheese and crackers.

My stomach growled loudly.

"Food first, and then a change?" Kellan asked me.

"What are you going to change?" Axel asked, craning his neck toward us.

Marilee shoved him, and he pulled his lower lip into his mouth.

"I meant her clothes," Kellan said, watching the exchange with as much curiosity as I was. "She needs to change her clothes."

"Right. Her clothes." Axel smacked his forehead. "That's what I meant, too, dude."

Marilee glanced at him with some sort of warning in her gaze, and he just lifted a shoulder. "Sorry," he muttered. "Slow sometimes, is all."

Marilee began to slice up the cheese and apples, using choppy gestures that had me seriously concerned for her fingers, at least until Axel pushed her aside and took over, utilizing the knife like a culinary chef, his movements so fast that his hands blurred.

His talent was clear, and a bit startling, given that I'd pegged him as slow and inept, but apparently there were some things he could do, and do well.

That one of those things was wield a knife somehow didn't make me feel much better.

He and Marilee had gone oddly silent. I knew there was something really weird going on, but I was so fried, I couldn't seem to summon the energy to get to the bottom of it.

Kellan pressed me into a chair, Marilee handed me a plate and, before I knew it, I was stuffing my face. Unable to help myself, I glanced at the freezer, concentrated and saw right through the door to the boxes of Girl Scout Cookies.

I think I had a miniorgasm.

"Do you have any dessert?" I asked as casually as I could.

"No, not yet, sorry," Marilee said with apology. "But I'm going to bake brownies tonight."

Axel choked out a cough that sounded like "God help us," and Marilee glared at him until he went back to being silent.

"So you have nothing?" I said. "Not anything like, say, *cookies*?"

"I'm sorry," she said again.

Damn it. I wanted to go to the freezer and whip it open, but I controlled myself—barely—promising myself a midnight sleepwalk to the freezer, and when I did, this time I wouldn't hold back.

I was going to eat them all.

Every.

Single.

Last.

One.

"I was thinking of calling Dot," I said to Kellan, "just to check in." And to see if she could help us make some plans to get out of Crazy Town.

Marilee shook her head. "Phones are down, too."

I pulled my cell out of my pocket. No reception. "I don't suppose you have wireless Internet?"

Both Marilee and Axel burst into laughter.

"Yeah." I sighed. "What about radio? We could call Jack and get him back here."

Marilee looked startled. "You want to leave early?"

Axel shook his head. "Not going to happen."

"Why not?"

"Jack never returns early."

"Oh," I said, and suddenly felt extremely powerless. Hated that.

Kellan put a hand on my shoulder, squeezing gently. "So there's no way to communicate with the rest of the world?"

"We're self-contained," Axel said. "That's what Gert loved about this place."

Of course she had. Oh God, this felt bad. Very bad.

"There must be some sort of evacuation plan in case of emergency," Kel said with quiet calm.

No sparks of temper, no kicking ass, not Kel. Just a cool, easy way that somehow soothed me.

Odd, since I'd always been attracted to the wildly passionate, temperamental sort. But I was extremely grateful that it was Kel at my side, because he gave me something few others ever had.

Security.

How he did it under such pressure was a big mystery, but I wished whatever it was would rub off on me.

"Oh, I can radio Jack," Axel said. "But it has to be life-and-death for him to respond."

"So other than one of us dying, there's really no way out?" I asked in a very small voice. "Because I thought this was the twenty-first century. How can we actually be stuck here?"

Axel smiled. "Now see, that's why they call this God's country, boss. No one gets in and out of here but God."

Marilee and Axel exchanged another long look.

And suddenly I wished I had gotten a lot closer to God over the years.

Chapter 7

After I realized how stuck here we really were, and that I wasn't going to get any Girl Scout Cookies until I could sneak them myself, things sort of caught up with me.

I was so tired that I had to prop my head up with my hand, my elbow on the table, and still I kept drifting off in the middle of eating my cheese and apples. I nearly snapped my neck while I was at it. I swear, my eyes just kept closing on me. The warm fire didn't help, nor did the lack of bright overhead lights—cookies would have helped—and I closed my eyes while Marilee and Axel talked to Kellan about . . .

The sexual healing powers of the mountain?

Huh?

I tuned into the conversation in time to hear Marilee say, "It's true, there's just something about this place. When people come here, they find a renewed spirit. It brings out the passion."

"*Wild* passion," Axel said, sounding like he'd experienced this firsthand.

"*Sex?*" Kellan said, sounding doubtful, clearly wanting to clarify. "You're telling me your guests all get sex?"

"Well," Marilee started. "Not necessarily—"

"Yes," Axel said over her. "Seriously, dude. I think it's in the water, dude."

I managed to concentrate, and by accident, I looked right through Axel. Damn, I could still do that. But his heart hadn't picked up speed, nor his pulse, which I supposed meant he actually believed every word, that this place was truly some sort of . . . sexual healing zone.

I drifted off for a moment, picturing that, getting sexually healed by . . . *Kellan*?

Damn, the guy needed to get the hell out of my fantasies.

"So," Kellan said, sounding amused now. "You're telling me what? That I'm going to have the sex of my life here?"

Axel laughed. "Hey, dude, don't knock it until you've tried it."

In spite of myself and my interest in this topic, I drifted off again, dreaming about Kellan getting the sex of his life. With that girl he'd dated a few times at work, that cute little blonde, what's-her-name—

No. I didn't like her. Too perky.

I tried someone else. Maybe that actress on that TV show he had such a crush on.

No, I didn't like her either.

Concentrate, I told myself. Concentrate on getting Kellan sex with . . .

Me.

I could see it so clearly, too: His long, rangy body towering over mine, him leaning in for a kiss as he sank into my body, taking us both to heaven and back—

Whoa. But it was too late. The image stuck. And not only did it stick, it was . . . hot. My face heated. I sighed dreamily.

And grinned stupidly.

"Rach." Kellan gently shook me. "Come on."

Come? Yeah, I think I could probably handle coming right about now . . .

"Let's get you changed," he said. "And then—"

"Yes?" I murmured hopefully, waking all the way up. "And then?" *More coming?*

"*Sleep.*"

Sleep. Right. Only problem? I think I was experiencing the sexual healing powers of the place already. My body was tingling from head to toe, and in all the good spots in between.

And then came the thump that made us jump. It came from directly overhead, and I jerked upright. "What was that?"

"What was what?" Marilee asked, careful not to meet my gaze.

I looked at Axel, who shook his head.

"You didn't hear that?" I asked.

"I did," Kel said, and stood.

Then the thump came again, louder this time.

Kellan raised a brow. "Was that nothing, too?"

Marilee looked at Axel. Axel looked back for one long beat before affecting a lazy smile. "Probably a raccoon."

"Doing what? Trying to sneak into one of the beds?" I asked.

Marilee laughed. "Oh, you never know." She pulled me out of my chair and nudged us toward the back door. "You look exhausted. Why don't you go catch some shut-eye?"

"I think we should look upstairs first," Kellan said.

"Oh, I'll do that." Axel opened the back door for us. It was pitch-black outside, and he handed us two flashlights.

"You two just get some shut-eye," Marilee said.

"And maybe some of that healing," Axel quipped, and shut the door.

Silence reigned.

Kellan looked at me.

I looked at him.

"They're up to something," I said.

"Oh yeah." He looked in the window. "They're already gone. Want to—"

"Oh, yeah."

And together, in mutual silence, we re-entered the kitchen.

Empty.

We moved to the hallway. Nothing. All around us, the B&B was dark, utterly silent.

"Up?" I asked, gesturing to the stairs.

"Definitely."

We tiptoed up the stairs, using the flashlights to cut through the dark, the beams piercing the blackness but not the silence. We kept bumping into each other in the dimly lit space. Apparently I wasn't exhausted or freaked-out enough, because I felt distracted by the feel of Kel's thigh brushing mine, his arm against my side. Distracted, and comforted, and . . . stirred up. I found that if I moved in closer, his arm brushed my breast instead.

Until he realized, and shifted slightly away. Damn it. I wanted him to pull me against him again.

And if he kissed me, I wouldn't mind at all.

And I really wanted to know why he smelled so good, even after all we'd been through today.

At the top of the stairs, he stopped me. We stood side by side, barely breathing, as we listened. Well, Kellan listened. I admit, I just scooted closer in order to get another sniff of him.

All four rooms on this floor were closed and, when we peeked in, empty. Same on the next floor up.

Marilee and Axel had vanished into thin air.

A little stunned, we made our way back to the kitchen, and stopped in shock.

Marilee and Axel stood at the back door, looking out into the night.

"Hey," I said behind them, making them both jump, "where did you go?"

They whipped around and stared at us. "Wondering where you two went," Axel said. "Did you change your minds about sleeping at Gert's place? Or about being together?"

I felt Kellan glance at me, silently giving me the option to change the sleeping arrangements if I wanted. I knew Gertrude's space had only one bedroom, but no way did I want to be out there alone.

Nor did I have any desire to be upstairs, where mysterious thumps and bumps ruled the night. I wanted, quite frankly, to be in my own bed, with the traffic blaring in the window, and the smog and the city lights choking out the stars.

But that wasn't going to happen.

God, I was tired, so tired. I knew we needed to press Axel and Marilee about the house, about the odd noises, but I couldn't seem to garner the energy it would take to do that.

"In the morning," I said softly to Kel, who nodded his understanding.

I looked at Axel. "He's with me."

If Kellan was surprised at this news, he didn't show it. He simply hefted our bags over his shoulder. Together we went out the back door and stepped into the black night. I wasn't afraid of the dark like I was of heights, but it was close. I tried to always paint my murals low to the ground, and in those rare circumstances when I couldn't, Prozac was my friend. I'd have been much, much happier if I'd managed to swipe a box of cookies from the freezer.

Beside me, Kellan lifted his flashlight. The beam of light didn't have a chance against the dark night. The air had chilled to a shocking suck-in-your-breath temperature. In L.A., summer nights never cooled down much. Here I could actually see my own breath when I exhaled.

And it was *August.*

There were all sorts of sounds out here. A distant howl of some sort that made me think of every horror movie Kellan had ever made me watch. The chirping song of too many crickets to count. A rustle in the bushes that might or might not have been a bear waiting to eat us in the same way I was waiting to eat those Girl Scout Cookies. I couldn't bring myself to look, and I slipped my hand in Kel's. He was too good a friend to comment on it. He just lightly squeezed my fingers.

"I'll make you breakfast in the morning," Marilee called out after us.

"Now why would you threaten them like that?" we heard Axel ask, and then came a smacking sound, as if Marilee had hit him upside the head.

"Dudette," Axel said mournfully, and then the door shut, leaving me alone with Kellan and the night.

I stepped up the two tiny concrete steps to Gertrude's door and took a deep breath, but I couldn't make myself go in. You'd think after my little woods adventure, I'd be dying to go inside, but no.

"Rach?"

"Yeah." I let out a heavy breath and opened the door. It creaked and revealed . . . more blackness.

No ghosts. No goblins. No extraterrestrials.

So why couldn't I shake the odd sense of fear, or get the hair on the back of my neck to go down? "You want the couch or the bed?" I asked, my voice seeming extremely loud.

He used his flashlight to look at the couch—a short, high-backed Victorian, green with tiny white flowers all over it, overstuffed and undoubtedly as comfortable as a bed of rocks. In silent agreement, we moved to the doorway of the tiny bedroom, and studied the bed there.

It was covered with a prim rose comforter, sported a single pillow and was as narrow as a pencil.

"Maybe we should have tried the guest rooms in the main house," I said.

"Complete with whatever goes bump in the night?"

I let out a low, disbelieving laugh. "My God, Kellan. What I have gotten us into?"

"Not sure. But I have a feeling we're going to find out, whether we want to or not."

"Yeah." I shook my head. "This place sucks bear balls."

He slid me an amused glance. "Bear balls?"

I closed my tired, gritty eyes and pointed to the bed and then the couch. "Eenie, meenie, miney, mo—"

"No, don't. You're taking the bed." He dropped the duffle bags to the floor.

"Why is that?"

"Because out of the two of us, you're the more freaked-out."

He had a point there. "Do you ever get freaked-out?"

"Yeah," he said. "Just ask me to relive going into that clearing and finding you on the ground, eyes closed, face completely colorless, with your clothes still smoking. You shaved years off my life on that one."

He'd been scared for me. It was quite possibly the sweetest thing anyone had ever said. "Yeah, sorry." My throat went tight. "And you don't know the half of it."

He was watching me in that quiet way he had. "Why don't you tell me."

I let out a laugh that sounded extremely close to hysterical, and clamped my hand over my mouth to stop it. "Okay, I'll tell you, but you should probably be sitting down for this."

Instead, he pulled me closer and leveled his intensely blue gaze on mine. "Your head? Or something else?"

"I have a headache," I admitted. "But I think that's just from the stress. Listen, I was serious about the sitting-down thing. Please sit."

He pulled me into the living room and sat both of us down on the couch, which was, yep, stiff as predicted. "Go," he said.

Yeah, only where to start? "Okay, something weird happened out there."

"You're not kidding. We are definitely not in Kansas any more, Toto."

"Kel." I put my hands on his arms and was immediately distracted by the tough sinew that made up his biceps. Yum.

No, not yum. Stick to the topic, Rachel. "Here's the thing. I can sorta see through stuff."

He blinked once, as slowly as an owl. "Okay."

"Like right now. I can see"—I gestured at his clothes—"through your clothes."

"Uh-huh. Rach, maybe you should lie down—"

"You're wearing plaid boxers. Size scrawny-ass thirty-two."

He blinked again. "Scrawny-ass?"

"Is that the part of this that you want to talk about? Really?"

He sighed. Scrubbed a big hand over his face. "Okay. So you can see through stuff."

"Yes." Desperate to sound sane, I twisted my neck, looking for some way to prove it to him. "See that closed case in the corner?" I pointed to a tall antique cabinet, complete with brass knobs and a pretentiousness that made the thing stick out, here in the wilds. "Inside there's . . ." I concentrated, looked through the wood, then gasped.

"What?"

I covered my mouth with my hand, which was suddenly shaking. "My God!"

Kellan looked at me oddly, and then got up, walking toward the case.

"Guns," I whispered, horrified at the row of guns within the closed cabinet. "It's filled with—"

Kellan opened the door. "*Holy shit.*"

Guns.

I don't know how long we both stared. Finally I stood, then walked toward the cabinet as well, reaching out a hand to touch the butt of a huge, wicked-looking rifle.

"Holy shit," Kel said again.

"What are these for?"

Kellan shook his head grimly. "I don't know." He shut the cabinet. "But I wish like hell I did."

I waited for the inevitable realization, which didn't take longer than a beat, because as laid-back and easygoing as Kellan might be, he was not in any way slow or stupid.

His eyes landed on mine, and held.

I lifted a shoulder.

"You saw through that cabinet," he said.

"I saw through the cabinet."

"And through my pants."

"Yeah, but if it helps, I didn't mean to." *Much.*

He just stared at me.

I tried not to look again, but he stood there, an intensely physical presence with something of an attitude—and boy, I was a sucker for attitude—in his faded Levi's and that borrowed sweatshirt, which only hinted at the broad shoulders I could actually see.

"What else?" he asked hoarsely.

"Well, your sweatshirt—"

"I meant, what else *besides* me can you see through, Rach?" he said in a low, rather frustrated-sounding voice.

"Oh." Right. "Uh, well . . ."

"Rach."

"Everything." I shrugged my shoulders helplessly. "I can see through everything."

"Do you see dead people, too?" he asked, trying to joke.

I shook my head.

And he nodded his, relieved. Then, in what was the nicest thing he could have done in that moment, he pulled me in for a hard hug. "This is fucking insane," he whispered against my damp hair. "I'm not crazy about insane, Rach."

I held on tightly and closed my eyes. "Me, either. What do you think is wrong with me?"

"Nothing."

"I can see through things, Kellan."

He tipped my chin up, his eyes dark, his voice low and quiet and incredibly soothing. "I can't explain that, but it's this place. I know it." He pulled back, and shivered.

I realized I was shivering, too.

He made a sound of concern and went to work on the buttons down the front of my pink, gauzy shirt.

"Hey," I said, holding the material closed, "I can do that."

"Okay." Backing up, he turned away and eyed the couch, no doubt wondering who could possibly sleep there.

Damn, he had a nice back, all smooth and sleek and tanned. Tanned? "When did you get sun?"

"Uh, every day of my life?" He kicked off his shoes. "I swim all day long in the tanks outside, remember?" He went still, and glanced at me over his shoulder, his eyes shadowed from me. "More seeing through stuff?"

I felt my cheeks heat, not because I'd been peeking, but because until now, I'd been mostly peeking south of his tanned back—waaay south.

"You getting into a hot shower?" he asked.

"Um . . ."

"Let me rephrase. You *are* getting into a hot shower."

This assertive Kel was new. "Maybe, things will somehow seem better, or different, when we're warm," he said, slightly less gruffly, but no less forcefully.

I couldn't tear my eyes off him. "Yeah."

"Let's go."

Let's. Yes, let's take a shower.

In fact, the image of just that flitted through my brain and stayed there—thank you so much, my overactive imagination—the two of us together beneath the spray, with Kellan naked and wet and gleaming as he pinned me against the wall to have his merry way with me.

Sexual healing, huh.

Oh boy. In my fantasy, he knew exactly how to sexually heal me. "Kellan?"

"Warm up first." He looked at me, and I had trouble breathing, mostly due to the fact that my cool, calm, laid-back and easygoing Kellan was not so laid-back and calm right now, no matter what his outside appearance said.

This knowledge had not come to me through my mysterious and newfound talent of seeing through things.

Nope, didn't need to see through his jeans to see he was aroused.

I actually had to lift my hand and fan my hot face. "You know what?"

His voice sounded a little gruff. "What?"

"Suddenly I'm warm. Very warm."

Chapter 8

Kellan sighed, and scrubbed a hand over his eyes. "I'm sorry, Rach. It's that kiss. It's messing with my head big time."

There, one of us had said it. Thank God. "The kiss?"

He cut those amazing eyes to me. "You forgot about it?"

Not likely. "No, I've, um, been thinking about it, too." I'd also been thinking about getting another. You know, just to see if it had been a fluke. "And then there was what Axel and Marilee said."

His eyes heated. "About the sex thing?"

I had to clear my throat to answer. "I believe they used the word 'amazing.' The 'amazing' sex thing. But yeah, that."

"Thought you might have been snoozing through that part of the conversation."

"No, I heard."

"Oh." He brushed past me and went into the bathroom. I heard the shower come on, and a moment later he was back, propping a shoulder against the doorway as if he owned it. "I lit some candles. The water's ready for you."

"Kel?"

He looked reluctant to answer. "Yeah?"

"Do you really believe that we're going to find some sort of a wild connection this weekend?"

"Rach, just get in the shower." He definitely didn't want to have this conversation with me, which perversely made me want to have this *exact* conversation.

"Go," he said. *Begged.*

I was doing pretty well without the shower regarding that getting-warm thing. In fact, just looking at his lean, muscular frame made me feel as if I had an inner fire raging. "Kel—"

"Look, I don't really want to talk about any cosmic connection."

"How about wild sex? You want to talk about wild sex?"

"No."

"But I do." I had no idea how those words made it past my inner editor. Oh wait, that's right, I didn't have an inner editor. Still, I usually had *some* pride—meaning I never made the first move on a man, preferring instead to be chased. I stood there a minute, trying to figure out how things had changed.

"Get in the shower, Rach."

"But—"

"Please."

"Fine."

He looked pained at my word choice as I stalked past him into the bathroom. I shut the door and stripped by candlelight, then stepped into the raised bathtub and pulled the curtain around me, reminding myself that, unlike me, Kellan couldn't see through the door or the curtain.

For now, I was utterly alone.

And because I was, maybe I could allow myself a few tears. Unfortunately, I wasn't one of those women who cried easily or well. I certainly didn't look good while doing it. My eyes always got all puffy, my nose ran unattractively and my cheeks became blotchy. Now was no different as I stood beneath the steady stream of hot water and let the pity party begin.

I sniffed noisily, then went still as I felt a whisper of movement. I stared at the shiny pink vinyl shower curtain surrounding me, then through it to the mirror on the wall reflecting my own astonished face right back at me, my hair plastered to my head, my wide, tear-reddened eyes. And then my eyes went even wider as I figured out what the sound had been.

Kellan opening the door. "Rach?"

I squeaked, then realized that while I could see him, he could not yet see me, since he hadn't gotten hit by lightning. I slapped my hand over my mouth to keep back any telltale sounds that might escape, like the remaining sob.

But he was looking right at me. Or at the curtain. I shrank back until my spine and butt touched the icy tiles, making me jump at the unexpected goosing. "Get out!"

"Rach."

I pointed at him, even though he couldn't yet see me. It didn't matter. I still felt like I was naked in front of a crowd. *"Out."*

He gave a low shake of his head, and with a frustrated sob, I whirled away so I couldn't see him, hugging myself tightly beneath the blast of hot water.

I felt another shifting of the cool air, and then the curtain was swept aside, and I squealed again, whipping back around. My quick movement sprayed Kellan with water right in the face.

"*Get out!*" I said.

"Are you crying?"

I swiped angrily at my eyes. *Had he even noticed I was naked?* "No, I'm not crying! And you're peeking."

But he wasn't peeking at all. He was looking directly into my eyes, his own full of things that made more tears leak out of mine.

Damn it.

"You are," he said, and clamped his hands down over my wrists, tugging me toward him. "You're crying."

"I'm going to be screaming in a minute," I promised, trying

to pull free to no avail. The hands that held me captive so easily were large and callused, and I liked the feel of them—too much—so I struggled to get loose before I lost all pride and threw myself against him.

"Christ." The word seemed to slip out of him as he tried to hold onto me without actually touching me. I realized how I must look—wet, soaped up, naked . . .

And yeah, he'd definitely noticed the naked part.

Through his drenched clothing, I could see his heart quicken, his abs tighten. I could sense the rush of blood to places that weren't thinking about the lightning or my new eyesight, or anything but this—just the two of us. "Go away," I whispered, thinking, *Don't do it; don't really go.*

Eyes dark—so very dark—he gently squeezed my bare hips. "It's going to be okay, Rach. I promise you."

At that, I felt a rush of new tears. "That's a promise you can't keep," I whispered.

"No, I keep all my promises. You know I do."

It was true. From the promise in first grade to hold my hand at the school's haunted house, to the one just last week to come here with me, and to all the promises in between, he'd never once failed me. "I'm okay," I said, and he slowly nodded.

"Yeah, you are."

I became incredibly aware of the steam rising around us, of the water hitting the tiles, of the way his clothes had become wet and plastered to his body.

"Kel?"

He blinked water out of his eyes. "Yeah?"

"I'm naked."

He finally let his gaze slip then, let it run over my body, from head to toe, and then back up again, his only obvious reaction a tightening of his fingers on my hips.

And suddenly I no longer felt like crying. "*Really* naked."

"I know," he whispered, his voice husky and thick.

"And you're not."

Gaze still on mine, he pulled the sweatshirt over his head. His wet hair stuck straight up, which he ignored as he kicked off a shoe, then the sock. His other shoe wouldn't come off, and he swore, breaking eye contact to bend and fumble with the wet, knotted laces. Finally he sent that shoe flying over his shoulder. It smashed into something on the counter behind him, and something hit the floor with a loud clatter.

He sent me an endearingly self-conscious smile.

I laughed, then gulped, as I let myself soak him up, my gaze trailing over his ribs, his abs and all those tightly defined muscles where his wet jeans sagged low. I wanted to kiss him there. Hell, I wanted to spread him on a damn cracker. I wanted—"You," I breathed. "I want you."

His hands stilled on the buttons on his Levi's. "God, I'm an idiot."

"What? Why?"

He backed up, his face tight in a mask of frustration. "I almost forgot."

"Forgot what?"

"This isn't right."

Are you kidding? "Yes, it is."

"No. It's whatever happened to you out there."

"I—"

"Listen to me. You've never wanted me like this before." He cupped my face, his own quiet and unreadable, and I shut my eyes to absorb the feel of his touch. "Just sleep," he said. "In the morning, it'll feel different."

"No, I—"

"Sleep," he repeated, and I felt his lips brush my temple.

I wanted to pull him against me, have him fulfill my shower fantasy. That would help dispel the fear, I was sure of it. But when I opened my eyes, he was gone.

I stood there for a few more minutes. *Slumped* there, actually, against the wall, in sudden exhaustion. Finally I got out and managed to wrap my hair in one towel, my body in another.

Kel was waiting for me, but not like I wanted—needed. "Lie down." He pointed to the bed as he passed me to take his turn in the shower. "Rest. I'll be quick."

But he wasn't quick enough, because in spite of myself, I was out like a light before my head even hit the pillow.

I woke up some time later in the pitch dark and have to admit to letting out a very childish whimper. I was still wrapped in the towels, but I was totally and completely alone in the bed and so chilled that I could hardly feel my toes or fingers.

There was only one thing worse than that: knowing that the cookies were in the inn waiting for me. Climbing out of the bed, I moved to the doorway of the living room and wondered where my flashlight was. Then I remembered. I didn't need it. I focused, and saw right through the dark. Kellan wasn't on the couch, and my heart stopped.

What if I'd scared him off, and he'd left? What if it wasn't the cookies all alone, but me?

Then I saw the long, lean length of him sprawled out on the throw rug in front of the couch, and I nearly collapsed in relief. He hadn't left me. He'd only moved to the floor, which must have been more comfortable than the Victorian couch.

I wished he'd have come to me. I'd have moved over for him in a heartbeat. I'd even have given him half my pillow, the ultimate sacrifice. Hell, for some of that delicious warmth I knew his body held, he could have had the entire pillow.

Motivated by my icy toes, I moved a little closer. He was flat on his back, one arm flung wide, the other over his eyes, his biceps taut and making my tummy taut, too. The blanket covered him up to his chin, but that was no deterrent for me and my X-ray vision.

I knew it was wrong, but I focused, and peeked. He wasn't wearing a shirt.

He wasn't wearing his jeans either.

Oh my.

All he had on was a pair of dark blue knit boxers, which meant they clung nicely to every little nuance of his body, and trust me, there was nothing "little" to be seen. I took a moment to think about all the things I could do with him in that position, sprawled out like some sort of fantasy treat.

Shame on me.

He wasn't snoring, which was good, but breathing deeply and slowly. His hair had fallen in his face as usual, and he hadn't shaved in a few days now. The thought of that stubbled jaw running over my skin made me tingle.

I realized I was starting to warm up very nicely. This time, I wouldn't give him a chance to think too much. "Kel?"

"Hmm?" he answered automatically, apparently still out cold, because he didn't so much as budge.

"*Kel.*"

"He's sleeping," he whispered.

"I know. I'm sorry."

Kel lowered the arm from over his eyes, and he stared blindly into the dark, clearly unable to see me. "Rach?"

Well, who else? The boogeyman? "Yeah."

He sat straight up, his expression unreadable. Blind, he reached out with his hands, coming into contact with my thigh, reminding me that while I could see everything, he could not. His brow shot up at the feel of my bare skin, and his fingers spread wide, as if to touch as much of me as he could.

Suddenly the towel didn't seem like much coverage at all.

"You okay?" he asked, his voice lower and thicker, and not from sleep, but from desire. Or so I hoped. I took my gaze on a little tour beneath his blanket and saw that I was right. He was excited.

"Nothing's wrong. I got cold."

"You need to get sleep," he said in direct opposition to what his fingers were saying, stroking my skin. I was still standing, so his hand was level with my belly.

The muscles there quivered.

His fingers were stroking up and down my legs now, his hair brushing against the towel at my middle. "Mmm," escaped me before I could help myself.

"Rach." His fingers tightened on me. "Sleep. You need sleep."

"Not tired."

"What then?"

What indeed? I knew exactly what. Possibly, I'd known from the moment I'd woken up after the lightning.

In the charged silence, he swallowed hard. "Rach."

"Kel," I answered and with a groan, he shifted even closer and, if I wasn't mistaken, inhaled deeply.

"Did you just . . . sniff me?"

"No. *Yes.*" He closed his eyes. "I didn't mean to. You smell good."

"Do I?"

"Yes," he said, sounding miserable. "I'm sorry you're cold, but you need to go back to bed. Like five minutes ago."

"Kel?"

"Yeah?"

I dropped my towel. Since it pooled over the hands he still had on my thighs, he knew what I'd done even though he couldn't see me, and he sucked in a harsh breath. "Rach, *no*—"

I leaned over until his lips were an inch from mine. "Are you going to fight me, Kel?"

"Oh God."

"Do you have a condom?"

He groaned again, and put his forehead to my bare belly.

"Condom, Kel."

"I don't have one." He let out a half-laugh, half-groan, his mouth brushing my hip. "I didn't think I'd need—"

"I have one. In my bag."

"Oh God," he said again.

I backed out of his grasp and made my way back to the bedroom. When I returned, he was sitting in the dark, blanket pooled in his lap, hair wildly mussed, looking befuddled and adorably sexy.

And aroused. "Am I dreaming?" he asked.

Laughing softly, I dropped the condom next to him. "If you're dreaming, then so am I. Let's not wake up."

"Rach—"

I dropped to my knees and pressed my torso to his. "The rest of this is such a nightmare, Kel. Let's at least make this part of the dream good."

With a rough groan, he wrapped his arms around me and buried his face in my hair. A sweet gesture in complete opposition to the impressive erection pressing into my belly. I think I actually whimpered at the feel of it digging into me. I couldn't help it. The feel of his bare chest against mine, his thighs tense, and in between them . . . All I could think was, *Hurry, God, hurry.*

But there was no hurrying Kellan. He was savoring me, stretching me out on the rug, touching every inch of me, lingering over each step, when I just wanted the final bang. Damn it, I needed to unleash him somehow, to make him, I don't know, primitive and wild, so that he'd lift me up and slam me against the wall, so he'd take me with a desperation and a hunger that knew no boundaries.

Yeah, now *that* would make me feel better.

He kissed me, and I sighed in pleasure, because he was so good at that part. For a guy *I'd* had to seduce, he'd jumped right in, kissing me every bit as hungrily as I kissed him. And then in the blink of an eye, his boxers vanished. Eyes glittering, he came down over the top of me, taking my hands in his, stretching them over my head . . .

Oh boy. "Um—"

"Shh," said the formerly mild-mannered Kellan McInty. He stared down at me, probably somewhat adjusted to the dark now, eyeing me sprawled out under his scorching hot gaze. "Are you ready for me?"

In answer, I arched up.

He put on the condom, then used a leanly muscled thigh to spread mine, stroking his hand down my exposed body. He slid two fingers inside me, making me gasp in pleasure and writhe for more, sheer sensual pleasure zinging through me.

"Yeah, you're ready," he said on a rough breath. Planting his hands on either side of my head, he braced his weight above me, arms trembling.

"Hurry, Kel."

He let out a short, unsteady laugh. "Yeah, that might not be a problem." Leaning in, he sank his teeth into the crook of my neck just as he thrust inside me, large and thick, with the exact right amount of rough.

I cried out and wriggled my hips for more, but he held me still with a grip of steel.

"Hold on." His teeth grated together. "Just . . . hold on a minute."

I spared a thought to wonder what I'd done with my easy-going Kellan McInty, because the guy towering over me, pressing me down with his weight, holding me where he wanted me, an edgy light in his eyes, was as far away from that guy as possible.

He pulsed inside of me, and I pulled my legs back and arched up.

"Don't move. *God*, don't even breathe."

I tried—I really did—but it was like what I'd been taught in every science class I'd ever had. The more effort I put into not moving, the more difficult it became. I couldn't regulate my breathing; I sounded ragged and out of control to my own ears. I couldn't stay still either; I just couldn't get over the feel of him, thick and hard and silky smooth inside of me, and I lifted my hips for more.

"Fuck," he said, sounding strained. "Oh fuck." And he began to move, slowly at first, but that didn't last, because I sank my nails into him, making him thrust deeply, bumping me up against the couch. But it was worth the rug burns, because his movements were sending shock waves of pleasure through me.

I bit his throat, and he groaned, sinking his fingers into my hair, tugging my head back, until I had no choice but to stare up at him, utterly imprisoned by his piercing, startlingly clear eyes.

"Rach . . ."

I already knew. He was gone, completely gone, and I couldn't tear my eyes off him. It was as if I couldn't just *see* into him, but I could also *hear* his thoughts, which were filled with me, with this, with what else he wanted to do to me . . . and how this was different for him than it'd ever been before.

Or was that *my* thought?

Oh God. It was mine. And it *was* different than it'd ever been with anyone else: deeper, stronger, *more.* Somehow so much, much more.

And as I stared up at him, aroused beyond belief, too stunned to speak, he somehow managed to smile down at me, and I thought, *Yeah, it's going to be okay. He's going to make it okay.*

And he did.

Oh, how he did.

I woke up slowly, stiff and desperate for caffeine, but that was nothing new. When I was growing up, my mother used to throw a pillow at me from the doorway of my bedroom and then bolt, leaving me to wake up slowly and alone, like I always seemed to need to do.

But I wasn't at my mother's house. I was as far from home as I'd ever been. And remembering, I sat straight up in the narrow antique bed of Gert's bedroom. The clock was blinking, so I knew the power had come back on. I looked up, startled by my own reflection in the antique mirror above the dresser.

Not a pretty sight, I can tell you that. Why was it that, no matter what the situation—and great sex the night before was one of the better situations I could think of—I still looked like death warmed over when I woke up? "Kel?"

No answer.

I slid out of the bed and realized I was naked. There was a towel on the floor, the one that had been on my head. I wrapped it around me and lifted a hand to my hair. Since I'd slept on it wet, I now resembled Little Richard. Perfect.

"*Kel?*"

The no-answer thing was sending little tendrils of panic down my spine because Kellan *was* a morning person, and always had been.

I ran to the bedroom doorway. The blanket was still on the floor, but there was no Kel.

He wasn't in the tiny postage stamp of a kitchen either. Feeling a bit like Alice falling down the rabbit hole, I hauled open the front door to yell for him, but that turned out to be unnecessary.

He stood on the bottom step, shoulder propping up the post, sipping at a mug, watching the sun rise over the line of trees. I caught him in profile, disgustingly alert and clear-eyed. His hair curled over his ears, past the nape of his neck. He wore a ragged old T-shirt and sweatpants that hung temptingly low on his hips, the drawstring barely knotted. Beneath those sweats, his body was hard and perfect, and after last night, I knew just how hard parts of him could be, and also exactly how perfect.

The rest of him was pretty damn fantastic as well.

So ridiculously relieved to see him, I went running out the door, ignoring that it slammed behind me as I leaped down the steps. I executed a little twirl to face him, relieved beyond belief. "We're even now, because you just shaved ten years off my life," I announced, then shivered in the chilly morning air. "Guess that sexual healing thing is dead on, huh?"

He didn't answer.

Oh boy. Awkward-morning-after alert. "I sure could use some caffeine."

He looked at my hair. "You need more than caffeine."

"Okay, so I need a brush, too."

"You really think that's going to help?"

"Funny." It wasn't fair that I looked like something that needed to be dragged to the curb, and he looked mouth-watering. He smelled good, too, damn it. But I shoved back the lust attack and got a grip. I adjusted my towel, and wished for clean clothes. Clean, *warm* clothes.

The morning was chilly enough to remind me that I wore nothing but a towel. In the light of day, the woods seemed just as close and impenetrable as they had last night, but a little less scary, thankfully.

Kellan didn't move, just stood there in the bright morning sun, his gaze on the towel that I was adjusting.

Or, more specifically, on me in the towel.

I was more than a little chilled in the sharp air, but at the heat that flared in his gaze, I once again began to warm up nicely. Odd that this strange, almost chemical-like attraction I had going for him hadn't resolved itself overnight. Odd and new. I had no idea whether it was the Alaskan air or the fact that, hello, he was damn fine to look at. Or maybe more than just my eyes had gone whacko out here in this high-altitude air. But all I could think was, *Was he up for round two?*

"You okay?" I asked.

"That was going to be my question to you." Setting his mug on the railing, he put his hands on my arms and rubbed them slowly up and down.

Mmm, now see, there was a nice way to assuage the morning-after awkwardness.

"Where are your clothes?" he asked.

"I forgot to put them on."

His mouth quirked. "My lucky day."

There he was, the funny, easygoing Kellan I knew. The men in my life tended to fall into two categories: those who sneaked out by dawn's light and those who wanted one more round before sneaking out.

Unfortunately for Kellan, there was nowhere to sneak to. For either of us.

Which left us in this awkward territory. We'd slept together. Actually, there'd been no real sleeping involved, and just thinking about it made me need to fan my face again. I shivered.

Mistaking the movement for a chill, he turned us toward the guest house and leaned past me to open the door.

It was locked.

"Kel," I said, fascinated by the muscles rippling across his shoulders and back. "Um, about last night."

"Huh," he said to the locked door, and tried again.

"Kel?"

He grunted, fiddling with the handle.

"I, um, hope it's not going to be awkward," I said. "Because that would be awful, you know?"

Ignoring me entirely, he tried the window, which was also locked.

"Stay here," he said. "I'll go to the inn and get a key."

"Right." I nodded agreeably. "I'll just stand here by myself, bear bait, in only a towel."

He looked me over. "I'll hurry."

"You never hurry."

He actually smiled. "I will this time."

I crossed my arms and blocked his path. "Last night. I want to talk about last night."

He made a face, like I'd made him taste bad medicine. Or Marilee's sauce. "Do we have to?"

This was new. Me being the one to want to talk. "Yes!"

He sighed. "Okay. Go ahead."

"All right." I looked at him, thrown unexpectedly off balance. "I don't want it to stand in the way of our friendship."

"Our one-night stand, you mean?"

"Yes."

He turned away from me and headed down the stairs. "No worries, Rach."

No? So why was I suddenly worrying even more? "Kel?"

"I'll be right back."

"But . . ." I bit my lip, trying hard not to say, "Please don't leave me out here."

Still, it must have been all over my face, because he sighed again and, coming back, pulled his T-shirt off over his head. Handing it to me, he said, "Here."

I scrambled into it gratefully, my body absorbing his heat, his scent, as the material fell to my mid-thigh. I nearly pressed the material to my face for more of his delicious scent, but I managed to control myself. "What about your sweats?"

"Keeping those on," he said.

"You're no fun."

"Wait here."

With that, he jogged off the steps and toward the B and B. Which was how I ended up standing there for the longest five minutes of my life.

I know it was five minutes because I counted.

At thirty, a bird squawked so loudly I nearly screamed.

At fifty-five, a squirrel dashed in front of me, chattering, nearly putting me into heart failure.

I got to three hundred twenty before Kellan showed back up. "What took so long?" I demanded, for once unimpressed by his half-naked state.

He held out his empty hands, perplexed and irritated, a rare look for him. "The inn's locked, too, which is weird, because I was just there."

"Locked?"

"Yeah."

"I thought Marilee gave you coffee."

"Axel did. He told me Marilee's coffee would burn a hole through my esophagus, and that his was far better, but I wasn't to tell her."

"What about the guns? Did you ask about the guns?"

"Gert never let anyone in her place, right?"

"Right."

"So telling them about the guns she kept there seemed unwise." He glanced back at Hideaway. "But why is the place locked up tighter than a drum, with no signs of life?"

Feeling very naked, I wrapped my arms around myself. "So I guess it's true then."

"What?"

"I'm really in the Twilight Zone. Without underwear. It's like every bad nightmare I've ever had."

Chapter 9

Locked out. I put my forehead to the front window, caressed at every movement by Kellan's shirt. "Kel? Remember that time in college when we played Truth or Dare?"

He moved behind me, rattling the front-door handle. "No."

"Yes, you do. Dot and I dared you to strip naked and run around the perimeter of the house, and you did, and then we locked you out. Remember now?"

He sighed. "Trying hard not to."

"You banged on the door, bare-ass naked, and then we flipped on the porch light, and all the neighbors came out. Someone took pics, and they ended up on the bulletin board in the coffee shop."

"I remember," he said tightly, rattling the window. "Is there a caboose to this story?"

"I was just going to say that suddenly I know how you felt."

"Are *you* butt-ass naked? With laughter ringing in your ears and light bulbs flicking on?" He peered in the window. "No, you are not."

I grinned.

"Yeah, you did that then, too," he said, and shook his head.

"Not at you. I didn't laugh at you."

"Oh yeah, you did."

"Okay, I did." I laughed now, too. I couldn't help it. He was pretty adorable over there, pouting.

"Damn," he said softly, his gaze holding mine.

"What?"

"Nothing."

But it had been something, and I had a feeling, given that he was watching my mouth, that it had to do with my smile. But before I could say anything, he turned away, again rattling the door handle.

Still locked.

"I'm going to break it."

"You can't break a door handle," I said. "You'd have to be Superman." I had my eyes closed again, my forehead to the window. I was pretending I was on a cruise to . . . somewhere warm, maybe the Bahamas. Yeah, that worked. With a hot sun and cute waiters carrying trays of goodies like—like *Girl Scout Cookies*.

At the sudden sound of wood cracking, I lifted my head.

And then gasped.

Kellan stood there holding the doorknob in his hand, staring at the hole he'd left in the door, looking a little unnerved.

"My God," I whispered. "How did you—"

"Don't know."

"Are you—" His hand was bleeding. "Kellan, are you all right?"

"Fine," he said tersely, and pushing open the door, he gestured me in.

"Your hand—"

"Just a scratch."

"The door—"

"Rach, just get inside."

I crossed the threshold and went directly to the six-pack of water on the coffee table before remembering that I hadn't been able to open one the night before.

Kellan reached past me, tore the first water out and opened

it without any effort at all. He handed it to me, looking a little bit sweaty and a whole lot tough.

Wow. He really had it going on. I still didn't get how I'd never noticed before.

Oh boy. Was I slow, or what?

In the guise of giving myself a minute, I drank half the bottle, then swiped my mouth and stared at him. "You were hit, too," I said with remarkable calm, given that my heart had just bounced off my other internal organs with the impact of a freight train. "We were both hit, and we were both changed."

He opened his mouth, but at that exact moment, Marilee—tall and lush and darkly gorgeous in black jeans and boots, and a black beaded leather jacket—appeared in the doorway.

"Morning," she said, and held out a steaming mug for me, not even blinking at the fact that I wore nothing but Kel's T-shirt and a towel.

Or that there was a brand-new hole in the door of her dead employer's private quarters.

She didn't acknowledge any of that because her eyes had locked on Kellan. Specifically, on the fact that his loose sweats hung low on his hips, and that he wore nothing else on his fabulous, mouth-watering body. She let out a slow smile as she leaned with easy negligence against the jamb, acting like sex on a platter, when only yesterday she'd completely ignored him.

Prelightning.

Presexual healing.

This made me mad, and it had little to do with the green-eyed monster.

Okay, it had everything to do with jealousy.

Marilee put her hands on her hips and thrust out her perfect breasts a little, demanding all eyes on her.

I would have liked to compete with that, but I was also still stunned over the realization that Kellan had been hiding a little secret.

A *big* secret.

"Where were you just now?" Kellan asked Marilee, and if I hadn't been so blindsided by his secret, I'd have fallen a little in love with him on the spot for not noticing Marilee eating him up. "The B&B was locked, and you didn't answer the door."

"I was busy," she said with apology but no excuse.

"We got locked out," he said.

"And the windows were locked, too," I said. "So he had to—"

Kellan shook his head at me. He didn't want me to mention the breaking-the-door thing. But if she so much as looked, surely she'd see the gaping hole.

"They were painted shut," Marilee said, not taking her eyes off him. "Don't feel bad. No human could have opened one."

I wrapped my chilled fingers around the steaming mug she'd handed me and considered different ways to get her to stop drooling. Strangling her seemed like a good option.

Apparently not much of a mind reader, Marilee moved toward Kellan and the couch, as if yesterday had never happened.

But no one messed with Kellan's head. Well, no one but me, damn it. Secrets or not, hot or not, Kellan was mine. I put down the mug. According to Axel, I wouldn't want to drink it anyway.

Before I could step between the two of them, Marilee put her hands on Kel's shoulders and rubbed. "Oooh, you're tense. We have some massage therapy appointments open today, if you'd like one."

And that green-eyed monster bit me hard. The bitch! Those were *my* shoulders to touch, not hers. "Okay," I said grimly, giving Kellan a dirty look. Damn men. They were such stupid, easy creatures, led around by a single appendage, which didn't even have the capacity to think for itself. Honestly, it was a miracle they managed to function on a daily basis. "Thanks for the coffee, but I really have to talk to Kellan now. Privately." I added a smile that could be called such only because I bared my teeth.

Marilee shot me a measuring look, which I returned, probably with some fire added, and she lifted her hands in a little gesture of surrender.

She moved toward the door, making sure to brush against Kel as she did, even stopping to practically purr, just before she pulled out her ace card, which was to stagger slightly, then put her hand to her head, letting out a quivery little sigh and saying, "Oh dear."

Kellan put his hand on her arm. "What? Are you okay?"

"Yes. Yes, of course . . ." But she wavered unsteadily, then fell right against him so that he had no choice but to catch her as her legs buckled. Her eyes rolled up, lashes fluttering, as she began to faint.

What a pathetic, novice move, I thought. Kellan could see right through that fake faint.

But no, his face had gone all tight with concern and worry, and he'd caught her up in his arms. *Clueless!*

I'd have let her head hit the table. "Oh, Axel," I said sweetly but loudly, aiming for the front door. "How lovely to see you this morning."

Marilee bolted upright in Kellan's arms, her gaze darting to the front door.

Which was open, and empty.

My eyebrows shot straight up as I sent Marilee a *top-that-beeyotch* look.

She lifted a shoulder as if to say she'd had to try, then she slid down Kellan's body. With a touch to his jaw, she smiled once more. "I'm okay now, thanks. I feel all better."

Uh-huh. I'll bet.

"You sure?" Kel asked, clearly still concerned.

Unbelievable.

"Oh yes. Really." Marilee smiled. "I'll be in the big house making breakfast."

"Uh . . ." Kel said, clearly remembering her sauce. "Yes."

"Give me about half an hour."

And then she was gone.

"Huh." He scratched his head and turned back to face me, looking like that rumpled, bemused professor again. A rumpled, bemused professor with no shirt and loose sweats slipping down his narrow hips, a gap between the string tie and his flat, firm stomach wide enough to dip a hand in—

My brain was out of control. "That was a fake faint."

"Rach, she was shaking."

"*I'm* shaking."

"You are not."

"Well, I could be."

When he shot me an even, patient look, I lifted my fingers and made then tremor. "See? And oh . . ." With dramatic flair courtesy of freshman high school drama class, I laid the back of my hand across my forehead. "I feel funny . . ."

Kellan's eyes narrowed. "Stop it."

"No, I mean it."

"Rach."

"I'm going to faint, Kel. You'd better catch me." I staggered backwards.

He crossed his arms. "That's not funny."

Damn it, why couldn't he look at *me* with all worry, catching me up against himself, as he had last night?

I wanted more of last night!

Trying for it, I let my momentum take me backwards, confident that he'd catch me.

Only I went down like a ton of bricks, smacking my head on the corner of the coffee table and seeing stars.

Kellan swore sharply and dove for me, firmly scooping me up against his deliriously warm chest, stroking a hand over my face to scoop back my hair, and everything was as I'd wanted before I'd found out that exactly *nothing* was as I'd thought.

Now he'd say how sorry he was. How much more beautiful and smart and wonderful than Marilee I was. And then he'd kiss me . . .

"You idiot," he murmured, and kissed my jaw.

You'd think I'd be happy with one out of three, but no. "You lied to me, Kel."

He didn't pretend not to know what I was talking about. "Didn't lie."

"You omitted."

"Okay, yes. I omitted. How's the head?" He slipped his fingers into my hair, cradling my head in the palm of his hand. "Hurt?"

"A lot. And for the record, omitting is as bad as lying."

He sighed and pulled back, denying me those arms. His hair was all over the place, and now he wore an unreadable expression, one that made me want to turn the clock back to last night, when he'd held me and made everything okay.

He rose to his feet and went straight to the window. He put his hands on the ledge, the muscles in his back and arms going taut as he pulled.

The paint gluing the window to the ledge cracked, and the window opened with ease.

Kellan stood there, utterly still, hands on the window, which was now lifted above his head. With the early morning sun slanting in over his gilded body, he made quite the picture, but that wasn't what had me walking towards him, gently putting my hands on his back.

"Kel."

Head bowed, he was breathing hard, as if he'd run a five-mile race uphill. Beneath my fingers, his body felt overheated and damp from exertion. I examined his hand.

"How bad is it? Are you hurt?"

"It was just a door."

"I meant from yesterday."

"I'm as okay as you are, I suppose."

"When did you figure it out?"

"Last night." He shook his head. "I'm just not quite used to it."

"Which begs the next question," I managed shakily. "Why didn't you tell me?"

He held still for another beat, then turned to face me. "You were a little wigged-out last night."

"So you were what? Trying to protect the little lady?"

"Rach—"

"No, you listen to me. You want me to freak out? Keep stuff like this to yourself. I mean, I can see through stuff, Kel." I let out a disbelieving laugh. "And you . . . you've gone from some mild-mannered and easygoing guy to . . . to Superman, for God's sake. I mean, what the hell?"

He winced at the Superman comment, as I knew he would.

And I could have added that his new strength came with an animalistic sexiness the likes of which I'd never seen before, but that seemed a little too revealing, so I kept that part to myself.

As if he could read my thoughts, he narrowed his eyes and said, "You know, I'm the same guy."

"Are you?"

"Yes! The same Kellan McInty. Nothing inside has changed."

"Okay." I went into the bedroom and grabbed my duffle bag.

Kellan followed me. "I haven't."

I pulled out fresh clothes and headed into the bathroom.

"We need to talk about this," he said to me as I shut the door.

In his face. Childish, I know, but *how could he have kept this from me*?

He knocked. "Rach?"

I turned away, and cranked on the shower. There. Could hardly hear a thing now, which suited me.

"Rach?" he called through the door. "I know you can hear me."

When I didn't answer, he turned the door handle.

Crap.

Leaping toward the door, I quickly locked it, not that *that* would stop Superman.

Satisfied at his silence, I eyed myself in the mirror. Huh. I looked the same as I had before coming into the Twilight Zone. Same brown wavy hair that always vaguely resembled a squirrel's tail when the air was dry, and it was very dry at the moment. Same eyes that needed mascara to look halfway good, but the mascara right now was somewhere in one of my two bags and not on my eyes.

I'd been told I had an okay mouth, but I didn't see it, mostly because it was down-turned at the moment.

Finally I gave up trying to see anything different, and I dropped both Kel's shirt and my towel to the floor and, naked, stepped toward the steaming shower—

Just as Kellan broke the lock on the door.

I put my hands on my hips. "*Hey!*"

"Oh, that's right," he said, sporting a new and oddly arousing bad attitude as he eyed me up and down, reminding me that I stood there in my birthday suit and all its glory. "Voyeurism is *your* specialty."

Oh boy.

Apparently, this was going to be a hell of a long few days.

Chapter 10

With some dramatic flair, I whipped the shower curtain closed. *There.* Now I could see him standing there, projecting a toughness that I had to admit was giving me a vicarious thrill, but he couldn't see me.

Fix that, Superman.

I did my business with the soap, enjoying the fact that Kellan was on the other side of the curtain imagining what I was doing.

Which didn't make any sense, because I was mad at him.

Wasn't I?

Hell, I didn't really know anything anymore except that I'd never been more exhausted, confused or frightened in all my life. Fact was, even though I was an artist, I still enjoyed logic.

And there was *nothing* logical about anything that had happened since the moment I had stepped onto that plane heading out of L.A.

Probably the worst part of all of it was that for as long as I could remember, Kellan had always been a rock. All the way back in kindergarten, he'd been dependable. Reliable. There for me to count on.

And now . . . now he was keeping secrets, which made me wary and . . . sad. I was sad.

How could he have kept it from me?

And that he'd managed to do so scared me most of all. And when I got scared, I tended to get pissy. Not particularly proud of that fact, but there it was.

P-I-S-S-Y.

I heard the bathroom door shut, and I knew he'd left.

Good.

Fine.

Damn it. How typical of a man, running from conflict. Never mind that I'd run first.

I turned off the shower and rung as much water from my hair as possible. I wished for a deep conditioner, but decided the hell with it. I'd just have squirrel-tail hair for the duration. Finally I opened the curtain, and let out a surprised squeak.

Kellan hadn't left.

Nope, he was leaning against the door, arms and legs crossed in a casual pose that did not come close to matching the extremely *un*casual look on his face.

A part of me tightened. The part with all the erogenous zones. The part that I didn't want to acknowledge, because I really wanted to hold on to my pissiness for a bit longer.

His hair was sticking up, probably courtesy of frustrated fingers. His jaw was tight, scruffy. His long, rangy body practically shimmered with tension.

Or maybe that was a lingering effect from the nice bolt of lightning he'd taken on, a fact that made me mad all over again.

"I was going to tell you, damn it," he said.

"Oh my God. Can you read my mind, too?" I asked in horror.

"No, it's just all over your face." His face grim, he tossed me a towel. "Hurry."

"Why? Do you have another revelation for me?"

"Jesus, let it go. No, no more revelations. But whatever you seem to think, I'm a regular guy, Rach, and you're standing there naked and gorgeous and oblivious. And if you aren't more careful, I'm going to—" At that, he clamped his mouth shut. A muscle twitched in his jaw.

"You're going to what?" I wrapped the towel around myself and lifted my head, inexplicably breathless for his answer.

He still hadn't put on a shirt. His sweats were no barrier to my new eyesight. He was aroused—hugely so—and it made me tingle. A lot.

He muttered something as he pushed away from the door, something that sounded like "You're a fucking fool, McInty." And then he was in front of me, yanking on my towel, tossing it over his shoulder, pushing me back into the shower and cranking the water on again, so that like last night, it rained down over us.

The bathroom was still steamy, and with his hot body pressing me back against the wall, all I could see was his eyes, glittering with intent. I blinked through the water and stared at him, mesmerized by his strength, by his intensity, by the utter alpha-ness he'd never possessed before yesterday's lightning bolt.

"What did you just say?" he asked hoarsely.

Had I spoken out loud? I hated when that happened. Shaking my head, I slid my arms around his neck, hitching myself up so that my legs could wrap around his hips and—

But breathing raggedly, he pulled away.

I tried not to cry from the loss. "I thought you were going to—"

"Say it again."

"That I thought you were going to—"

"The other part," he grated out. "You said you're mesmerized by my strength, my intensity, my—" He broke off, then winced, looking a little embarrassed. "My alpha-ness."

I crossed my arms. He looked at my breasts, plumped up by my stance, which elicited a darkly erotic sound from his throat, which in turn caused an answering tug deep in my womb.

"You said I'd never possessed any of that before the lightning bolt," he said thickly. He hadn't moved toward me again, though the water was hitting him at chest level, running down his body, soaking into the sweats, which had to be damned uncomfortable now.

"I didn't mean—"

"Yes, you did." Shaking his head, he stayed just out of reach. "This . . . this heat between us." He shoved his fingers through his hair, and turned away. "It's because of what happened here. The lightning, or whatever it was."

"You are not walking away from me in this shower for the second time."

But he didn't come back. The water sluiced over his broad shoulders and back, down all that sleek sinew, and then he stepped out of the shower, dripping bad attitude and water everywhere as he went.

"You are," I said in shock. "You're walking away from me in the shower for the second time."

But I was talking to myself. I dried off and dressed, then with no small amount of bad attitude myself, I entered the living room. Kellan was dressed in his beloved old Levi's and a T-shirt, and was pacing by the broken front door.

"Finally," he groused. "Let's get a move on." Then he walked out the door.

Gee, sorry, Rach. Sorry that I didn't trust you. Sorry that I hurt your feelings. Sorry I left you hot and bothered.

"Where are we going?" I asked.

"What, you can't see the thoughts in my brain?"

Okay, he was definitely still attitude-ridden. "No. But actually . . ." I forced him to a stop, and pulled him around to face me, having to tip my head way up to look into his eyes, because he was trying to avoid me. "We should talk about this."

"Which part? The weird tendency you have for X-ray vision, mine to put my hands through things or your temporarily lusting after me?"

I swallowed. "That last one. You're . . . lusting, too."

"But my lusting isn't anything new, Rach."

Oh boy. I had no idea what to say to that.

Kellan waited, one hundred eighty pounds of edgy, unhappy, sexy-as-hell male.

"Kel—"

"You know what?" he interrupted. "Let's not talk." Turning, he headed toward the big house, where lo and behold, the back door wasn't locked. "Of course not," he muttered, and glanced back at me. "Stay close."

Oh yeah, I planned on staying close.

We entered the kitchen. Axel was sitting on the counter in the same pose we'd found him in yesterday, chanting "ohhhmmm" and occasionally stopping to reach for a steaming mug near his hip.

We hadn't been particularly quiet when entering, so he had to know we were there, but he didn't stop his chant.

"*Dude*," Kellan finally said.

Axel turned, the tassels from his hat smacking him in the face as he smiled broadly. "Dudes."

The normal Kellan would have smiled back, patient and easygoing, but this Kellan had run out of patience. "What's going on?"

Axel blinked. "Well, I was just about to come and get the two of you to take you fly-fishing. You can't come to Alaska and not go fly-fishing."

Fly-fishing? I pictured guts on a hook, and shuddered. "I really don't think—"

"Go with that." Axel hopped off the counter. "That's the beauty of fly-fishing. You don't think; you clear your mind. It brings you peace, and all that."

"What we want is answers," Kellan said.

Axel nodded. "Yep. And answers. Fishing can get you all kinds of answers, trust me. Stay there. I'll be right back."

And he walked off.

I looked at Kellan.

He looked at me.

"This is crazy," I said. "I don't know how to fish. Do you?"

"You wanted to learn new things."

"Yes, but I was thinking spa-treatment new things."

"He said there are answers out there. I intend to get them," Kel said grimly. "And I'd really like it if you were with me so I wouldn't have to worry about what you were getting into while I was gone."

Before I could retort to that, Axel came back into the kitchen, now sporting a khaki vest with a ton of pockets and carrying three fishing rods and a small case.

Thanks to my super vision, I could see all sorts of things in that case, including hooks and, ick, something that looked like it might be . . . flies.

Double-ick.

"Let's go." Axel pulled open the back door. We followed him, right up to the woods, and stopped.

Axel looked back at us. "It's not far. Just back where Jack left you off."

That quarter-mile trek had seemed like at least two hundred miles. And then there was the lightning problem. I looked up. No clouds.

Marilee stuck her head out the back door. "Where are you guys going?"

"Fly-fishing," Axel said.

A long glance was exchanged between Axel and Marilee.

"Stay on the trail," Marilee said firmly, mostly to Axel. "You have your map?"

Axel slapped his hip pocket, frowned, then slapped his back pockets and frowned some more.

With a sigh, Marilee came down the steps and walked up to him. She barely came to his shoulder. She tapped a finger over his left pec.

Paper crinkled.

Axel grinned.

Marilee rolled her eyes and started to turn away, but Axel grabbed her hand, still smiling down into her face. "I knew it was there."

"Sure you did."

"Maybe," he said, leaning in just a little, his gaze roaming over her face as if he wanted to memorize it, "maybe I just wanted you to touch me."

Marilee laughed as she planted her hand on his chest and shoved, sending him staggering back a few feet. She whirled away to hide her smile, hair flying around her head like a halo of silk as her hips swayed with her graceful, feminine walk.

I wondered if my hips swayed like that, but I had to doubt it. When I was at work usually I wore a tool belt with paintbrushes hanging down, slapping against my butt and thighs. Hard to sway gracefully under those conditions.

"Stay safe," Marilee called out.

"Yeah." Axel rubbed his chest and watched her go. "You, too."

"Why wouldn't she be safe here at the inn?" I asked.

"Because it's the in-between. Never all the way safe in the in-between."

Kellan and I looked at each other. "Um, *what*?" I asked.

Axel jumped a little, as if realizing what he'd just said. Then he let out one of his low easy laughs. "Oh, listen to me rattle on. Keep up now."

He started walking down that trail we'd trudged up only yesterday. That time, my biggest worry had been carrying our stuff. Now . . . I glanced up at the sky again. Still pure azure.

I hoped it stayed that way.

After a few minutes, Axel stopped, and pulled the map out of his breast pocket.

Uh-oh. Bad sign that he needed the map already.

"Marilee drew this for me," Axel said. "And also this." He flipped the map over and began to read. "Alaska is a land of immense beauty and diversity. Behind us, you'll see dramatic capped mountains. Follow me for a morning of fly-fishing that will be an unforgettable experience." He looked up. "Damn, I was supposed to read that part before we left the B&B."

"How about info on *other* areas," Kellan said.

"By the water," Axel said, then began moving down the trail again. "It's peaceful there."

Kel's expression said he'd find peace wringing Axel's neck.

I had to admit, I felt the same way. "Axel—"

"Hang on. Almost there."

Indeed, within another few moments, we were back on the banks of the river where Jack had left us yesterday. The water rushed over the rocks and sediment, glinting in the sun, steaming into the early air. If I hadn't been so on edge with all that was happening, I might have actually stood there in awe of the beauty around us.

Axel handed Kel a fishing rod.

"I want answers, Axel."

Axel patted him on the shoulder. "All in good time, dude." He also handed me a rod, which might as well have been a power tool, for all I knew what to do with it.

"Now," Axel said. "Putting on the flies."

"No," I said, and shook my head. "No torturing flies for me, thanks."

Axel laughed, then pushed us down to sit on the rocks along the shore. "Not real ones. Look." He pulled out handmade "flies," and I had to admit, their colors and feathers and materials were interesting.

Kellan took a fly and copied Axel, his fingers working deftly, the tendons and cords of muscles on his forearms fascinating me as he applied the same easy concentration that he did to every task he took on.

I tried to do the same, and poked my finger. "Damn it."

Axel laughed. "Don't rush it, dudette."

Easy for him to say. He never rushed anything. I tried again. Another stab into my finger. "Damn it!"

"Here." Kellan took over, doing it the way Axel had showed us, his head bent, the material of his shirt stretched taut across his shoulders, his arm brushing mine. "See, like this." He turned his head and caught me staring at him, caught me thinking, *Even though you make me mad and sad and crazy, omigod I want you.*

So much . . .

"Here." He handed me back the rod.

I looked down at the feathery fly. "Pretty."

Both men laughed, united for that one moment in my ridiculousness. Kellan was smiling at me in a way that started my heart beating faster, and when I dropped my gaze, I could see that his heart had sped up, too. In complete opposition to that, time seemed to come to a stop, and for that one lovely beat, I had the most inane thought.

It was going to be okay.

Somehow, despite everything and the insanity that went with it, it was going to be okay, because Kellan was here, and he would make it so.

Or so I could only hope.

Chapter 11

"Okay, dude and dudette, it's easy stuff. Angling is all in the flick of your wrist, see?" Axel demonstrated with his fishing rod, winging his pretty fly and line way out into the water. "Let's get some dinner for tonight."

Kellan went next, and with little-to-no effort, sent his fly and line sailing out like Axel's.

On my first try, I caught the seat of my own pants. While Kellan nearly busted a gut over that one, I tried again, and then snagged his shirt, which was an accident.

Mostly.

On my next try, I did get the fly into the water, but it caught on something, and when I tugged, the only thing that moved was me, toward the river. I'd have fallen on my ass if Kellan hadn't snagged me by the back of my shirt and held me up.

"Thanks," I said. "That was a little scary."

Kel shook his head. "Rach, your entire life is scary."

Axel had moved down the bank a bit, giving us some privacy. We were standing pretty close, and Kel was still holding onto my shirt. His hair was falling into his eyes as always, and without thinking, I reached up and pushed it back. He caught my hand in his, and looking pained, leaned in. Eyes open, on mine, he shook his head, and then kissed me.

Oh yeah. That worked for me. And when his tongue touched mine, every erogenous zone in my body perked up and stood at attention.

Then he let go, and turned away.

It took me a moment to get my brain to click back on. "What was that for?"

"I don't know."

"You don't know?"

"No!"

I studied his face, filled with carefully banked frustration. "If you figure it out, are you going to let me know?"

"Rach, with you, I never figure anything out."

I tried again to cast out the line, or whatever it was called, and nearly got Axel in the face. He came back and took the rod from me, casting it himself before handing it back. "Safer that way," he told Kellan.

Kellan's lips curved at that, and I rolled my eyes. Axel began to move away again, but Kel stopped him. "Where are those answers?"

"Uh, yeah." He scratched his head. "They're . . . coming. Listen, it's chilly here. Hang tight. I'm going to walk down-river a little bit and see if there's a warmer spot in the sun."

Kellan looked at me as Axel walked away. "He's good at avoidance. Must have learned it from you."

"*Me?* I'm not the one who won't talk."

"Ha."

"What does that mean?"

"Nothing."

The length of his thigh pressed against mine, warm and solid. He was warm and solid all over; I had reason to know.

"Kel, what if I told you that what happened between us last night had nothing to do with the lightning?"

"I'd say you weren't thinking clearly."

I grabbed his sleeve and tugged until he turned from the water to face me. "I'm thinking plenty clearly."

He was quiet. All around us was the sound of rushing water, the buzz of insects, the dry warmth of the sun. Thankfully no kamikaze squirrels though.

"I'm glad it's you with me," I whispered.

That got a ghost of a smile. "Don't tell Dot."

I managed a smile, too, but suddenly my throat felt tight as I stared into his beautiful eyes. "We've never really spent a lot of time alone."

He slowly shook his head.

"It's nice."

"Rach." He took the rod from me and recast, his movements easy and graceful, the muscles in his arms and shoulders flexing as the line flew in an arch to the water. When he handed the rod back to me, our fingers touched, but he pulled back. "Don't mistake the adrenaline from all the fear and excitement for something more."

"What does that mean?"

"It means that up until about twenty-four hours ago, you weren't interested in me this way."

"Things change," I said.

He was shaking his head. "Not that fast."

I thought of the lightning. "It can happen in a second. In a blink."

"We've had a lot of seconds, a lot of blinks, and it's never happened before," he said stubbornly.

"You've never kissed me before."

Or sent me skittering into a mindless orgasm . . .

He stared at me. Then, as if he couldn't help it, his gaze dropped to my mouth. I could almost see him remembering last night, how amazing it'd been, how it had escalated out of control with one touch of our tongues, how he'd pressed me into the floor, his hands . . . God, his hands.

Seeing it all in my eyes now, Kel closed his, and swallowed hard. "Okay," he murmured, "we're going to have to agree to disagree here, or I won't be able to think rationally."

I ran my gaze down his body and saw his reaction to where his thoughts had taken him. "Thinking rationally is overrated."

He was shaking his head. "I'm not going to have an affair with you."

"Well, don't look now, because it's too late," I pointed out. "Besides, you were long past due."

His eyes narrowed. "Are you keeping track of my sex life?"

"You went nearly a year without sex before you started seeing your last girlfriend. I don't think that even qualifies as a sex life, Kel."

He flushed. "So, I'm not a smooth operator. I work with dolphins all damn day long. What do you expect?"

I put my hand on his chest. Beneath my fingers, his muscles leaped, and so did my belly. "Maybe you're smoother than you think."

He met my gaze, his own dark but getting a little hotter by the second, which in turn heated me up.

"Don't." His voice was hoarse now, barely audible over the water. "I'm not going to play with you. Not like this. Not now."

"Because it would be bad?"

Those eyes positively flamed as he pressed his lower body hard against mine, letting me feel the hard bulge between his thighs. "First of all," he said, sliding a hand up my torso to find the soft mound of my breast, "it would be great."

I had to let out a breathless laugh, even as I arched up into his touch, my nipple begging for more attention. "Yeah. Um, Kel? I think you're far smoother than you give yourself credit for."

"Shit." Voice hoarse, he stepped clear of me, reeling in his line, recasting like a pro. An extremely frustrated one.

"Forgot for a minute you don't want me there, huh?"

"Damn it, I do want you, and you know it. What I don't want is a casual thing. Not with you." His motions were uncharacteristically jerky. "I'm not going to risk the best relationship in my life for one night of . . ." He searched for a word, and apparently, given the sound that escaped him, failed to find it.

"Greatness?" I whispered in jest, even though what he'd just confessed had hit me with the impact of . . . a lightning bolt.

A shadow of a smile crossed his mouth. "Yeah. But I mean it, Rach. We're not doing this."

"Not, as in never?"

He didn't answer, and I stared down at the rod in my hands. "Never's a long time. That's all I'm saying."

I didn't get a response to that either. "What if I was the only woman on an island with you?" I tried. "*Then* would you still say never?"

His jaw jumped. "Jesus, Rach."

"I mean, there's just some things you can't put a time limit on, you know?"

"Where's Axel?" he asked, clearly needing to be saved.

"He said he'd be right back."

"No, he didn't. He said to wait here—*Shit.*" Kellan glanced up the path. "He's not coming back. This was all a stalling technique to keep us busy so he wouldn't have to come up with answers."

"And it worked."

"Shit," he said again.

We both looked at the trail and knew we had to go back up it. Again. We walked mostly in silence. Well, Kel was silent; I kept asking questions, because I couldn't help myself. "What do you think Dot is doing right now?"

"Not asking me a million questions."

I decided not to take that personally. "I bet she's eating cookies," I said.

Kel just sighed.

When we got back to the inn, we went straight to the kitchen, where Axel was sitting on the counter doing his "ohhhmmm" thing again.

"You always ditch your guests on a fishing expedition?" Kel asked him.

"I thought you two wanted to be alone."

"What we want is answers. You know that."

"Huh. Sorry."

Kel put the fishing gear down on the table. "What the hell is with you?"

"Like I said, just trying to give you two some privacy."

"We don't need privacy!"

"Don't mean to contradict you, man, but if anyone ever needed privacy, it's you two." Axel waggled a brow. "I mean, you look at each other with such heat that trees spontaneously combust when you two walk by. You might want to do something about that."

Kellan pinched the bridge of his nose. "Just tell me what happened to us yesterday."

"What do you mean?"

"I mean, when that storm hit, something weird happened, and you know it. Marilee knows it, too."

I've never seen Kellan demanding like this. But slacker dude didn't seem to respond well to demanding, and remained in his yoga pose on the counter, his smile fading.

Marilee walked in, took in the unusually tense expression on Axel's face and did an about-face, ready to walk right out again.

"Oh hell no." Kellan slapped a hand on the kitchen door above her head, holding it closed so she couldn't escape. "Someone's going to start talking. *Now.*"

Marilee bit her lower lip and looked at Axel, who shrugged, sending the tassels on his hat sailing. "Maybe we should—"

"No, Ax. We promised we wouldn't. You know we did. It's not up to us."

"Whom did you promise?" Kellan broke in.

Marilee and Axel stared at each other, silent.

"I'm sorry," Marilee finally, said. "but there's nothing we can say."

Axel, gaze locked on Marilee, nodded slowly.

"Bullshit," said the man who used to be so laid-back. "Total and complete bullshit."

"Look," Marilee said softly, "the timing of your arrival was bad, and I'm sorry for that, but what's done is done." Again she reached for the door. "Now, if I can arrange some fun for you, a hike or maybe bird-watching . . ."

Kellan slapped his hand back on the door, holding it closed over her head. Or that's what I think he meant to do, but instead, his hand went right through the door, leaving a perfect handprint in the veneer.

Everyone stared at the hole.

"Wow," Marilee whispered, and looked at Kellan as if seeing him for the first time.

"Holy shit, dude," Axel said much more eloquently. "*Sweet.*"

"Oh, you think so?" Kellan's voice was silky quiet but vibrating with frustration. "Because I don't think it's *sweet.* I think it's pretty damn freaky."

I had a lot of thoughts going through my mind, but I couldn't help being utterly fascinated by Kellan's display of temper and strength, not to mention his new forcefulness. Of course, I'd never admit such a ridiculous thing out loud, but I was thinking it plenty.

The silence between us all began to go from stunned to extremely awkward. And then another of those odd and inexplicable thumps sounded, from the other side of the door that Kellan had just put a hole through.

Kellan glanced at Marilee and Axel, then at me. Everyone in the house was supposedly accounted for. Narrowing his eyes, he whipped open the door, and there stood a young couple—the same couple I'd seen yesterday looking out the window at me when we'd first arrived.

The guy was tall and thin, and still resembled a grown-up Harry Potter. Holding his hand was the pretty blonde, with a sweet, relaxed smile. In fact, they were both smiling, as if completely unconcerned with the hole that had just been punched through the kitchen door not two inches from Harry's nose, not to mention the four of us standing close, the tension in the air so thick you could cut it with a knife.

There was something off about the two new people, something I couldn't quite put my finger on. They were dressed as one would expect out here, in jeans and T-shirts—normal clothes—but all their clothes, right down to their matching athletic shoes, looked shiny, brand new. They were no longer glowing, as I'd clearly imagined yesterday, and they had their arms around each other.

"Hi, there," the guy said. "We were just wondering . . . is breakfast going to be served soon? We're hungry."

The young woman wrapped herself around him like a pretzel, and giggled. "*Starving.*"

Marilee moved past Kel, and smiled the smile of someone who'd just been delivered a get-out-of-jail-for-free card. "I *just* baked a special breakfast casserole. You're going to love it!" She beamed and expertly nudged the couple down the hall. "I'll serve it to you in the dining room," she called after them. "I'll be right there . . ."

"You've got guests," I said when she turned back to us. "You told us there weren't any."

"No, I didn't. When you asked, I didn't say anything either way. You just assumed."

"Not a good thing, assuming," Axel said to me. "A-S-S-U-M-E makes an ass out of you and me. Get it?"

"I get it," I said through my teeth. "What I don't get is why you both tried to hide from us the fact that we have guests."

"I didn't want to upset you," Marilee said primly.

"Why would it have upset me to have *paying* guests?" I just couldn't fathom the reasoning.

"Well, you seemed so uptight. I didn't want to make things worse."

"I was upset because I was hit by lightning! And, as it turns out, so was Kellan."

Both Axel and Marilee looked at Kel.

"We don't have lightning here," Marilee said after a full minute of silence.

If I could have torn out my own hair, I would have. Kellan put a hand on my arm, probably trying to tell me to keep my cool.

But I didn't have any cool!

"Look, I need to serve breakfast," Marilee said. "If you'll excuse me?"

"I'll help you," Axel said quickly.

"But I want some answers," I said, watching as Marilee bent to the oven, Axel helping her pull out two casserole dishes, which I sincerely hoped he'd helped put together.

"Rach." Kellan tugged me out of the kitchen and into the hallway. We took a moment to stare at the handprint he'd left in the wood.

"I'm really confused," I said in a smaller voice than I'd have liked.

"That makes two of us." Kellan took my hand. "Come on."

"To the couple?"

"Oh yeah."

They were sitting in the dining room. Well, the guy was sitting. The woman was straddling his lap, kissing him as if she planned on sucking his lips off and making them hers.

"Ahem," Kellan said, and they jumped apart. "Hi."

The young woman stood up and straightened her blouse with a sheepish grin. The blouse was already buttoned crooked.

And because I was now Supergirl, I could see that her bra was all askance. Yeah, definitely seeing *waaay* more of people than I'd like.

"Serena," she said, and thrust out her hand.

The Harry look-alike stood and pushed up his glasses. "William."

We shook their hands and introduced ourselves, too. And then Kellan asked where they were from.

"Far," Serena said. "Took forever to get here."

William nodded.

"Far like . . . back East far?" Kellan probed.

"Farther," William said, and took Serena's hand. "So what about you two? How long are you staying?"

"Until Monday," I said. "You?"

"Same," was the noncommittal answer.

I wanted to ask if they'd seen the lightning yesterday, if they'd suddenly found themselves equipped with odd, inexplicable *powers*, but something about them sort of said "Don't ask."

And I got goose bumps all over again.

"We're starving," William said. "I bet you guys are, too, given all that you've been through since the swap."

The swap.

The swap?

Kellan and I looked at each other. We'd been doing that a lot since we'd gotten here.

"The swap?" Kellan repeated.

"You know." Serena simulated either having an epileptic seizure or being zapped with a bolt of electricity.

Or . . . *lightning.*

Kellan tightened his grip on my hand. "The swap of what exactly?"

Serena glanced bemusedly at William, as if she couldn't believe we didn't immediately grasp what she was saying. "Um . . . nothing."

"No," I insisted, "you meant something."

Serena, chewing on her lower lip now, shook her head.

And my goose bumps grew to full-fledged mountains as a deeply rooted certainty grew in my belly: We were truly the only ones who didn't know what the hell was going on.

"Kellan?" I said as casually as I could, gesturing to the door. "A minute?"

"Oh, absolutely."

I tugged him out of the dining room and into the hall, where we stared at each other for yet another long beat.

"Okay, I'm now officially freaked out," I whispered, and started to have trouble drawing air into my lungs.

Kellan pulled me around a corner and pinned me back against the wall, lifting my chin with his hand. "Deep breaths."

I realized I was panting, nearly hyperventilating. "They know what happened."

"Yeah, they do. Keep breathing, Rach." He waited me out, holding me between him and the wall, stroking his thumb over my jaw, holding my gaze with his incredible blue one, until I could breathe without feeling like I was going to pass out. Finally I nodded.

"We're going to figure this out," he promised, his hands still on me, wrapping me in a hug I desperately needed.

I'm not sure when I felt the nature of the embrace change from comfort to, well, way more than comfort, but suddenly I became vibrantly aware of how he had me sandwiched between the hard wall and his equally hard body. Taking his bloodied hand in mine, I ran my thumb over his knuckles.

He made a sound of pain, and I met his gaze.

"I'm fine," he said.

A new mantra with us apparently.

"You don't sound—"

"*Fine*," he said again, letting out another rough sigh when I pressed up against him. Hmm. Maybe that hadn't been a moan of pain at all.

Kellan shook his head. "Ignore me."

But I'd spent a lot of time ignoring things I shouldn't. My own heart, for instance. Kellan's heart. It was easier, far easier, to do that, because when it came right down to it, I was one big, fancy chicken with my feelings. Always had been.

Not exactly a pleasant revelation to have about myself. "Kel—"

"No." He made a rough sound of exasperation, and if I wasn't mistaken, there was also some humor in there as well. "Not here."

"But—"

"Later, Rach."

I squirmed a little, and he made the dark, erotic sound again, the one that melted my bones. He had me pinned, the length of him against me, so that I couldn't move a single muscle.

Not that I wanted to move a single muscle, because Kellan's body was to die for, and in this position—that is, me flat against the wall and him flat against me, one thigh between mine, his hands holding me still—there was no place I'd rather be.

Well, except alone with him somewhere, with him buried deep inside me . . .

"Listen," he whispered, and I realized William's and Serena's voices carried from the dining room through the wall.

I looked at the plaster, and gasped. "I can see through the wall!"

"What are they doing?"

It took me a moment to focus. I still wasn't used to being able to do this. "They're hugging."

"Hugging?"

"He's backed her to the wall. He's going to kiss her. Omigod, he's going to—"

"*What?*"

William cupped Serena's face with a gentle tenderness that

made me feel like a voyeur. "They're looking into each other's eyes and talking," I whispered. "But I can't hear what they're saying. Too bad my ears didn't get the superpowers."

"Yeah, just what we need. More insanity. Here." Kellan pressed his ear to the wall, and I followed suit.

"They didn't know." Serena's voice came through clearly. "How could they not know?"

"Marilee didn't tell them." William sounded surprised. "That seems highly unlikely."

"Not to mention unethical," Serena said. "You can't pass off an ability to an unsuspecting. That's just bad form."

"Honey, not everyone is as open as you are. Maybe . . ."

"Maybe what?"

"Maybe Marilee had her reasons," William said.

Reasons?

Abilities?

An unsuspecting? *My god, I really had ended up in the Twilight Zone.*

I might have gone running into that dining room to demand answers, but one, Marilee came down the hallway.

She looked as cool as ice, as always, carrying a tray that was loaded with freshly cut fruit and the promised casserole.

"Sorry," she said, slightly breathless, still not looking at us. "Here's some—"

Kellan yanked me close.

"What—" I started, but saw his warning, and his intent.

He didn't want Marilee to realize we'd been eavesdropping, and there was only one way to explain us standing there.

He kissed me.

Hard.

Deep.

Wet.

"Oh!" Marilee gasped, apparently finally looking up. "Um, excuse me."

She vanished into the dining room.

And yet Kellan kept on kissing me. And kissing me. And kissing . . .

The guy so knew his way around the inside of my mouth that I actually lost track of things, pulled him close and enjoyed.

Chapter 12

Kellan's view of things

If anyone had told me in high school that someday I'd have Rachel Wood pinned against a wall, kissing her as if she were the next best thing to air, I'd have laughed up a lung.

Yeah, she was *that* far out of my league.

But then again, here I was, kissing her, *inhaling* her. I kept telling myself to slow down. Slow. Down. It was self-preservation, a necessity, because this wasn't just any woman, but Rach, the one who could so easily break my heart if I let her.

And yet, I couldn't keep my distance to save my life, because there were her hands, racing restlessly, possessively, over my body, beneath my shirt, touching my bare skin. Plus, I'd been inside her now, just twelve hours ago, and I wanted to be back inside her more than I wanted my next breath.

She pressed herself closer, grinding her hips against mine, going still for an imperceptible beat when she felt me, so hard that the buttons on my Levi's were threatened.

I had no idea what I thought I was doing—we were in the hallway, for God's sake—but I held her head still for my mouth, plundering and pillaging, loving how her hands slid up my chest, to my face, then in my hair. In fact, she held on so tightly, it was possible she was going to snatch me bald, but I'd gladly give up my hair rather than have her let go.

How was I supposed to walk away from this? From her? It would take a stronger man than me, and thanks to our "abilities," I was as strong as it got at the moment.

I'd only meant to shut her up, to make sure she didn't give away anything we weren't ready to give away, but like last night, I'd gotten thoroughly lost in the taste of her, in the feel of her lithe, curvy body plastered up against mine. And the sounds of sheer pleasure she made . . . *God*.

In yesterday's storm, aka "the swap," I'd been changed. It hadn't been immediately evident to me how, but I'd felt it. I'd always been lean, skinny lean. Even scrawny lean, as Rach liked to tell me.

But there was nothing scrawny about me now. Every muscle had toughened, hardened, and I could do things I'd never even thought of. Hell, I did them without realizing I could, hence the whole hand-through-the-door thing.

And of course, the coup de grâce: making Rach come.

Yeah, I'd really had no idea I could do that.

So I kept kissing her. It felt amazing. *She* felt amazing. And those sexy little sounds she made deep in her throat really did it for me big time. Finally needing air, I pulled back just for the sheer pleasure of taking her in.

She looked right back at me, her eyes huge and dark, her mouth pretty much an open invitation to sin. I loved her mouth. I wanted her to do things to me with that mouth. Without intending to, I went at her again, and she met me more than halfway, sucking my tongue right into her mouth, gripping me so tightly I couldn't breathe, but that was fine. Breathing was overrated. I moved my hands up to tangle them in her gorgeous, silky hair, holding her head, not that she was trying to get away.

But despite the roaring of my own blood as it all drained

south to my raging hard-on, I remembered that this was all for show, for Marilee, and she'd gone into the dining room.

We could stop kissing now.

Yeah, any time.

Instead, my hands swept down Rach's body, mindless now, seeking more of her, all of her. And thankfully, Rach seemed to know what she wanted as well.

Me.

Loved that.

I still had her pinned to the wall, one of my thighs thrust hard between hers. And somehow, I'd managed to grab one palmful of sweet ass, the other palm cupping her breast, my thumb playing over her nipple, which had pebbled in my hand. It wasn't enough, not nearly, so I skimmed my hand beneath her shirt, seeking hot skin to hot skin, and when I encountered a light satiny bra, I simply tugged it down.

She let out the sexiest little sound I've ever heard, and pressed her breast harder into my palm. "Oh God," she whispered, as I continued to rasp my thumb over her nipple, back and forth, listening to her pant. I was out of control, and utterly unable to stop my other hand from slipping inside her panties, from spreading her wet folds and sinking two fingers deep inside.

"Omigod," she gasped, as I found the right pressure to send her arching into me. "*Omigod.*"

I wanted to put my mouth on her *there.* I wanted that so much, I shook with it. But barely, just barely, I remembered we were still standing in the hallway, where anyone could come upon us at any time. One of us needed to get a grip fast, and judging by the dark, needy sounds escaping from Rach's throat, it wasn't going to be her.

Damn. Because that left me, and I was prepared to offer the devil my very soul in order to let me continue touching her like this, to strip her down to nothing, to tear off my own clothes and then to bury myself in deep . . .

A sound from the other side of the wall brought me back, as it did Rach, given the way she jerked.

I was breathing like a lunatic as I lifted my head. Rach staggered a step, as if she could barely stand, and leaned back against the wall.

"You okay?" I asked.

"Um." She licked her lips and looked adorably dazed. "Yeah." Her nipples pressed against the material of her top as if begging for attention, and since I knew what they liked and how amazing they felt in my mouth, it was everything I could do not to give them that attention they wanted.

Yeah, so much for keeping my distance.

I could still feel her, the way her skin had been so soft beneath my work-roughened fingers, and as if my brain had disconnected from my body, I stepped close again, sliding my fingers into her hair, holding her head for just one more kiss. And then one more . . . I ate her startled murmur, and then her soft acquiescence, letting out a groan when she entwined her arms back around my neck and held on tightly.

When we ran out of oxygen, we blinked at each other, chests rising and falling rapidly.

"Love this new Clark Kent–to–Superman thing you've got going on," she whispered.

The Superman comment made my jaw twitch uncontrollably. My *exact* reason for needing to keep my distance. It wasn't *me* she was attracted to, but whatever had happened to me. If I had any hope in hell of keeping my heart in one piece when this was over, I needed to find my control and use it.

"Are you going to tell me that was all a diversion?" she asked.

"Yes."

"So that Marilee wouldn't catch us eavesdropping?"

"That's right."

She laughed a little. "Yeah, okay." She nodded. "Nicely done.

I doubt she realized that wasn't real." She bit her lower lip. "Um, Kel?"

It was in her tone, something warning me to back away. Hell, to run for my life. But my feet were glued to the floor as she came toward me. "What?"

"You should see the look on your face. I'm not going to hurt you, silly man."

Right, she was only going to rip my heart in two, but it wasn't going to hurt a bit.

"Don't worry, Kel. I'll be gentle."

Gentle, my ass.

She slid her hands up my arms, entwined them around my neck and tugged my head down. Her lips just barely brushing mine, she looked into my eyes. "Can I have just one more diversion?"

I tried to back up, but she held on tightly. "Rach, no."

Eyes sleepy and soft and sexy as hell, she stuck out her lower lip until I wanted to lick it. "Why not?" she whispered.

Yeah, you idiot, why not? "We need to focus." I sounded desperate even to my own ears. "There's something strange about those guests."

"Well, duh, Kel."

"And about Marilee and Axel, too. Everything's strange, and we need to figure it out."

Turning, she backed *me* to the wall now, staring at my mouth, and I nearly groaned.

She blinked those gorgeous eyes and licked her lips. *Ah, man.* "Rach—"

"Love the way you say my name," she whispered, leaning her body into me. "As if I'm killing you and giving you your greatest fantasy all in one."

"Bingo," I managed. "You win."

"Good. I do like to win." Tugging my head down, she kissed me, long and slow. And she did something with her hips, just a little wriggly oscillation thing, rubbing against me in a way that made it impossible for me to think about anything except tearing off our clothes and burying myself inside her.

"I had no idea you were such a good kisser," she murmured, nibbling at my jaw. "No idea at all . . ." She rocked against me some more, and my eyes rolled back in my head.

Okay, time to get a grip, McInty. Tearing free, I held her away from me. "Don't."

"Why not?"

"Because . . ." Think, man. "Because the coast is clear."

She went still. Her eyes slid to the door to the dining room. "Gotcha. The coast is clear. After all, why else would we kiss?"

"Rach—"

"No, I understand."

I pointed at the wall. "What's going on in there?"

She was very quiet as she turned to face the wall. She put her hands on it, standing very still as she concentrated.

"What do you see?" I tried not to let my gaze fall down her body, to the unintentionally submissive pose she presented, legs slightly spread, hands up to the wall, leaning in slightly to listen.

I could shift behind her right now, came the unbidden thought. I could pull down her jeans and—

"They're coming," she whispered, and whirled around to face me as the door opened.

"Axel's going to take Serena and William on a hike today," Marilee said as she emerged.

"A hike," Rach repeated, in a tone that said hiking was pretty much the last thing on Earth she'd voluntarily do.

"We'll join you," I said.

"We . . . will?" Rach shot me a death look, which served to shrivel my erection nicely.

"Yes."

"A hike." She sighed. "Sounds . . . lovely."

"Sorry." Marilee gave an apologetic shake of her head. "This is a prebooked hike. Just Serena and William."

Axel appeared in the hall. "Ready for the hikers."

"I could book you for later perhaps," Marilee said to us. "If there's room in the schedule."

"If there's room?" I said. "The B&B isn't even full. How could there not be room in the schedule?"

"Oh." Not easily flustered, Marilee kept her composure and smiled. "It's best to see the area in small groups. You know, individual attention and all." With that, she hustled Serena and William out.

Axel stayed back a moment. "I'll be right there," he called to Marilee with an easy smile, which faded when she was gone. "Look," he said to us—specifically, to *me*. "Yeah, okay, so I lied about you getting your answers. But trust me, you don't want to know. You need to just relax and—"

"No," Rach said with a shake of her head. "Not relaxing."

Axel sighed. "Dudette."

"You tell us what's going on," I said, "or I'll get Marilee to talk."

"You'll get Marilee to talk?" Axel repeated slowly.

Even Rach looked as if she didn't like the sound of that, and they both gave me a long, measuring look.

"She's mine, you know," Axel said.

"Okay, wait a minute." Rach laughed a little harshly. "I must have just gone back in time to the dark ages. To before women's rights. Getting women to talk, owning women . . ."

Axel flushed. "I meant, I *want* her to be mine."

"What does this have to do with us getting our answers?" I asked. "*Nothing.*"

"You want her," Axel said. "Marilee."

"Kel wants Marilee?" Rach looking at me. "Really?"

"No."

"Yes, he does," Axel said.

"No, I don't," I said.

"Great, because she's mine," Axel repeated, not looking so slackerish at all at the moment.

"I'm telling you, I'm *not* interested."

"What, she's not hot enough for you?" Axel asked.

"No, she is, but—" But I zipped my mouth because Rachel was eyeballing me with that ball-shriveling expression.

"So, you *do* think she's hot," Axel said.

I sighed, caught between a rock and a hard place. Was it possible for a head to just blow right off its shoulders? Because it felt like maybe mine was going to.

"Look, all I want is information. Can we stick with the subject? Please?"

"Kel, that's not very sensitive of you." Rach touched Axel's arm. "Have you told Marilee you're crazy about her?"

"Not yet." Axel looked miserable. "Working on it."

"How?" Rachel asked.

I couldn't see how this was relative, and opened my mouth to say so, but Rach glared at me.

Axel scratched his head. "Oh, you know. A bit of this and that. By telling her how to cook."

"A woman doesn't want to hear that she sucks at something," Rachel said. "You have to compliment her. Show her you're interested."

"Hey, I've shown her lots of interest," Axel claimed.

"Have you told her she's pretty?"

"She already knows that she's pretty."

"Then tell her you like to be with her," Rach suggested. "Tell her you want to date her. Then, you know . . . take it from there."

"You mean . . . in physical ways?"

"Sure."

Axel looked hopeful. "Yeah. Thanks, dudette. I owe ya." With a quick grin, he leaned in and gave her one smacking kiss right on the lips.

Then he was gone.

Yeah, definitely, my brain matter was boiling. "The next time you play good Samaritan," I said with remarkable calm, given I was so *not*, "maybe you can make a bargain for, oh, I don't know . . . *answers*?"

"I did," she said. "Now he's going to try to romance her tonight." Her eyes sharpened. "While we snoop."

Okay, maybe she was sharper than I'd guessed. "Just promise me you're never going to turn your powers against me."

She smiled. "How about *on* you?"

My poor body went from at-rest to ready-to-party again in five point five seconds flat. "Stop."

"Okay, but only because I have another plan."

I was almost afraid to ask.

"Come on," she said, and tugged me along to follow Axel into the kitchen, leaving me to wonder what exactly the plan was and if it involved her seducing me.

I'd like to say I hoped not, but in spite of myself, hell yes I hoped the plan included some seduction.

And a naked Rach.

Chapter 13

Still Kellan's view . . .

When we entered the kitchen, Rach right behind me, Axel whipped around from where he'd been standing in front of the open fridge.

"I'm just checking the temperature—" he began, and when he saw it was just us, he sagged. "Whew. Close one. She hates it when I dip into the food in between meals."

"Where are you taking Serena and William?" Rachel asked.

"Told ya. On a hike."

"Where to?" I asked.

Axel scratched his head and shifted his big feet. "Oh, here and there."

"Can you be more specific?"

"Winging it, to tell you the truth."

Marilee poked her head in the kitchen doorway right behind us, took in the scene with one glance—including Axel in the refrigerator—and sighed. "You hated breakfast."

"No," Axel promised. "I just . . ."

"Truth. You hated it."

Axel glanced at Rachel, then back at Marilee. "You look really beautiful today."

She raised one brow and crossed her arms.

And he folded like a cheap suitcase. "Ah hell, Mari, don't make me tell you how bad it sucked."

In a rare unguarded gesture, Marilee's mouth fell open. "Sucked? It was *that* bad that it . . . sucked?"

"Damn." Axel shot another glance at Rachel. "Have I mentioned I'm, uh, crazy about you?"

Marilee looked at him as if he'd grown horns. "You been smoking again?"

"Not once all year, since you asked me to stop."

"We were talking about my cooking," she said. "I followed your directions for that casserole to the last letter."

Axel shook his head. "The eggs tasted like you drowned them in salt and pepper. No way did you use half a pinch of each."

"Half a *pinch*?"

"I wrote it out for you."

"I thought it said half a pint. Which is a cup. I looked it up."

"Who in their right mind would use a cup of salt or pepper in one casserole dish?" he asked.

Marilee's face froze. "Apparently only an idiot."

Axel scrubbed a hand down over his face. "I didn't mean—"

"Go ahead and say it," she said stiffly. "I am an idiot. Might as well let it all hang out, and also mention that I don't belong in the kitchen."

"I like you in the kitchen."

"I noticed you didn't say I wasn't an idiot."

Axel slid yet another desperate glance at Rachel, who waved him closer to Marilee.

"This is one of those no-win situations for me," Axel said, touching Marilee's shoulder, "so I'm going to do one last thing."

Marilee looked wary. "What's that?"

"This. Hold on tight, Mari." And he hauled her up to her toes and kissed her.

She let out a squeak, her hands straight out at her sides, but Axel didn't let go, and after a few seconds, Marilee let out another sound, not a squeak this time, but more of a . . . moan. Then she wrapped her arms weakly around Axel's neck.

Rach looked at me and arched a brow.

Finally Axel stepped back and cleared his throat. "Yeah. Um . . ." He tripped over his own two feet. "So. It's time to take Serena and William out."

Marilee nodded faintly. "Right."

He nodded, and turned away.

"Take the map I left for you on the foyer table," Marilee said, her voice softer than it'd been since we'd met her.

"Thanks." Axel glanced back at her. "And for what it's worth, you are a *pretty* idiot. You're the prettiest idiot I've ever known."

Marilee startled all of us by laughing. It was a nice sound, actually, I thought, as she threw her oven mitt at Axel.

"A pint," Marilee said on a sigh when he'd left. "Can you imagine?" She tapped her own forehead. "I'm so doing the wrong job."

"Yeah," I agreed, then blinked when both women glared at me.

What had I done but agree with them? Weren't you supposed to agree with them?

"So why don't you want us to spend any time with Serena and William?" Rachel asked Marilee without preamble. She put her hands on her hips for emphasis, looking extremely serious. And gorgeous.

And sexy . . .

How could she ever have thought I wanted Marilee after I'd had her? I was fairly certain I'd never want another woman again.

Marilee opened her mouth, but Rachel narrowed her eyes and focused on a spot right between the other woman's breasts.

"What are you doing?" Marilee asked, crossing her arms over her chest.

"Watching your heart. If you lie, your heart is going to speed up."

"You can't see my heart."

"Wanna bet?" Rachel asked, her eyes glittering with what I knew to be bad temper. Whenever she looked at me like that, I tended to duck for cover, but Marilee didn't know better, and she took a stand.

"You're just going to have to trust me," Marilee said. "There are some things you're better off not knowing, and what's going on here is one of those things."

"I'm the owner of this place," Rach reminded her. "I have a right to know."

Marilee looked at her for a long moment. "Gertrude always said that out of all her relatives, you were the one most likely to just keep things status quo. We knew you'd come visit, and then we counted on you going away and not coming back."

"Why wouldn't I come back?"

But Marilee had busied herself with the dishes.

"Marilee?"

"Because maybe you wouldn't have such a good time."

"Maybe?" I interjected. "Or certainly, because you'd make damn sure I wouldn't."

"That," Marilee admitted. "The second one."

Rachel looked at me and shook her head in shocked amazement. "Okay, so your job as hostess was to make us so miserable that we'd leave. And then what? The place would just run itself?"

"Yes."

"Well, no one's leaving, at least not until Jack gets back," Rach said. "Your own words, right?"

"Right."

"So you might as well talk to us."

To this, Marilee said nothing.

"Look, Serena told us some things," I broke in, trying a new angle. "About the swap, for instance."

Marilee's lips tightened. "Sounds kinky."

"Whoa." Rachel pointed to Marilee's chest. "Your heart just sped up."

"Yeah? Well, washing dishes is hard work."

"She knew about our 'abilities,' Marilee."

"Poor Serena," Marilee said. "She desperately needed this vacation. It's a good thing for her mental health that William got her away."

"Okay, you know what?" Rachel stepped to my side and took my hand. "I've just decided I don't want you to tell us anything, because I wouldn't trust it anyway. We'll figure this out on our own. Where's the office?"

"What?"

"The office for the inn, where all the paperwork is kept."

Marilee lifted her shoulder. "Hey, I'm just the cook."

"And the maid."

"Only when strictly necessary."

"I know Gertrude had an office," Rach insisted. "She was as anal as they came."

"Did you see an office when you walked through the house?"

Rachel bit her lip, thinking back. And it occurred to me, I hadn't seen an office either. Strange for a business. There had to be files, a computer . . .

"Never mind. We'll find it ourselves," Rach said, and led me out the back door, with Marilee standing there pensive in front of the oven.

We walked away from the house to avoid being overheard and ended up on the edge of the cleared property, staring at the trees.

"I wanted to talk to you in private," she said, looking at the woods, "but I'm finding myself a little unnerved by the thought of going in there again."

"We did okay fishing."

"But we had Axel, at least at first." She tipped her head up further, eyeing the blue sky. "No clouds at least."

"Maybe clouds would actually solve our problem."

"You mean, if we were hit again, then everything would go back to normal?"

"Something like that. Normal being relative, of course."

"Turns out I'm awfully fond of normal." She laughed a little, then startled me by setting her head on my shoulder. "I'm so glad you're here with me, Kel."

I looked down into her soft eyes and sweet smile, and promptly forgot about the office. She dropped her gaze to my mouth, and I nearly forgot my own name.

Not good.

"The answers are down that trail," she said, still looking at my mouth, "in that clearing where we were hit. I say we go there now and just look around, then tonight, when everyone is asleep, we get the cookies and then search for the office."

"The cookies being necessary for the search, of course."

"Of course."

We took the trail, in silence at first, if one could call it silent when wind whistled through trees, insects buzzed, and birds chirped. Several times we had to push branches out of our way or brush off our clothes after a pinecone—and accompanying dirt—fell on us from the trees above.

"What if we get lost again?" Rach asked after a few minutes, pushing yet another branch out of her face.

She had a streak of dirt over her jaw, and I traced it with a finger, tucking a wayward strand of her hair behind her ear, just for an excuse to touch her. *Yeah, way to keep your distance there, champ.*

"This was your idea," I reminded her.

"I really need to stop that."

"Tell you what. You take your shirt off this time," I said, my brain apparently disconnected from my mouth again. "We'll tear off strips and tie them around the tree like yesterday."

Without hesitation, she reached for the hem of her shirt and pulled it up over her head.

Ah hell. *Don't look*, I ordered myself, but I might as well have just tried to stop breathing. No luck. My gaze lowered and took in her bright pink bra, the way it pushed her perfect breasts up, barely covering her nipples, which were hardening into two tight pebbles as I watched.

I made a low, rough noise and squeezed my eyes shut. "Jesus, Rach—"

"Just in case," she said, and tried to tear her shirt but couldn't. She let out a sigh of frustration and tried again, the motion making her arms tighten and her breasts plump up even more, so that her nipples—God. Another fraction of an inch, and they were going to pop right out. "*Rach*—"

"Almost got it."

She jerked hard, and it happened.

Nipplegate.

Oblivious, she kept yanking at her shirt, one rose-colored nipple bouncing and swaying with the motion, just this small, delectable treat in an otherwise shitty day, and I couldn't take my eyes off it. "Rach—"

"Yeah?"

She kept tugging, and I put a hand over hers, noting that mine was shaking. "You, uh . . ." I waggled a finger at her chest.

Her gaze followed the motion, and she let out a little laugh before tugging her bra back into place. "Oops."

I stood there wishing I hadn't said a thing. But I had, and my poor overtaxed brain, not to mention other parts, parts way south of my brain, couldn't seem to recover, especially with her standing there in that pink bra, breathing a little harder than her exertion dictated, each little pant threatening another exposure, which my body wanted with every fiber of its being. I grabbed her shirt, turned it right side out again and handed it back to her. "Here."

"But—"

"Rach, I'm begging you."

She slipped the shirt on over her head, then straightened it out.

Her nipples were like two gumdrops waiting—no, *begging*—to be tasted.

And I was a man suddenly starving. I think I even let out a sort of growl, which sounded more like a whimper than anything else. I stepped back a few feet because I suddenly remembered: *distance*, *control*.

I started walking, and she had to practically run to keep up. In no time, we stood in the clearing, me as far away from her as possible. Both of us looked skyward.

Still no clouds.

"Whew," she said, and smiled at me. "Hey, you can come closer if you want. I won't take my shirt off again. Even though you've already seen everything."

Yeah, that didn't seem to matter.

"I don't bite, Kel."

No, but I might.

"Kel?"

"I'm fine right here, thanks."

She nodded, then looked around, trying to be cool but not quite managing to hide her apprehension. "So. This is it." She pointed to the spot where she'd been hit. "Doesn't even have a mark."

There were no answers here, no hint of what had happened. Nothing.

"Looks almost . . . pretty out here, huh?" she asked softly.

She was scared, damn it. I gritted my teeth and reminded myself: distance. That was key here. If I wanted her in my life, which I did, I wanted her to want me, the Kellan who was usually a little too thin, the Kellan who was a lot more laid back than I'd been here. The Kellan who was definitely not a badass. The *real* me.

Only I wasn't even sure who that was.

My eyes locked on the tree to which I'd pinned Rach when I'd kissed her for the first time. I got hard just looking at it.

Her gaze followed mine. "Hey, isn't that where we first kissed?"

"It was the swap," I said. "The abilities. Not us." I shook my head. "Jesus. I sound like I almost believe this, don't I?" I rubbed my suddenly aching temples. "Look, my point is, whatever's happened to us here, it's all temporary. Soon as this is over, we'll be back to normal. Back to friends only." I paused at this, giving her a chance to jump in and say that she'd realized she was madly in love with me and couldn't live without me or my body, and that I had to promise to do her every day for the rest of her life.

But she didn't say anything.

Okay. Nice one for the ego. Still, it's what I'd expected.

"I don't see any answers here. Let's go back." Turning away, I began walking.

"Kel?"

My heart leaped. "Yeah?"

"Best friends. You forgot that part. Right?"

"Rach—"

"Say it."

"Best friends," I repeated softly, and meant it.

She reached out a hand for mine.

I sighed, and took her fingers in mine, leading the way back to the inn.

We decided to split up. I was to try to get Marilee by herself and flirt my way to some serious answers. Rach was going to keep Axel occupied.

Which is how I ended up in the kitchen, up to my elbows in flour and chocolate, making cookies with Marilee.

Or, I made cookies while Marilee did her nails.

"Look," she said, delicately blowing on a newly painted purple nail while I pounded butter into mush with my new and improved muscles. "Pretty, huh?"

High from the scent of the lacquer, I agreed. "Very nice." I pounded more butter. "I think I have some of this figured out, by the way."

"What's that?"

"The whole ability-swapping thing." I watched her stiffen. "Are you the one in charge?"

"You know what? I find that music is instrumental in making good cookies." Careful of her nails, she cranked up the radio.

I waited until Kanye West stopped rapping before turning the radio off again. "It's just that I don't see Axel being in charge."

"Axel is a good man," she said, surprising me by responding. "He's just not into . . ."

"Subterfuge? Lying?" I set aside the bowl of dough. "Manipulating?"

"Hey, there's no manipulating going on here. We just . . . didn't expect you, that's all."

"Yeah, I get that part. What goes in here next?"

She blew on another nail. "Whatever you think is best."

"What would you have put in next?"

She blew on another nail. "Oh, this and that."

I'd bet my next breath she'd never made a successful batch of cookies in her life. "Chocolate . . . or pepper?"

"Either."

"There is no pepper in chocolate chip cookies, Marilee."

Suddenly she got very busy applying daisy decals on her thumbs.

"You're not a chef," I said.

"You know what? Thanks for your help, but fun time's over." Careful with her nails, she guided me to the door, then gave me a little push, nearly shutting my nose in it. "Appreciate it," she said through the hole I'd caused earlier, "but I'll take it from here."

Ten bucks said she'd screw up those cookies. "No pepper," I said.

"I know."

Uh-huh, right. Hoping Rach had fared better than I had in the getting-answers department, I went looking for her.

Only she was nowhere to be found, and I know this because I searched the entire inn, up and down and up again, a very bad feeling growing in my chest.

Axel was in the foyer with Serena and William, the three of them talking about their hike. "Have any of you seen Rach?" I asked.

"Dude, hopefully she's taken a chill pill," Axel said.

Yeah. A chill pill. I went out the back door and stared into the woods, my concern growing by leaps and bounds.

She wouldn't have gone out there again, not alone, would she?

Then I heard it, a low humming noise, of a compressor or pump or something mechanical. I followed the sound around the corner of the house, to a side deck.

Rach stood next to a hot tub. The water bubbled enticingly from the jets, the steam rising into the air behind her like a halo.

"Look what I found," she said. "Inviting, don't you think?"

What was inviting was her. Too bad she wasn't in the tub, all wet and flushed and . . . wet. But my mind could plug in the picture, no problem. Her bare skin would be gleaming and slick, her breasts just above the water, nipples hard and wet—

"Kel?"

I shook it off, barely. Extremely relieved to see her, naked and gleaming or otherwise, I nearly yanked her into my arms and kissed us both stupid, but luckily, some sort of common sense prevailed.

"Later," she whispered, and if I wasn't mistaken, she smelled like chocolate mint.

It took me a minute to realize she probably didn't mean that later I could kiss us both stupid and maybe get to that naked-and-gleaming part of the program, but that later she'd show me whatever she'd found on her search.

"Why do you smell like chocolate?"

She tightened her lips and looked guilty, but she didn't say a word.

She didn't have to. I'd have bet every last penny that her search had yielded a cookie stash.

I leaned back against the edge of the tub, but I didn't realize she'd put all her weight against me. Strong as I was, I hadn't received any grace in the swap, so when I lost my balance, tumbling back into the water, Rachel came with me, clothes and all.

The hot water closed in over my head, engulfing me in its cocoonlike warmth, and when I broke the surface, so did an equally drenched Rach.

She tossed her hair out of her face and looked at me blandly as she swiped beneath her eyes to clean away streaked mascara. "You know, there are easier ways to get me wet."

"I'm sorry, I wasn't trying to—"

"No?" She sighed. "Well, that's just a shame."

With that she rose out of the water, just like in my fantasy, except in clothes, her pale shirt clinging to her like the hottest wet T-shirt I'd ever seen, her jeans also clinging to her every single curve and dip.

"Nice water temp," she said. "Maybe we can come back here tonight, and stargaze."

I couldn't respond because my tongue had become stuck to the roof of my mouth.

She pulled her shirt away from her skin. The material broke free with a suction noise that tugged at my groin and made me want to drop to my knees and worship her body. Then she merely walked away.

Pretty much the story of my life when it came to her.

Chapter 14

Still Kellan's view . . .

Marilee burned the bottoms of my cookies and then blamed the oven, bringing us into the kitchen to taste them anyway after we'd changed out of our wet clothes.

I knew her hospitality wasn't kindness but a way to keep us from snooping.

"Is there something that you'd like us not to find?" Rachel finally asked so politely, it took Marilee a moment to realize what she'd said.

"Of course not," Marilee said. "*Mi casa es su casa.*" She laughed. "I'm learning Spanish on tape."

Rachel smiled. "*¿Es usted que planea en dormir con Axel?*"

Marilee looked at her blankly. "Um, I don't think I got to that chapter yet."

"I asked if you planned on doing Axel."

Marilee folded, then refolded, a kitchen towel. "That's something we haven't quite worked out yet."

"But you want to," Rachel said.

"Yes," Marilee admitted. "But to be honest, I was hoping he'd make the first move. That boy is as slow as molasses; nothing can rush him. Drives me crazy."

"Yeah." Rachel sighed as if she commiserated greatly.

I looked at her. I wasn't as slow as molasses.

Was I?

But she *had* made the first move . . .

Fine. I still wasn't as slow as molasses, because there'd never been a first move to make before now—at least, that I knew of.

"*You* could make the first move," Rach pointed out to Marilee, carefully not looking at me. "I know it's always preferable when *they* do it, but sometimes, a girl's gotta do what a girl's gotta do."

Really? Had I been a "gotta do"?

"You're being awfully nice," Marilee said, sounding just a little unsure.

"I'm not used to being at odds with someone," Rachel said. "I hate that we got off on the wrong foot."

The women looked at each other. Rach smiled, and then, unbelievably, so did Marilee.

Bonding right before my eyes.

"Well, this is good," I said. "Except for the whole missing-information part."

Marilee looked at her watch, and moved to the door. "Oops, would you look at the time? I've got to—"

"Go," I said in unison with her. "Yeah, imagine that—" But I was talking to myself, because Marilee had vanished.

"I almost had her. Before you screwed it up," Rach said.

"What? You had nothing."

"She's not so bad, Kel."

I stared at her. "Is this a girl thing?"

"Probably."

Marilee popped her head back in. "Oh, I forgot. William and Serena want you to play a game with them in the den."

More conspiracy. "What game?" I asked, but Marilee was already gone.

"Probably Monopoly," Rach said. "Come on. Maybe we can wheedle something more from them."

Not Monopoly. No, William and Serena wanted to play Sensual Truth or Dare, a game for couples, that was pretty much self-explanatory.

"Oh boy," Rach said, and glanced at me.

"Come on," Serena said, and patted the couch.

I stood there. "Uh . . ."

"Oh, don't be shy," Serena said, and got up to pull us to some seats.

Truth or Dare. Fine and dandy for her and William, a couple obviously at ease with their sexuality in regards to each other.

But I felt like I was sitting on a time bomb with a lit fuse.

William went first, and picked truth. "Tell a secret to the person on your right," he read.

I was on his right. "Tell me about the swap."

"Dare," William decided, switching, and smoothly turned the card over for his resulting dare. "Instead of telling a secret to the person on your right, do something to them."

"Wait!" Serena hopped up from his left and squished herself in between us so that now she was on his right.

"Go," she said breathlessly.

William smiled at her, then slipped off her sandals and gave her a slow, languid foot massage, which had Serena melting boneless into her chair with a moan so sensual, it got to me. She lay back, eyes closed, breathing shallow, nipples hard. I glanced at Rachel, who looked as turned on as Serena.

At her turn, Serena chose truth. "Choose a secret to share."

"I know which secret I want to hear about," I said.

Still looking hot and bothered, Serena smiled. "I'm glad it was you two."

I looked at Rachel, who looked back at me. "What do you mean?"

But Serena's smile became mysterious, and she shook her head. "That's my secret. That's it."

And there was no getting her to say more.

When it was my turn, I picked truth, afraid of the dare.

Yes, afraid. I was no fool.

Rachel drew the question, read it first, then gave me a long, measuring glance.

Uh-oh.

"What's your greatest fantasy?" she asked.

Ah hell. "How about my greatest irritation, which is when people won't talk to me."

"Fantasy," she repeated, clearly forgetting that we were supposed to be on the same side here.

"Greatest fantasy? Uh . . ." *You naked. Me naked. You naked, pinned by me also naked, against my shower wall.* "Uh . . ." *Think, man.* "To go skydiving."

"Sexual fantasy," Serena said, laughing. "Unless you'd rather have the dare."

"Dare," I said, deciding I was less afraid of that.

"Fine." Serena turned the card over. She read it in silence, then stood and opened the coat closet door. "Take a partner of your choice and kiss her for five minutes."

"You are joking."

"No."

I looked at Rach for help.

"I thought it was seven minutes in the closet," she said.

Some help.

"Sorry, you only get five," Serena said. "Get moving, you two."

Rachel smiled into my eyes, took my hand and led me to the closet.

I knew this was just a stupid game. But that didn't explain why my heart was suddenly racing, or why my palms had gone sweaty.

I didn't want to do this.

Right. I was already hard as a rock, and I hadn't touched her yet. Hell yeah, I wanted to kiss Rachel for five minutes.

I wanted to kiss her for the rest of my life.

Rachel went into the closet first, then pulled me in as well, shutting the door, leaving us in complete darkness.

Actually, it was just me in complete darkness, because she could see right through anything, including the inky black. A soft scarf brushed my cheek and the padding of a down coat pushed at my back, but all I could think about was what we could do with five minutes. I didn't know about Rach, but *I* could think of a lot.

"Rach."

She put a finger over my lips. "Not talking. Kissing. Unless . . . you don't want to."

I let out a rough laugh, and pulled her hand from my mouth, pressing it up against the vee of my jeans, loving the soft little "oh!" that escaped her at the feel of me. "Yeah, feel how much I don't want you—"

She kissed me, diving in with such unexpected fierceness that I fell backwards.

A pile of coats broke our fall as her arms entwined around my neck, pressing closer, straddling me with those glorious legs spread on either side of my hips so that she could arch against me.

I think my eyes rolled back in my head.

"Mmm," she said when I ran my hands down her spine to hold onto her ass, pressing her closer, urging her on, as her hips rocked both back and forth, and my world.

I couldn't stop kissing her, kissing her with everything I had, hoping my five minutes would never come to an end, that I didn't ever have to let her go.

And then far too soon, a laughing voice called through the door, "Time's up!"

No.

Rachel stood, and I nearly cried. Seriously.

She reached a hand down to help me, then went to open the door.

But I held it closed, as gently as possible so as to not destroy my third door in two days. "I need a minute."

"You do?" She outlined me through my jeans with her fingers. "Oh my," she breathed, doing it again, making me jerk and grab her wrist.

"That's not going to help," I said tightly.

With a soft laugh, she kissed the side of my neck.

"Neither is that."

"I'm sorry." But she didn't sound sorry. "What can I do to help?"

Take off all your clothes and drop to your knees. "Wear a potato sack. Stop smiling at me." I sighed, and attempted to make adjustments, but there was no way to get comfortable. "Stop breathing."

"You're so cute when you're sexually frustrated." And she kissed me again, softly, sweetly, right on the corner of my mouth.

All I could do was pull her in for a hug, and sigh.

"Better?" she murmured.

"Much," I lied, and buried my face in her hair, still painfully hard, still painfully aware that in spite of everything, there was nowhere on Earth I'd rather be.

Dinner was a bit of a strained affair, mostly because Marilee ruined her chicken dish and Axel rescued her with a steak barbeque that was so successful, it made her pout and threaten to lead all his fishing and hiking expeditions.

Axel laughed, which made her madder.

"Why don't we just switch jobs, Mari?" he asked.

She stared at him. "Seriously?"

"Why not?"

"Yeah," she said slowly, "why not?" And she began to glow with happiness as she talked about some of the expeditions she wanted to plan.

Axel glowed as well, over a mouth-watering pan of brownies he'd baked for dessert.

"So you're really swapping?" Kel asked.

"Just jobs," Axel said. "Not . . . you know."

Silence fell.

"Now see, I would know, if you'd tell us," Kel finally said, but Serena and William quickly excused themselves to go upstairs, and Marilee did the same.

Axel sighed. "Guess it's good night." He opened the back door for us, then ended up wandering to the guest house, too, which I thought was strange.

He plopped himself down on the couch, kicked his feet up on the coffee table and bogarted the remote.

Since we only got one channel, a fishing channel, there wasn't any reason to feel resentful, but I sank into the couch next to him and felt it anyway.

I wanted that remote.

Rach glared at Axel. "Don't you have your own room?"

"Thought you might want some company. But if you two want privacy or something, I can go."

Privacy. My entire body leaped at the thought, especially since Rachel sent me a quick speculative glance.

But Axel kept watching the fly-fishing team on the TV.

Finally, I kicked his feet off the table and snagged the remote. "You want to stay? Fine. All you have to do is explain some things."

Axel stood up, and sighed. "Dude, you really gotta learn to chill."

And then he finally left.

Rachel followed him to the door (with the hole still in it), and locked it. She looked at me, and crooked her little finger to come close.

When I did, she wrapped her arms around my neck, making me moan and haul her close. "Rach—"

"I found the office," she said in my ear.

This information took a moment to soak into my brain, but when it did, I went still. I told myself this was what I'd been waiting for, all day *not* for night to get here so she could jump my bones again. I pulled back, and tried not to feel stupid that I'd thought she'd wanted me.

"Where?"

"Soon as everyone's asleep, I'll show you."

We waited two hours, an eternity in a small room, alone with the woman I'd been drooling after for so many years, especially since I now knew exactly how good it could be.

She changed into a camisole, sans bra, and matching pj bottoms, thin and insubstantial enough that I could see she'd gone commando beneath.

Seriously. She was going to kill me, and I was going to die with a hard-on. I could only hope they wouldn't ask my mother to identify me.

Finally, the lights went off in the main house. Rach pulled on a sweatshirt—mine—and out we went into the night.

Damn, the nights were pitch-black here, and the first thing I did was stub my toe on the porch step. Hopping up and down, I swore the air blue, while Rach laughed breathlessly and bent down to try to see the damage.

I looked at her crouched in front of me, in an extremely erotic position, and could only groan.

"Is it broken?" she asked anxiously.

"No." I hauled her up. "Not broken. It's just too bad my superpowers don't extend to seeing in the dark."

"Mine do." She bit her lower lip as she took me in from head to toe, stopping at one particular spot in the middle. "And, um, wow."

Yeah. Wow.

We sneaked into the dark inn together. She led the way, clearly seeing with ease, while I felt like a bumbling idiot, still limping because of my toe. Having her warm, curvy body pressed up to mine didn't help much either, and she seemed to know it. Every time I stumbled, she threw her arms around me, pressing her breasts into my ribs, holding on tight, until I began to wonder how long a male could have an erection and not die from DSB—deadly sperm buildup.

In the kitchen, Rach went directly to the freezer and grabbed a handful of cookies. "For strength," she said with utter seriousness.

We moved through the living room, Rach pulling me to safety before I could fall over a big chair in the way. Past the living room we went, down the hallway.

Rach stopped at a coat closet, then quietly opened the door and shoved me inside.

"Um—" I started to say.

"Shh."

She closed the door. In the dark, coats and sweaters brushed my face, and then Rach was plastered up against me.

"I can't see," I whispered.

"Scared?" she asked, sounding amused, and smelling like chocolate mint.

"Rach, we don't have time for this."

"For what?"

For all the wicked things running through my head.

"Silly man." She pressed me through the coats and opened another door. Which is how I found myself in a small room just off the living room, facing a tiny, cramped desk, a row of metal filing cabinets and stacks of files everywhere—strewn haphazardly across the desk, on the floor, on top of the cabinets—basically everywhere but where they belonged.

"Apparently Gertrude wasn't so great with the paperwork," Rachel said.

"A hidden office."

Rachel smiled. "Suits Great-Great Aunt Gert, believe me. Where should we start?"

Hard to say, given the state of things. "The file cabinets. Since the files all appear to be scattered out here, what's in them?"

She tried to open one, and couldn't. "They're locked."

Frowning, she concentrated on the first one, then blinked. "Kellan."

The tone of her voice alerted me, and I remembered what she'd found in the guest house: guns. "What do you see?"

"Whiskey in the bottom drawer. Good to know," she said softly. "And a laptop in this one." She pointed to the next. "But that one? It's got . . . cash. Lots of it."

"Well, isn't that just fascinating."

"A bit, yeah. And the top one—" She gulped. "A pistol."

"Okay. Give me some room."

There wasn't much room to be had in the small confines of the office, but she sat on the desk, while I pulled open the locked drawers with my new muscles, finding a laptop, a Blackberry, a gun and, indeed, a drawer full of cash.

"Jackpot," Rachel whispered, and put a hand to her head.

"What? What is it?"

"I feel weird."

I think my heart stopped. "Headache? Piercing pain?"

She shook her head.

"Dizziness?" I set everything down, and strode toward her, which took all of two steps. Putting my hands on her arms, I waited until she looked up. "Talk to me."

Her eyes shimmered brilliantly, and she shook her head. "I'm sorry. Not sick weird."

"What then?"

"Hard to explain."

"Try."

Instead, she pulled me in for a hug and held on tightly. "An I-need-you weird."

Need me. That should not have meant so much. She was scared and had no idea what she was saying.

"Am I making any sense at all?" she whispered.

"No."

But Christ, she was. And unable to resist the pull of her see-all eyes or the tremor of her lush mouth, I compounded my errors and held onto her tightly.

"This is nice," she whispered. "But by 'need you,' I mean naked."

"Uh . . ."

She squeezed her eyes shut, and if I wasn't mistaken, she blushed. "Have you ever noticed that it's always me coming onto you?" she whispered.

"Is that right?"

"Yes," she said very quietly, looking . . . embarrassed?

No. No, I didn't want that. "Let's fix that right now," I said. Clearly I'd lost my mind, but she was right.

How was it that I'd never even attempted to make a move on the most beautiful woman in the world? Oh, that's right, because we'd never been on the same plane before, much less both yearning and burning.

But there we were, on the same plane.

Yearning and burning . . .

I cupped her face and leaned in, watching her watch me as I touched my lips to hers, keeping it quiet and warm and intimate. And only when her eyes flickered did I kiss my way up her throat, making my way to the sensitive spot beneath her ear, then over her jaw, her scent and taste driving me wild, and by the time I got back to her mouth, she had her hands fisted in my hair and was helping.

"No, let me," I whispered.

And she did.

Chapter 15

My name is Rachel, my name is Rachel . . . I had to keep repeating this to myself as Kellan kissed me halfway to orgasmic bliss, because I'd discovered that if I didn't repeat my own name when he had his mouth on me, I could actually forget it.

That's how good he kissed.

We needed to get out of the office, obviously, before we were discovered, but the feel of his lips brushing my earlobe, then the sensitive skin beneath it, locked me into this weird place. Our close proximity, the dark, the danger . . . it all gathered together, like a cloak of intimacy, and I turned and put my face into the crook of his neck.

How was it he always smelled so orgasmically good?

Finally he pulled back, eyes so hot they were flaming, and breathing hard enough that he could have generated his own electricity. "Damn it, you are distracting." Then he pulled his hands from me and shoved them both into his pockets, turning away to stare glumly at the file cabinet.

"Do you really think . . ." I licked my lips and asked the question that had been haunting me. "Do you think this . . . animal magnetic attraction is just a part of the swap?"

He was quiet for a moment. "I think your attraction to me is a result of what happened to us, yes." He stood there, all tall, long and edgy, broad shoulders hunched, the muscles of his back rigid, tension coming off him in waves.

I wanted to touch him, to turn him to face me, but something held me back. Maybe it was how quickly he assumed that what I felt for him wasn't real.

So instead, I opened the laptop and hit the power button. When the thing booted up, Kellan, apparently unable to help himself, turned around and came to join me.

Just as he did, Marilee stuck her head in from the closet. "*Sheee-it,*" she muttered at the sight of us and what we were doing. "I should have known."

"You should have told."

She took in the open laptop. "I suppose you found the petty cash, too."

"More than petty."

Marilee lifted a shoulder. "Gert hated checkbooks and credit cards."

"Good thing for you, as now paying you and Axel won't be a problem."

She looked insulted. "I wasn't worried." She sniffed. "Just so you know, Gert didn't like people in her stuff."

"Gertrude is gone," I reminded her. "And I'm here now."

"For the weekend."

"For as long as I want."

"So you're going to stay here indefinitely?"

"What if I did?" I felt Kellan look at me in surprise, but I just kept my eyes on Marilee. "You have a problem with that?"

"Why would I?"

"You tell me."

"It's just that Gertrude was so sure you wouldn't. That you'd go back to Los Angeles, because that's who you are: an L.A. artist."

"Maybe I'm more than that."

"She said you weren't."

The Wood family of overachievers loved to make me the butt of their jokes, the odd duckling in their roost. Without my dad around, I was the only nonconformist, the artist. No career path, no real plan. I'd always smiled and taken it, but right now I didn't feel like smiling. "Maybe Gertrude was wrong."

Marilee glanced at the computer again. "Maybe you won't be able to get in."

"Why don't you just save us some time and trouble, and tell us what it is we're going to find?" Kellan said.

Marilee cut her eyes to him. "I think I hear Axel calling me."

Of course she did.

When she was gone, Kel pulled the laptop toward him and began clicking on the keys. "It's password-protected. Any guesses?"

I stared at the screen, and focused. "Bite me," I said, startled at how fast the words came to me.

Kellan went still, only his gaze moving as it slid over my face, stopping at my mouth. "Excuse me?"

"It's the password," I said, and then laughed at the expression on his face. "Did you *want* me to bite you?"

"You have no idea."

My body heated, but I pointed to the keyboard. "Bite me."

His eyes positively smoldered as he leaned in close enough that I could see each individual dark, long eyelash over his gorgeous baby blues.

Why were men allowed to have such pretty eyelashes? It just didn't seem fair. "*Bite me,*" I whispered again.

"Say it one more time," he promised in a low voice that sent tingles down my spine and to other places as well, "and I will not be held responsible for my actions."

I was tempted. Oh God, how tempted. There was just something about this new alpha-ness, the quiet fierceness of it and the utter confidence. He seemed both alien to me and yet almost unbearably familiar at the same time, and I stared at his mouth, the words on the tip of my tongue.

"Say it," he dared silkily.

A dare, damn it. I couldn't pass up a dare. "How about I do it instead?" Holding his gaze, I cupped his jaw and sank my teeth into his lower lip.

Shock held him immobile as I lightly tugged, then stroked my tongue over the sting of the bite.

When I straightened, I was breathing unsteadily, and he was looking pretty flustered.

"Um," he said.

Yeah. Um.

He brought his fingers up to touch his lower lip, which was still wet from my tongue. "You take every dare that comes your way?"

"You know I do."

His eyes went soft and dark and dreamy, and my thighs tightened in reaction to that. He went to push his glasses high on the bridge of his nose before remembering he wasn't wearing them. "We're not kids anymore," he said carefully.

"Did anything about that feel childish to you?"

He let out a rough laugh, but his amusement faded quickly, and he hauled me close, making me gasp as his teeth sank into the flesh between my neck and shoulder, the bite a definite aggressive sexual claim.

I shuddered with need, but he gently set me away from him and turned me toward the laptop. "Now we're even," he said, and typed in the password.

I had to blow out a breath before I pushed his fingers away and clicked on the main menu, and then on the financial application, and ran right into another password-protected area. "Huh."

He leaned over my shoulder, his arms on either side of mine, surrounding me with his body. "What?"

It would be appealing to turn in his arms and let him bite me again, then kiss me, then . . . And yet it was one thing when I was chasing him. Then it was fun, it was easy, it was playful.

A game.

But more than that, and it scared me. He scared me, because I knew he wasn't playing at all.

And if I did this, got involved heart and soul . . . *God*, what would I do without him when it was over? I couldn't bear to think about it, so I tried the password again, but it didn't work here. Incredibly aware that our faces were close enough that a strand of my hair had caught on the stubble of his jaw, that he was watching me and not the screen, made breathing difficult, if not impossible. I closed my eyes and concentrated on another password. *Nothing.* Just like old times. I tried typing in Gert's name, Marilee's name, Axel's name—

A sticky-note program suddenly opened, and a pop-up sticky appeared in a pretty pink color and fancy font:

Did you really think it'd be that easy?

Stunned, I sat back, staring at the computer screen. "She knew. Whatever's going on here, Gertrude knew all about it."

"Strange family you've got, Rach."

"Tell me." I chewed on my lip for a moment, considering. My great-great-aunt Gertrude had always been a loner. I could remember my mother sighing in frustration when another invitation to a family gathering was politely declined.

"Just as well," my mother had always said. "She's too looney to mainstream."

"Looney how?" I'd asked on any number of occasions.

"We don't discuss it," my mother had always replied. "Let's just say she thinks she can . . . do things."

I had to wonder what things. Like see through stuff? Like using superhuman strength? I picked up the Blackberry and turned it on.

"Check her calendar for the entries before she died," Kellan said.

Not surprisingly though, her social engagements were nonexistent. She'd kept track of her grocery list, and of requested supplies, of the number of guests going in and out—

"Are you seeing what I'm seeing?" Kellan asked over my shoulder.

I looked at the entries again. "What?"

Reaching his arms around me, he took possession of the Blackberry, pointing out the Fridays of the last month. "Each has a star."

"So?"

"So yesterday was Friday. What happens on Fridays that would warrant starred entries?"

We looked at each other.

"The swap," I whispered.

"And there are dots on Sundays. Fuck." He shoved his fingers through his hair. "What's going to happen tomorrow?"

I got up, went to the bottom file drawer and pulled out the whiskey. We each drank two fingers straight from the bottle.

"Jesus," Kel said, blowing out a breath. "Strong stuff."

I could have used two more fingers. "Kel?"

He'd gone back to fiddling with the Blackberry. "Yeah?"

"Let's get the hell out of Dodge."

He looked up, grimaced at the fear that had to be written all over my face and pulled me in for a hug that felt more real than anything had since . . . since he'd kissed me. Burrowing in tightly, I closed my eyes and just held on. "I mean, maybe we could hike out of here."

"Rach, it's too far."

On the other side of the closet, door someone rattled the handle.

Kellan set me aside and quickly moved through the clothes in the closet, putting his hand on the door handle, holding the door shut. With his other hand, he lifted a finger to his mouth, signaling me to be quiet.

Marilee had just walked in, not concerned with being seen. Whoever this was clearly didn't want to be seen.

I put both my hands over my mouth and concentrated on breathing. We watched the handle turn from side to side as someone very quietly tried to come in.

Kellan kept his hold, his T-shirt stretching at the shoulders, his jeans falling off his narrow hips, his hair wild as always, easily preventing the door from opening in such a way that the person on the other side of it probably imagined it was a jammed lock.

"Who's there?" Kellan mouthed to me

I focused on the wood, and gasped. "Serena and William," I mouthed back.

Kellan blinked. He hadn't expected that, and truthfully, neither had I. What would two guests want in Gertrude's secret office?

And, if they'd never been here before, how did they even know this office existed?

On the other side of the door, the two of them looked at each other, shrugged and walked away.

"They're gone," I whispered.

Kellan came out of the closet, looking lean and rangy and spoiling for a fight. "I want to know what the hell is going on." He paced the small office, which meant he could stride two whole steps before having to whip around and repeat the process. Tension and grimness rolled off his broad shoulders, and so did unused adrenaline.

I stood, and stepped into his path. "Hey."

He didn't look at me, so I held on when he started to stalk past me. "*Hey.*"

He wasn't happy when his gaze met mine. Not even close. "What?"

"Maybe we're keeping the new abilities. You ever think of that?"

"What? *No.*" He thrust his fingers into his hair, making it stand straight up. "I am not putting my hand through doors for the rest of my life, or worrying about how I touch things for fear of breaking them. Jesus, Rach." He looked me straight in the eyes, letting his own worry show, and behind that, the fierceness of his desire for me, and something deep inside me physically ached.

"What?" I whispered. "What is it?"

He looked away, then back. His jaw tightened. "What if I accidentally hurt you?"

There was an actual tremor in his voice, and in tune with it, my heart quivered. "You wouldn't," I said softly, shaken by his fear.

"I'm not thrilled with any of this shit. I'm not."

I was beginning to see that. I just didn't know what to do about it, or about another, new revelation I had. "Truth or dare?" I whispered.

"What? Rach—"

"Pick one."

He sighed. "Truth."

"Okay, here's my truth. I really like the Kel you are, right here, right now. So much that *that* scares me more than anything that's happened to us so far."

Chapter 16

He stared at me for a long beat, then turned away. "I'm different here."

"Kel, you have the same heart." I put my hands on his arms and tried to turn him back to face me. I say tried because the guy dug in his heels and was nearly impossible to budge. Only when I made a sound of frustration did he allow me to turn him. "I want you," I whispered. "*You*, Kel."

His baby blues met mine, and I let him see everything I was feeling. With a groan, he dropped his forehead to mine, his broad shoulders eclipsing the light so that it was just him and me and nothing else.

His hands came up and gripped my waist, not pulling me in, but not pushing me away either. His eyes were stubborn, but softening, as he just looked at me.

"This thing between us is temporary," he said, in the old refrain.

"How do you know?"

"Your own motto, Rach. Nothing good lasts forever. Remember?"

I stared at him. "I remember," I whispered, wishing I didn't, wishing that I'd never believed such a thing. But I did . . . "I want this to be different. God, I wish this could be different. Just this one thing."

He closed his eyes, then opened them again. "Don't you dare regret this," he said fiercely, his hands already gliding down my back, cupping my butt, pulling me close so that I could feel his reaction, at which it was impossible to hold back my sigh of pleasure.

"Love that sound," he murmured, and lifted his head, noting the desk behind him. Turning me, he used his body to press me back against it, those eyes darkening with things that made my belly quiver.

Other things quivered, too, and I bit my lower lip. "Are we going to . . ."

"Up." Then he lifted me, plopping me down on the desk.

I could tell myself he was the same guy I'd always known, the slightly goofy, always sweet, unfailingly steady Kellan, but the evidence told me otherwise. The old Kel wasn't this bold, this daring, this sexually sure of himself.

And God help me, I liked this bold, daring, sexually-sure-of himself Kel.

Very much.

In fact, I could hardly breathe, I liked him so much.

"Here, Kel?"

Reaching around me, he swiped a hand across the surface of the desk, knocking the telephone, files and paperwork all to the floor in one motion, then looked at me, silent, letting me draw my own conclusion.

Oh. My. "Okay, here," I said shakily.

He pulled off one of my tennis shoes, tossed it over my shoulder.

"Hurry," I whispered.

His eyes cut to mine as he gave the other shoe the same treatment.

"So you like it when I completely lose it?"

I liked it so much, I couldn't speak. I think I managed a nod.

"Yeah? Then try this." Putting a hand on each of my thighs, he nudged them open, then stepped between so that I couldn't close them.

He'd turned into every badass I'd ever fantasized about. "Um. Kel? Now?"

He pulled off my sweatshirt.

I couldn't breathe. "Are you going to say anything at all?"

"*Now.*"

The air stuck in my throat, and a shiver of thrill raced down my spine, as I gripped the desk on either side of my hips for dear life.

Kel reached for the hem of my camisole. "Arms," he said in a gruff whisper.

I lifted my hands up and felt my breasts spring free as he pulled off the shirt. His gaze was still holding mine, but then he let it drop, drinking in his fill of me with a sigh of pleasure so real, so deep, that I felt the answering tug in my womb.

His fingers went to the waistband of my pj bottoms.

"Um," I said, momentarily sidetracked by the thought of being bare-ass naked to his fully clothed self, but he didn't give me much time to dwell on this, because he slowly but firmly began to tugg my pj bottoms down over my hips.

"Um—"

"You already said that."

Another tug had the pj's to my thighs.

Then to my knees . . .

I was wearing a smiley-face thong with lace trim that made him go utterly still for a beat.

"Oh man," he groaned, and abandoned my pj's, dangling off one ankle, to trace a finger over the lace. "You take my breath. Every single time."

"There's been only one time."

"Every single time I look at you."

I stared down at his bent head, a little stunned by this revelation. "Kel—"

But he surged up and kissed me, long and wet and deep, and that, combined with his questing finger, drained any thoughts right out of my head.

Then he dropped to his knees, scraped my thong to one side and leaned in and put his mouth on me.

Oh. My. God. I fell back against the desk, gripping the wood at my sides like an anchor, as he took me on a rocking ride that left me unable to control my senses. Lights burst behind my eyeballs, my blood rushed through my veins, roaring in my ears, so that I couldn't hear a damn thing. I think I probably cried out, maybe even screamed his name, but I didn't have enough self-awareness left to be embarrassed. All I could do was ride it out, wave after wave, only to have him bring me up yet again, and again . . .

Finally I came back to myself, only to hear what sounded like Frankenstein gulping air in and out of a set of taxed lungs. "Someone's breathing loud," I whispered.

"That's you."

I opened my eyes. Kellan was leaning over me, a hand on either side of my head, bracing his weight off me.

He'd just given me the most amazing oral sex of my life, and I think, given the way his eyes glittered, he probably knew it.

And the crazy breathing? It *was* me. Damn, how mortifying. But the more I tried to control it, the more ragged it sounded. "Sorry." I tried to sit up, but he held me down.

"Don't be sorry. I like knowing I can do that to you."

I ran my gaze down his body, stopping at the unmistakable bulge behind his button fly. "Tell me you have a condom."

With a sheepish smile that said he wasn't all Superman all the time, a fact that possibly endeared him to me all the more, he pulled one out of his pocket. "It's one of yours."

"You were hoping—"

"More like praying."

I laughed, and realized that was a first—laughing with a man I wanted so badly, I was shaking for him. I took the condom out of his hand and tore the packet open.

He opened his jeans.

I slipped my hands inside.

He hissed out a breath.

"Good?" I murmured, melting all over again.

"Cold," he muttered. "Christ, your fingers are ice."

"Baby."

He hissed again, but since I could feel him growing, swelling, even more, I didn't worry. In fact, I grinned. "You still want me."

"Go figure."

Watching him put on the condom, his jaw tight enough to be jumping, the tendons in his neck standing out in bold relief, his arms and shoulders tense, was an experience I'll never forget. I pushed up his shirt for the sheer pleasure of watching his abs contract beneath my fingers, and had barely pulled the material over his head when he eased himself into me.

The pure gratification of the connection stunned us both into immobility. I could feel him, thick and pulsing inside me, could feel his tremors, and knew how rigidly he controlled himself. I didn't want that, so I wrapped my legs around him, driving him forward, deep enough to make me gasp.

"Jesus." His gorgeous eyes went blind, and he dropped his forehead to mine. "Am I hurting you?"

"Only if you don't move."

"I'm trying to make it last longer than two seconds," he managed.

"It's been longer than two seconds."

"Rach—"

I dug my heels into the small of his back, and I bit his jaw.

"So violent," he murmured, but still held back.

"Kel, I want you as out of control as I was!"

His eyes softened. "Ah, Rach. Don't you know that you look at me and I'm out of control?"

"Love me," I whispered. "Please? Just love me."

That did it, and finally, finally, he began to move, watching himself fill me in a way I couldn't remember ever being filled before. I closed my eyes to savor the feeling, and also, maybe, to hide a little.

"No," he whispered, open and honest in a way that didn't come as easily for me. "Rach, look at me."

With a struggle, I opened my eyes, struck by the combination of tenderness and affection and heat I found in his.

"Yeah," he breathed, his own beautiful gaze holding mine prisoner now. "Love that."

I'd never done this, connected like this, eyes open, heart open . . . and by doing so, I found myself giving so much more than I'd ever given before. I gave him all of me, everything I had, and a bit afraid, I clutched at him.

"I'm right here with you," he promised softly, and bending for a kiss, finally took me where I wanted to go.

Oblivion.

And he was right next to me the entire way.

When I could breathe again, I realized I had my face plastered into Kel's neck and my fingers embedded low on his back. I pulled back slowly, and blew the hair out of my face.

Kel looked no less shaken as he pulled me upright on the desk. "What the hell *is* that?"

"Don't worry," I said, smiling into his unsmiling face. "I don't think it's fatal."

He looked at me for another long beat, then nodded. "That's a relief."

But then he turned away, leaving me vaguely uneasy.

"Kel?"

"Truth or dare."

"Truth," I whispered.

He didn't turn to face me. "You really think this would be happening between us if we hadn't come here? You know, to the sexually healing B&B from hell."

I opened my mouth, then closed it, not wanting to lie. I honestly had no idea how it was that I'd not been so attracted to him before. It had taken this trip, being within such close proximity—

"Never mind," he said, again fiddling with the Blackberry. "We have more important things to do. Such as figuring out what the dot means for tomorrow."

Our gazes met, and the somber knowledge flitted between us. As bad as things were, we both knew it could get worse, so much, much worse. I tried to think about it, but I was so tired, I yawned widely.

Kel tucked both the Blackberry and the laptop beneath his sweatshirt. "Bed," he said in a quiet, authoritative voice that I was beginning to react to like I suspected his dolphins did. Kellan McInty, animal whisperer. *Rachel* whisperer.

"You need some sleep before we figure out the rest of this swap thing," he said. "And so do I. Back to the guest house."

"With one little pit stop on the way."

"Let me guess. The freezer?"

"Problem?"

"No. I don't care if you eat every last cookie in the place. As long as Marilee doesn't find out."

"Why? Are you afraid of her?"

He stood there, shirt a bit wrinkled from the time it'd spent wadded on the floor, his jeans disturbingly low on his hips, looking good enough to jump. *Again*.

"Actually, I have bigger things to fear at the moment," he said.

Which left me to wonder. Did he mean the swap, the impending dot . . . or me?

Chapter 17

We escaped the office and made our way through the dark inn, me in front leading the way with my night-vision abilities in order to save Kellan's toes and shins. I steered us through the living room and into the kitchen. The wood stove was still hot, with embers glowing red. We were halfway across the floor when a creak sounded from above.

"Did you hear that?" I asked.

"Yeah." Kellan had one hand in mine, and he was so close behind me that I could feel his warm breath brush my temple, blowing bangs into my eyes. He felt big and warm and safe, and right then and there, I experienced a warm fuzzy the likes of which I'd never experienced before.

Or I *would* have felt warm and fuzzy if I could have shaken off the sense of impending doom.

"What was it?" I asked.

The sound came again.

Someone was moving around quietly, not wanting to be heard.

Kellan squeezed my hip, putting his mouth to my ear. "Can you focus on it? Who is it?"

Damn, I kept forgetting I could tell. I looked up, and sighed. "Marilee. She's pacing her bedroom."

"Why?" he wondered.

"I don't know."

"Let's get out of here."

"Yes, but first . . ." I headed straight for the freezer and grabbed a few cookies, offering one to Kel, who shook his head. Damn, that was probably how he stayed so much leaner than me.

We went out into the night. Again, that odd sense of noisy silence surrounded us—air rustling through the trees, a coyote calling in the distance . . .

Or some other wild animal that I didn't want to meet.

The stars scattered across the black-velvet sky lit our way, but I'd have rather been home, with so many city lights, they drowned out the stars.

Inside the guest house, Kel set the laptop and Blackberry on the coffee table, and took me straight to the bedroom, where he pulled back the covers on the prissy, lacy bed and waited until I obediently slipped between the sheets.

"You coming in?" I asked, and batted my eyes.

"Bad idea."

"I'm cold."

He pulled the covers up to my chin, tucking them in, as if looking at me would weaken his resolve. "I'm not falling for that one."

"I *am* cold."

He put his hands on his hips, looking tense, rough around the edges and slightly temperamental. "You want me to crawl in there with you and share my body heat."

"Uh-huh."

"And other things."

"You're quick, Kel."

"I need to think. And I can't do that when you're near me."

"Ah, that's the sweetest thing anyone's ever said to me."

If possible, he looked even more tense. "I'm not feeling particularly sweet, Rach."

Well, if that wasn't arousing. Tossing the covers aside, I came up to my knees on the mattress. I cupped his beautiful face and looked deep into his drown-in-me eyes. "I want you."

"For now."

"At the moment, now is all we have." And besides, thinking ahead to what I'd want tomorrow, or the day after that, wasn't in my genetic makeup. "Can't that be enough?"

A shuddery sigh escaped him, and his hands came up to my hips, squeezed. His voice, when he spoke, sounded tortured. "No."

He said it so gently, it took a moment for it to sink in.

"But—"

His arms came around me, and I felt the softening in him that I needed, even as his body became harder than ever. The hug clogged my throat with emotion, because I knew it was a good-bye hug. I held on, and closed my eyes. "You make me feel so safe, Kel."

"You are safe. I'll make sure of it. Even when—or if—I change back."

I blinked back tears. "Another promise."

"I mean it."

No one had ever said such a thing to me before, in a voice so fierce I didn't doubt he'd keep me safe if it meant his own life.

I'd never wanted anyone to say such a thing. I don't know if I was ready to want *him* to.

I wasn't.

Of course, I wasn't.

I was young. Twenty-seven. I was a modern woman who could take care of herself. I always had.

But a small part of me stared at him with a bunch of what-ifs suddenly flowing through my head.

But before I could finish processing, a shockingly loud *BOOM* sounded, shaking the ground beneath us. The shelves rattled, the furniture jumped.

Not to mention us.

With an oath, Kellan grabbed me off the bed and dragged me to the doorway, but as fast and loud and hard as the Earth had rumbled, it stopped.

Everything went completely, almost unnaturally, still. Not a sound, not a remnant shudder, nothing.

And then, from out of the darkness and through the windows, came a high-pitched scream.

"Marilee?" I gasped, reaching for Kellan. "Was that Marilee?"

I'd never seen him so grim. He pushed me back into the bedroom while at the same time flipping off the light, flipping off all the lights. "Wait right here," he said urgently. "Stay still, and don't make a sound, all right?"

"Kel—"

"Say you'll do it." He pushed me behind the door, thrusting something into my hands.

I stared down through the dark at his flashlight. "I don't need—"

"Listen to me. This thing is heavy. If you swing it just right—"

"*Kel—*"

"A nice hit to the head will make an assailant kiss the floor long enough for you to get away."

"Oh my God."

"Promise me you'll use it if you need to."

"I don't—"

"*Promise me.*"

He was so fierce, so serious, and I think that scared me more than anything else had so far. "You think something very bad is happening."

"Promise me, Rach."

"I promise," I said very quietly, instead of clinging, as I really, *really* wanted to do.

And then he was walking away from me, hands out in front

of him, staggering slightly, heading directly for the coffee table instead of the door. "Kel—"

Too late. He tripped right over it, going down flat on his face.

I ran to his side just as he rolled over.

"Out of all the abilities I could have gotten," he said through clenched teeth as he rocked back and forth holding on to his shins, "I had to get worthless superstrength, when a little grace would have done me."

"Are you all right?"

"I will be." He got up, felt around for me and pulled me close for one beat. "Stay here."

I let him get to the front door, fumbling, limping now, before I called his name softly. When he turned around, blind in the dark, I walked to him and slipped him back the flashlight. "You need this more than me, Superboy. And here's something else to chew on. I'm going with you."

"You are not."

"Am, too."

"Not."

"Kel."

"*Rach—*"

The front door whipped open, almost slamming into us. In the doorway stood Serena and William, both with their clothes askance, hair mussed, eyes wild, looking as if they'd been interrupted right in the middle of a good time.

"Thank God," Serena said at the sight of us, and pushed her way inside the dark guest house. "We don't have a lot of time. I assume you have the laptop. Can I have it, please?"

"No," Kel said.

"It's imperative."

"I'm sorry." Kel said this with genuine regret as he shook his head forcefully, not looking at me, while I—the only one with clear vision in the dark—very carefully and slowly backed away, slipping the laptop from the coffee table to beneath the couch, out of sight. The Blackberry, being smaller, fit beneath my shirt. I didn't know why I needed it, but it felt important.

"I don't know what the hell is going on," Kel said to Serena and William. "Or whom to trust. Until I do, you're SOL."

Serena looked in my direction.

"Shit out of luck," I translated for her. "And I think he means it."

"You don't understand—"

"That would be correct," Kel agreed. "We don't understand. A point that pisses me off greatly."

She sighed, and William shut the door, then locked both the handle and the bolt. "No, no lights," he said urgently when I reached for the lamp. "We have to hide you. Now."

"And get the laptop," Serena said, turning on a small penlight, using it to search around, single-minded in her mission for the computer. "I know you have it."

"Why do you have to hide us?" I asked.

"You're going to have to trust us," William said.

"No, we're not." This from Kellan.

"Oh, we don't have time for this!" Serena pushed her way through the living room toward the kitchenette, searching there as well. "This is serious. You must trust us. Now!"

"Why?" Kellan asked. "Because you've been so honest so far?"

Serena had the good grace to look a little ashamed. "I know, it's hard."

"What was that loud boom?" I asked. "Who screamed?"

"Now see, that's what we don't have time for." Pressing himself flat against the wall, William craned only his neck and peeked out the window, seeming satisfied with whatever he saw.

Or didn't see.

He nodded at Serena, who frantically waved for us to follow her into the kitchen.

I looked at Kellan, who stood firm. "Tell us what that loud rumble was."

"If you hide right now, without further delay," Serena said without answering, "everything will be okay. I promise you."

"If you ever answered a question," Kellan countered, "things would be better."

"There's no time for questions," William said grimly.

"Or answers." Serena gestured us close. "Please. You must come with us."

William still had his back to the front wall, silently keeping watch out the window. He turned his head and looked at Serena. "Still clear. But not for long. Cut the flashlight."

"Please," Serena begged us, slipping her flashlight into her pocket, then resorting to grabbing first my hand, then Kellan's. "Just come. It's your lives that are in jeopardy here."

It was that, and her palpable fear and undeniable desperation, that ultimately reached me.

Our lives were in jeopardy?

We let her pull us into the tiny kitchen, where she opened the pantry door. Inside the small closet were shelves filled with stock and enough dry goods to last for months, and as a result, there wasn't room for the four of us to stand.

Serena shoved us all in there anyway, with William taking up the rear. To shut the door meant plastering us all up against each other, which she did. I had my nose in Kellan's armpit, my elbow in William's ribs, my butt to Serena's.

And then I saw what I hadn't taken the time to see yesterday. What I couldn't have seen yesterday because I'd been in here before "the swap."

There was a trap door, similar to the one that led to Gertrude's hidden office, which led down to a basement that I could already tell I wasn't going to like because it was dark and cramped and quite possibly filled with spiders.

"In," Serena said, and opened the door and pushed us onto the stairs landing. She and William followed.

The stairs creaked and trembled beneath our weight, which didn't make me happy. "I don't know—"

"In," Serena repeated firmly.

Once at the bottom, Serena flicked her small flashlight on, and we surveyed our surroundings.

Just as I'd seen from above, the basement was small and cramped, basically empty but for a few crates and boxes. It had a high, narrow window, through which moonlight flitted in. It was a gorgeous night, clear and bright.

"This way," William said, and pointed to what looked like a paneled wall but was really—

"Great," Kellan said. "Another door."

Which opened to a big, yawning tunnel.

"Are there any normal, plain doors in this place?" Kellan asked, but it must have been a rhetorical question, because no one answered.

William gestured for Serena to go first, which she did without hesitation. Then he looked at Kellan and me. "I'm sorry. I know you don't understand, but this is for your own good, tr—"

"Yeah," Kellan said grimly. "Trust you."

The two men looked at each other for a long beat, Kellan's face steely and pensive, and most definitely not trusting.

"Okay." William scrubbed his hands over his face. "This is going to sound pretty whacky, and you're going to think I've been sharing some funny tobacco with Axel, but I swear to you, it's the truth."

"Just spit it out," Kellan said. "How exactly are we in danger?"

"This place is . . . special."

"Will—"

At Serena's protest, William took her hand, then continued with his explanation. "It's special in that people—people who are different—come here because this is the only place they get a break from their lives."

"Different how?" Kellan asked.

"They have . . . abilities," William said. "And when they come here, they're relieved of these abilities for the duration of their stay. Like a vacation of sorts."

"And you . . . you're *special*?" I asked, wondering if humoring an obviously insane person could be dangerous to my health.

"Yes," Serena answered. "We have—*had*—abilities. William could see, um"—she glanced at him—"everything, and I had a special strength."

"Past tense," I said.

Kellan nodded. "Because in the so-called swap, you gave them to us."

"Yes."

Kellan looked at me. "Well, take them back. We don't want them."

Even as I knew he was right, a part of me wanted to say, Let's not be hasty . . .

William shook his head. "Sorry, but we don't want the abilities back."

"What?"

He smiled at me with both regret and joy as he took Serena's hand. "Yeah, we weren't going to take them back. We planned this. We don't want the abilities."

"You planned this," I repeated.

"Well, not this. Not ever this."

"And what is *this* exactly?"

William looked at Serena, who shook her head slightly. "Let's just say, we didn't want to go back." He pulled Serena close, and she leaned her head on his shoulder.

"We like your plane," she said to us.

"Plane," I said weakly. "You mean . . ."

"Your plane of reality."

"Uh-huh." I was *not* swallowing this. "And how many 'planes' are there?"

"Oh, there's an infinite number of levels," William said

calmly. "None more real than the next, of course. But this one is good."

Boggling.

"We just want to stay here, but to stay, we have to pass off our abilities."

I stared at them. "You can't just do that. I mean, what would you do without them?" Jesus, I really sounded like I was buying all this.

"Oh, you can keep them. But you can't stay here on this plane if you do."

"Oh no," Kellan said before I could respond. "Hell no."

"We just don't want to see you killed for them," Serena said. "So we have to hide you."

"Yeah, about that killed thing," Kellan said.

Serena wrung her hands, and looked worriedly over her shoulder. "We'll get to that. But we really need to get—"

"Let's discuss the killed thing first," Kellan said tightly. "And when I say 'us,' I mean you. You discuss. *Now.*"

"Look, this was supposed to be a safe zone," Serena said quickly. "The in-between. But . . ." She winced. "Once in a blue moon, pirates get through. They're tricky bastards."

Pirates. *Pirates?* "Is that why Gert had guns?" I asked in horror.

"Yes," William said, and shuddered. "Though I don't believe fighting is the answer."

"Exactly how many safe zones are there?" Kellan asked. "And how fast can we get to another one?"

"There are only two. The other one is brand-new. It's in the Bahamas. We wanted a warmer climate," William explained.

"The Bahamas." Now why couldn't Great-Great-Aunt Gertrude have owned a B&B in the Bahamas? See, that would have been a location I could have really gotten behind! "Are there . . ."

"Pirates?" William supplied helpfully.

"Yes." I swallowed hard, and tried not to let the words take root in my brain for fear I'd start laughing hysterically and never be able to stop. "Are there pirates there, too?"

"Probably not. They don't know about the new location yet."

"So none of that killing thing happening there?"

William shook his head.

I nodded as if this all made perfect sense. "Let's go there then."

"Okay." William nodded in relief. "Good. Outside, quickly."

"Where we'll call Jack?" I asked. "Radio him back up here? He can get us to the closest airport, and off we'll go to the Bahamas, right?"

Serena bit her lower lip.

William slowly shook his head.

Ah hell. I didn't think so. Because nothing was going to be that damn easy.

"We'll take you, but we need the laptop."

"Why?" Kel asked.

"That's the power-source director."

"Power-source director?" Kel said.

"It's . . . like a TV remote," William explained. "Gets you set up to go right where you want to go. Otherwise, well, there's some guesswork involved, and that's never a good thing."

Okay, this was just getting weirder and weirder. I looked at Kel, who sighed. "I'll be right back," he said.

"Kel, no—" I said.

"I promise, I'll be right back." He squeezed my hand, giving me a long look that said to trust him.

While Kel and Serena ran back upstairs, William and I held our breath, not so much as moving, until they returned. *Safe.*

For now . . .

Serena held the laptop.

Kel looked at me again, silently telling me it was going to be okay.

Then I saw the bulge at his hip I had no idea how he'd done it, but he'd grabbed a gun.

Oh God. I tried to keep cool and calm, tried to remain normal, but nothing was normal at all . . .

Then, from far above came the crash of a door slamming open. Serena jumped, and covered her mouth with shaking fingers. "We don't have time to get outside and make the emergency swap right now," she whispered. "They're here. *Hurry.*"

William looked so grim and frightened that I stepped into the tunnel with Serena, and after a moment's hesitation, Kellan did the same.

William shut and bolted the tunnel from the inside, and brought up the rear. It seemed like we walked forever, but in reality, it was probably only a minute before we came to another door. We all went through it, to another small landing and a set of stairs going straight up. William locked the door behind us, and we began to climb.

And climb.

At the fourth landing was another door.

"Getting tired of doors," Kellan said.

William cautiously opened it, peeked, then gestured Kel and me in ahead of them. As I turned to protest, the trapdoor shut in my face.

And then came the sound of the bolt sliding home.

"This door can't hold up to my strength," Kellan warned them on the other side. "You know that."

"Listen to me," Serena said urgently through the door. "I know you can burst through this, but you mustn't. We're hiding you. We're trying to protect you. Please, please, believe me. Don't turn on the light. *And do not come out this way!*"

Kel put his hand on the door as if tempted to break it down regardless.

I put a hand on his back, and felt his hot, damp muscles leap.

"Just don't make any noise," William urged through the door. "They've already searched up here. They won't think to come back. They don't know about the tunnels. They're not smart enough to think of it on their own."

"Let me guess," Kellan said tightly. "The pirates."

"Trust me, I hope you never meet them. They can't stay past dawn's first light. Plus, they don't have the abilities you have, so if you just remain quiet and wait them out, it'll be all right. I promise you."

It was insane, it was all so insane, and I moved closer to Kellan. Through the door, I could see Serena shift closer to William as well, and bury her head in his shoulder. He hugged her tight, as if comforting her, then looked worriedly at the door. At me. "It's going to be okay," he said again, as if he knew I was watching. "Just stay quiet and hidden. We'll be back for you at dawn." He looked over his shoulder, peering down the stairs, then took Serena's hand and vanished back the way we'd come.

Leaving us alone, in the dark.

I was able to see through dark, of course. We were in Hideaway now, I realized. In the attic, which was surprisingly large and stuffed with old furniture and boxes, as if Gertrude maybe had never thrown a single thing away in her very long, ninety-year lifetime. Above us hung a heavy light, some sort of glass chandelier, but I left it off.

Kellan sneezed, then turned on his flashlight. Dust danced eerily in the narrow beam of light, and he sneezed again.

Neither Kel's flashlight nor my vision were able to penetrate the far-reaching corners, where shadows seemed to lurk, and I scooted toward him.

With a sigh, he tugged me close. "What's this?" He reached beneath my sweatshirt, pulling out the Blackberry. "Ah, good thinking." He slipped it in his back pocket, and hugged me again. "Never a dull moment with you," he said, and pressed his cheek to the top of my head.

Chapter 18

"I've decided there's something to be said for dull," I said. "Dull's the new excitement." My voice wavered. It was all getting to me. My stomach jangled, my knees wobbled. "I really miss dull," I whispered.

Kel tried to study me in the darkness. "What's going on, Rach?"

"I'm cursing the day I thought I needed adventure and got on a plane. And when I say 'plane,' I mean airplane, not level of reality. You?"

"I meant, what can you see?"

"Oh." I sighed, and looked around with my new-and-improved vision. "Well, we're in the attic."

"Where is everyone else?"

I looked at the floor and saw through it. Nothing on the level beneath us. And nothing on the floor below that. But on the bottom floor . . . "Omigod."

"What?"

"Two men in the kitchen, standing in front of the freezer, eating—*Hey!* They're eating the cookies!" Then I saw more, and fear froze me to the very core. "They're armed."

"Okay." Kel sounded unhappy about this news. "Where are Axel and Marilee, and William and Serena?"

I searched. “I don’t see anyone else. My God, do you think they’re all okay?”

“Well, they have the laptop.”

“Yes.” My voice sounded small. “I hope they don’t go to the Bahamas without us.”

“I don’t know if they can. We have the abilities.” He grimaced. “That’s getting easier to say, which scares me.”

“Kel, what’s going to happen to us?”

He reached for something tucked into his waistband: the gun he’d taken from Gert’s.

“Kel.” I swallowed hard. “Can you actually use that?”

“Maybe not with any finesse, but if it comes right down to it, I’ll do what needs to be done.” He said this with just enough grimness that I knew he meant it. “I need you to keep an eye out. If our unwelcome guests start upstairs—”

“Oh my God.”

“Will said they already searched up here. Let’s just try the stay-quiet thing.” He tucked the gun back into his waistband and pulled out the Blackberry. “Time to make this thing give us some answers.”

The glow from the small screen lit up the dark. Kel’s face became visible, and I looked at him, so familiar, so damn important to me. *I’d* gotten us into this. If we died here . . . *God.* My throat closed. “Kel.”

“Hang on.” He was working the buttons, oblivious. I could see his fingers, and the cuts on them from putting his fist through two doors now, and I took his hand.

He glanced at me, eyes blind in the dark. “What?”

“Just making sure you’re okay.” I ran a finger over his palm. “It’s you I’m worried about.”

“I can take care of myself,” I said softly. “Always have.”

“I know. But that doesn’t make it easier.”

“You’re not alone in worrying, you know. I do it, too.”

His gaze searched mine in the dark. “Do you?”

I could barely speak past the ball of emotion. "So much, Kel."

His eyes never wavered. "I'm never sure what you think, when it comes to me. And you and me."

"I guess that's fair," I managed to say with a little smile. "Since I've pretty much been confused about that since we got here. You're, um, not my usual type."

"Yeah, you've dated some real winners."

I opened my mouth, but at the look on his face, and the knowledge deep down inside that he was right, I shut it again. "So I've had some wild oats to sow."

"A few."

"As my friend, you're supposed to give me unsolicited opinions. It's an unspoken pact of our relationship. You could have tried to talk me out of a few of them."

"Rach, has anyone ever successfully talked you out of anything?"

"Okay, I'm a little stubborn."

"A little?"

"Kel." I shook my head. "Sometimes . . . I'm not sure what it is you want from me."

His smile faded, his eyes letting the heat shine through, just plain, primitive, raw emotion that told me exactly what he did want: me. On a platter.

The man made my knees wobble without saying a word. "Kel—"

"No," he said, shaking his head. "I don't want to go there again."

"But . . ." I put words to my biggest fear. "If we don't get out of here—"

"We're going to get out. Trust me, you're going to live to torture me another day."

I'd always been aware of him having a crush on me, but he'd never put it to words, and I certainly never had. I think the truth was, I'd always felt terrified that if he did say anything, it'd mean the end of our relationship, which had always meant everything to me. *Everything.*

And now I could lose him anyway. "You want—"

"Nothing. I want nothing from you."

"No, don't do that. I want to be honest; I need you to be honest. You don't want to have a causal thing with me, and my first instinct is to run, because I haven't done anything deep when it comes to men. The deepest I've ever done is—"

"Cade."

A fellow painter I'd dated for three months before finding him in bed with his roommate. For me, it'd been a passionate affair, and I'd mistaken lust for love. Hindsight was always twenty-twenty. "No."

"Devlin, then."

The Harley-driving bartender. I'd met him after I'd painted a mural in his bar. We'd burned hot and cold for a few months, before his intensity had scared me away. Well, that, and his habit of drinking himself into a coma at night. "No."

"Then—"

"You," I said, and drew a deep breath at that admission. "You, Kel."

His startlingly blue eyes didn't waver. "But we never mixed friendship with anything more."

"But our friendship . . . it's the deepest, most important relationship with a man I've ever had," I admitted. "It's why I'm afraid to screw it up by adding . . ."

"More." He shoved his fingers through his hair, and turned in a slow, frustrated circle. "So you can't give anything else, and I can't take less. Hell of a place to be."

Oh God. I was losing him. "Good things don't last, Kel—"

"Bullshit."

"Oh really?" I put my hands on my hips, not that he could see me. "What was the last relationship you had that lasted?"

"My relationships have all been good ones."

"But none lasted," I persisted.

He stared at me. "You're saying what then? That you can sleep with a guy but not get to know him, or you can get to know him but not sleep with him?"

Well, when he put it like that, I sounded as crazy as my great-great-aunt Gertrude. "It's made for some pretty limiting relationships," I allowed.

"This weekend is a bit of a departure for you then. Sleeping with a good friend."

"You knew it was."

"So when I told you this was a bad idea . . ."

"I know." I covered my face. "I'm sorry, but . . ."

"But what? You were just carried away? By my . . . what did you call it? Animal magnetism?"

He sounded frustrated and hurt, because that was the part of himself that he'd gained here, with the swap. Or so he thought. I was beginning to see he'd had it all along, though I had no way of proving that to him. "Kel—"

"No, it's all right. I get it." He went back to the Blackberry, jabbing at it a little harder than necessary.

"It has nothing to do with you," I insisted. "It's me, and my inability—"

"More BS." He looked up, his eyes dark and full of temper. "You have the ability to do anything you want. Look, let's talk about something that's helpful, like how to access some info— Well. Look at that . . ."

"What?"

"Did Gert ever e-mail you?"

"No, I doubt she even knew how."

"Oh, she knew how." He showed me the screen, which revealed e-mail files for Gert, Marilee and Axel. He opened Axel's.

I stared at it for a moment as the ramifications fell into place. "But Axel said he didn't know how to use a computer."

"Read," Kel suggested, and I turned the screen more fully toward me so I could.

To: Marilee
From: Axel
Subject: Trouble
Gert was right. Her niece e-mailed me from the Web site, and has called several times. She's coming.

To: Axel
From: Marilee
Subject: Trouble
Be ready. And remember your part.

Kel pulled up the reply.

To: Marilee
From: Axel
Subject: Trouble
I know my part. Be the stoner. It'll be fun, delving into my past.

A smiley-face emoticon came after this, animated and bouncing up and down.

To: Axel
From: Marilee
Subject: Trouble
It wasn't so in your past.

To: Marilee
From: Axel
Subject: Trouble
Fair enough. Don't worry, I won't regress.

To: Axel
From: Marilee
Subject: Trouble
Let's just do this. Show the place off, and then get her to go back to L.A. Then things can continue status quo. I like status quo, Axel.

To: Marilee
From: Axel
Subject: Trouble
Status quo, and all that it implies, works for me.

To: Axel
From: Marilee
Subject: Trouble
Implies?

To: Marilee
From: Axel
Subject: Trouble
You know, the you-wanting-me thing.

To: Axel
From: Marilee
Subject: Trouble
Oh, delusional one. I do not want you.

To: Marilee
From: Axel
Subject: Trouble
You're such a beautiful liar.

To: Axel
From: Marilee

Subject: Trouble
Stop e-mailing me.

And he must have, because there were no more e-mail messages in the file. Kel clicked on Gert's file.

To: Marilee
From: Gert
Subject: This weekend's guests
This weekend's guests are Serena and William, regulars, as you know. Are we ready?

"What did Marilee reply?"

Kellan looked, but eventually shook his head. "I don't think she did before Gert died."

"They all talk about this swap thing like . . . like it's normal," I said unevenly. "And what the hell happened? How did we become the unwitting hosts? They can't just do that."

"But they did. Look at this one."

To: Gert
From: Perry Dickenson at All Travels
Subject: 4 stars!
Once again your B&B has been nominated for Favorite Alt-Uni Mini-Vacation. It's also been upgraded from a 3-star to a 4-star destination. Congrats, and keep up the good work!

I stared at it. "Alt-uni?"

"No idea," Kellan said, then combed through some other files. "Huh. Look at this. It's labeled Alt-Uni: Rules."

Iron-clad rules, punishable by banishment:

- No swapping with unsuspectings.

- No stealing of abilities.
- No swapping for longer than three days.
- Pirates are to be shot on sight.

I gulped hard. "Pirates."

Kellan scowled. "Unsuspectings."

"Shot on sight. What the hell is that?"

Kellan slipped an arm around me and shook his head. "Really don't know. And really don't like not knowing."

"It's like we're in some Harry Potter world. And I want out."

"Where is everyone? Can you see?"

I focused, then felt my heart kick hard. "I don't see anyone. Nothing moving at all."

"Really?"

"Yeah, but why?" Panic filled me again. What was happening to the others? Were they okay? Damn, I was so darn tired of the fear. "Kel, maybe we should make a run for it."

"Where to?"

Good point.

"We're better off waiting for dawn," he continued, running a hand up my arm, his eyes peering through the dark in my general direction. "Serena said they'd have to leave then."

"Can you see me at all?"

"Not so good," he admitted, and let his fingers do the walking, stroking my jaw, my cheeks, wiping away a tear I hadn't even realized I'd shed.

"Hey," he murmured, tugging me with him as he sank into the closest piece of furniture, a high-backed Victorian couch. Dust rose, enclosing us, and Kellan sneezed a few times "We're going to be okay," he promised, his hands staying on me.

Which was good. I liked that part a lot. With his hands on me, and the dark all around us, the adrenaline and fear turned into something else as I snuggled up to him on that dusty couch. "Kel?"

"Yeah?"

I slipped a leg on either side of him, straddling him.

He went completely and utterly still, only his face lifting to mine. "What are you doing?"

"Well . . ." I'd been kind of hoping he'd know. "Looking for comfort, I guess."

"Feels like more than that. And anyway, didn't we just do this?"

"Again."

"Rach," he said cautiously, and set the Blackberry aside. The screen went dark, robbing him of even that small bit of light. He blinked like an owl.

"You really can't see anything?"

"Nothing."

"Hmm."

His voice went even more cautious. "This is not going to happen."

"Work with me here." I loved the look on his face, that wary arousal. "It made us feel better before, remember?" I leaned forward, and he put his hand out to feel exactly where I was, coming in accidental contact with my breast.

"Damn it," he said, and yanked back.

I took his hands and put them on my hips.

"*Rach.*"

I loved it when he said my name like that, as if I was both torturing him and yet was his next breath of air. "I'm just taking us back to where we were at the guest house, before we were interrupted."

"We were not doing this."

"No, but I wanted to be."

"Yeah, but—Oh God."

I'd leaned in, and because I was straddling him, the movement brought us flush together in a specific spot that had him breaking out an oath and me sucking in my breath.

I wriggled a little bit, just to get even closer. A rough sound escaped him, and I think I heard him grinding his back teeth into powder.

"You're wrong," he said in a tight voice. "We were not going here. Not again."

I leaned down and kissed him, making a liar out of him, when his arms came up and surrounded me, holding tight, as if he didn't want to let go.

As if maybe he didn't want to ever let go.

Chapter 19

"This is not going to happen just because we're here alone," Kellan said into my hair.

I held him tight. "How about terror? Can it happen because of the terror?"

"No."

"Okay." I tightened my legs on him. "How about in case we die?"

He groaned. "We're not going to die, damn it." His arms gathered me in even closer, and he buried his face in the crook of my neck.

God, I loved the feel of that, his rough jaw skimming over my tender skin, his mouth pressing against my throat, tasting me as if he couldn't help himself. I loved the feel of his body, all six feet two of lean hard muscle and hot libido. Plus he had this way of moving, sort of like a cat, at least when he could see. Had he always moved like that? Hard to believe I'd never noticed . . .

And then there were those liquid, sky blue eyes, or how about the coup de grâce, that always, no matter whether we'd been lost in the woods, flying in a tin can or just plain running from unknown bad guys, he always smelled warm and sexy and one-hundred-percent pure, yummy male?

Slipping my fingers into his unruly hair, I held his head close. In reply, he kissed my throat, then my jaw, while his hand, low on my spine, urged me even closer. He felt so good against me, and I turned my head so I could nibble at the corner of his sexy mouth.

His fingers curled into the back of the sweatshirt I wore. "I no longer have enough blood in my brain to make a rational decision here. Rach . . ." he said when I tightened my fingers in his hair.

I kissed him, and he responded, and in that moment, all alone with him like this, adrenaline flowing, fear wild, there was nowhere else I'd rather have been.

Kel made a low, rough sound in his throat again, the one that said he had to be inside me, buried deep, now. *Yesterday.* Then he lifted his head, his eyes revealing everything he felt, all the pent-up need warring with careful restraint. "You're killing me."

Because he loved me. He loved me, and I knew it. The knowledge bathed me, and something deep within me opened to it for the first time.

"Jesus." His laugh was wry as his hands came up to my hips, rocking them to his most impressive hard-on, which was nestled nicely between my legs. "I'm like Pavlov's dog with you. Touch me—hell, just look at me—and I get hard."

I leaned forward and kissed his jaw, then nipped the same spot. "Love me," I whispered against his mouth, running my hands up and down his tense arms, taut with strength and quivering with rigid control, which I intended to shatter. "Please love me, Kel."

With a groan, he kissed me deeply, thoroughly, until I curled, warm and totally aroused, around his body, feeling the sensual pull of his mouth, of his hands as they ran restlessly up and down my back.

Straightening, I pulled off the sweatshirt, then let the straps of my camisole top fall. The top slipped to my waist. Lifting his hands, I put them over my bared breasts, so he could tell in the dark what I'd done.

His fingers knew what to do, and in no time I was out of control, melting with desire, and needing him to get on with it. But he just keep kissing me, deep, melting, languid kisses, along with those slow, sure strokes of his hands over my ribs, my breasts.

"Rachel," he breathed, as if I were something special, something to treasure. He slipped his hands down the back of my pj bottoms, tracing a finger over my thong, the long line of which he traced down, down, down . . .

"Still not doing this," he said, panting a bit now.

"Okay."

Oh, he was wrong, so very wrong. In fact, if he stopped now, the very tips of his capable, long-fingered, work-roughened hands a fraction of an inch from where I needed them more than I needed my next gulp of air, it was possible I would cry.

"Look for them again," he said.

"Huh?"

"The pirates. The others. Anyone." He slid a finger beneath the thong. "Where are they?"

I tried to focus, barely managing it. "I—I don't know."

And another finger. "Look, damn it."

Not easy, but I tried again. "I still don't see anyone." Reaching down, I pulled on the fly of his Levi's. Pop.

Pop.

Pop.

I revealed a wedge of his tanned, taut, flat abs, and spread the jeans open as far as I could. Slipping my fingers inside, I found more hot, silky, smooth, hard flesh, and realized something I hadn't realized in Gert's office, because I'd already been too far gone then. "Commando, Kel?"

I could see his blush lighting up the night. "Yeah, uh, yeah."

I let out a breathless laugh, and stroked him, loving the sound of pleasure it tugged from deep in his throat. His sexy eyes were at half-staff, the expression on his face an image I figured just might dictate my fantasies for a long time to come. "Maybe I'll adopt the policy."

A low sound rumbled from his chest as he continued to stroke those fingers over me. "Look again."

"Kel—"

"*Look.*"

I tried to focus to do just that, but what I really wanted to know was how the hell he'd learn to touch a woman like that.

"Rach?"

"Still nothing," I gasped, but then I couldn't talk because he was doing things to the inside of my mouth with his tongue, to the inside of my body with his fingers . . . I wanted more, so much more. I wanted that tongue on my breasts, my belly . . . I wanted it all.

Still straddling him, I lifted up on my knees and straightened a leg, trying to get my pj bottoms off, all in tune with his low, rough groan. The sound inspired me, drove me on. Unfortunately, with my desire and hunger leading the way, all finesse went out the window. So did grace. I did get my thigh out, and then bent my knee and—

"Oomph," Kellan said as I nailed him.

Yeah, there was the way to seduce a man: knee him in the nuts. "Oh my God. Did I get your—"

"No."

"Are you sure?" I ran my hands down his belly, lower, cupping him.

Another sound escaped him, this one not of pain. "I'm okay."

"Whew." But I didn't move my hands. He was aroused, hugely so, and I have to admit, I couldn't get enough of that either. I struggled with my pj's for another moment, before Kellan's hands held me still. Wrapping one arm around my waist, he effortlessly hoisted me up, freeing my leg.

I took advantage of the freedom by wrapping my fingers

tighter around him and stroking the very tip of him over my damp flesh.

"*Jesus.*"

Then I let the very tip of him inside.

Gripping my hips, his head fell back against the couch. His eyes were shut, his jaw tight, the tendons in his neck standing out in bold relief, much like the part of him I held in my hands right this very minute. It excited me, knowing what I did to him, and as unbelievable as it seemed, given our precarious, unknown situation, I was so turned on I couldn't stop squirming.

"Look again," he demanded, jaw tight.

"Nothing," I gasped, wondering how it was he managed to keep his wits, when I couldn't keep mine.

The darkness continued to swirl all around us, creating that sense of intimacy that felt startling. Before Kel, it'd been a while since I'd been with anybody. Maybe yesterday I could have attributed some of my urgency to that most basic human need of being held, swept away, loved.

Comforted.

But, now I knew it was more than that; it was Kel. *Kel* did this to me. I'd already learned he was an incredibly earthy and giving lover. His kisses were heart-stopping, as were his roughened hands, busy exploring every inch of me, urging me even closer, so that my world became a blur of bare skin, rough sighs and a building hunger I needed assuaged.

He stroked a hand down my belly, then lower, lazily rasping a thumb just where I needed it, making me rock my hips against him with a dark, needy sound.

"Good?" he whispered.

"*So* good."

He kissed me again, keeping his fingers in tune with the kiss, until my world shrank, until nothing else mattered. The sound he made when he sank a finger into me and found me so wet nearly sent me over the edge all by itself.

"See anyone yet?"

"*Kel.*"

"Check. Please?"

Not easy, but I tried. I could still see nothing, and when I said so, he rewarded me with more of those mind-blowing strokes of his thumb, over and over, slowly first, then speeding as my hips began to pump, when I finally lost it, coming completely undone all over him. "Oh my God," I gasped, clinging to him as the shudders took me. "*God.*" I sagged down over him, forehead to his shoulder, panting for breath in his ear.

Beneath me, he was still hard, gloriously so, and I lifted my head, finding myself a little unnerved and embarrassed by how fast I'd gone off.

He kissed my shoulder, my neck. "Better?" he murmured.

Did he think that was it, that I'd just needed the edge taken off, and we were done? Not by a long shot, big guy. "*More.*"

Game, he slid his hands back down my body, but I shook my head, lifting up, wrapping my fingers around him and then sinking back down so that he slid deep inside me.

Instantly I was back on the edge. He hadn't even begun to move, and already my toes were curling, my body tightening. I rocked my hips and gasped in pure pleasure.

"Rach—" He gripped my hips hard, holding me still, when I didn't want to be still. "Don't—"

But he was filling me to bursting, and the heat and joy of it took over. My insides trembled as much as my fingers when I cupped his jaw, stroking his chest with palms that felt hot and achy. He was just so magnificent, I couldn't stop. I ran my fingers down to his abs. I loved touching him there, loved the sound he made, the way his breathing went all ragged, as if he couldn't control himself.

"If you move," he grated out, "I'll—"

"If you don't move, I'll—"

"No, Christ! I'm not—" He groaned. "We can't—"

I rocked my hips.

Swearing, he laced his fingers through mine, as if he couldn't handle my touching him, my name another rough rumble from his chest, as he eased my legs farther apart by spreading his.

Now I couldn't move, but it also caused him to thrust up even higher within me, and I clutched at him, gasping in pleasure.

"Oh fuck," he said in a strained voice. "*Stay still.*"

Was he kidding? Stay still, with him buried to the hilt inside of me. It was all too much, seeing him sprawled beneath me, jaw tight, muscles quivering, flesh and hard sinew damp, breath coming in short, choppy bursts . . . "*Kel.*"

"No condom," he ground out.

How bad was it that I'd completely forgotten? Very bad. Very, very bad! "Why don't you carry condoms, damn it?"

"I did! Yours. We used it."

"Why didn't you take two?"

His laugh was self-deprecating. "Because never in my wildest dreams did I think I'd need that one, much less more. But believe me, when we get out of here, I'm going to carry a damn box around for the rest of my life. Now please God, Rach, get off."

"But you didn't get to—"

"No, but I'm going to—"

He sounded so desperate that I was overcome by an unexpected blinding rush of affection. Slipping off him caused another ragged groan from his lips, but I just whispered "shh" and sank to my knees between his thighs.

"Rach—"

"Shh," I said again, and put my lips to his hip.

And then a few inches over to the right.

His head thunked back against the couch, his fingers tunneling into my hair, as if he couldn't help himself. "You don't have to—*Jesus.*"

I'd moved my mouth again.

"We need to get up." His voice was weak now, a mere whisper.

"Hmm." I loved the taste of him. "But you're already up, Kel."

"Funny."

"I try." My hair fell over my shoulder and stroked his belly, making him jump a little and his muscles quiver.

The power of that—making this long, rangy, leanly muscled man quiver—rushed through me. Suddenly I felt like a superhero, like I could do anything.

And what I wanted was to drive him right off the edge of sanity, the way he'd done me.

"Rach."

"Right here." I took my tongue on a little tour, and his fingers tightened in my hair. He said something completely unintelligible, the rough sound turning me on just as much as what I was doing to him did.

"You need to look out for—"

"We're okay. I've got you," I promised, trying to give him back some of the security he'd given me.

And as he went over, he held on to me, the both of us lost. Just as together we were found.

As simple and as terrifying as that.

We were still breathing like absused racehorses when he stroked a damp strand of hair from my cheek. "Every time we do that, it gets harder."

I stood up and looked for my camisole. The last I'd seen it, it'd been sailing across the room. "Thank God for hard."

"I don't want to joke about this."

Where the hell was my top? "What do you want?"

"You."

I turned back to him. "You just had me."

"You know what I mean."

I did know. Just as I was beginning to know how deep my feelings for him really were, despite my hang-ups.

But I really liked how things were right now. The close friendship. The new benefits. Everything that made a good relationship, without the *word* "relationship" attached to it, so that nothing could be taken away.

Not one single thing.

But I looked into his gorgeous eyes, saw the wanting, the yearning, and felt my heart crack, because he didn't—wouldn't—understand.

Proving it, he stood up with a long sigh, his shirt wrinkled, pants opened, looking unfairly sexy.

As he'd been doing all his life, he shoved his fingers through his hair in lieu of a comb. "Look, next time, well, there shouldn't be a next time."

My stomach clenched. "So you're saying what? You don't want to see me anymore?"

"Not if we're only going to play at this thing."

"But—"

I broke off at the sudden pounding of a fist on the door. "Omigod." *I'd forgotten to keep looking*!

"Here." Kellan tossed me my pj bottoms. "Goddamnit, I knew it."

"Really?" I hopped on one leg while shoving my other into the bottoms. "You knew it, huh?"

"Yes."

"You knew we were going to come to the Twilight Zone and get hit by lightning, then locked in an attic by a couple of crazies whose favorite words are 'the swap' and 'abilities.'"

He threw me my camisole, which had ended up on the floor. I caught it in the face. I pulled it away and scowled at him as he buttoned up his jeans and grabbed the gun.

"Hurry," he said.

I opened my mouth, but he clapped his hand over it and

pulled me flush to his body. The body that had just sent me into screaming ecstasy and back. "*Shh.*"

The pounding came again, making the door shudder.

Hell, the walls and the floor shuddered, too. And in spite of being mad and hurt, I allowed myself to cling to Kel.

"We know you're in there!" yelled a terrifyingly gruff and angry voice. "Open up!"

Whoever it was, he was furious, and I somehow managed to focus on the door—

"Uh-oh," I whispered.

"Yeah," Kellan muttered. "Definitely uh-oh."

"What do we do?"

"You open the fuck up, that's what you do!" yelled the scary voice from the other side of the door. "Open now, or you'll be sorry."

Kellan tried to see in the dark. "We need a better place to hide."

"You think?"

"Any more of those handy closets-that-aren't-really-closets around?"

How he remained calm, while the hair on the back of my neck was standing straight up and my knees and teeth were knocking together, was beyond me. I searched the room and tried to focus.

But a gunshot rang in the night, shattering both the unnatural quiet and the bolt on the door, not to mention shaving a few years off my life.

Chapter 20

The shot-up door swung open to reveal the two men I'd seen stealing the cookies, both of them just as huge as I'd thought, and just as beefy, each carrying enough armor to free a third-world country from terrorism. Kellan could see all this as well thanks to the lantern that one of them wore on his head, the light in the center of his forehead like the eye of a cyclops.

I'm pretty sure my life passed before my eyes, but since I was also seeing gray spots and thought I might throw up, I really couldn't be too sure of anything.

Kellan hadn't revealed his gun. There wasn't much point, with all those big bad-boy guns in our faces. He shoved me behind him, then managed to effortlessly hold me there despite my attempts otherwise.

Didn't he know I cared about him every bit as much as he cared about me, even if I'd been a bit stingy with my feelings?

And I had been stingy. I hated that about myself, and I promised God and the saints, and anyone else who could read my thoughts, that I wasn't going to hold back.

Not ever again.

"Who are you?" Kel demanded of the two men. He'd managed to get his jeans buttoned, but he still wore no shirt, no socks, no shoes—nothing to protect himself.

Who was this brave man standing between me and certain death, and why did he have to be brave *now,* when it was stupid to be so? "Kel—"

He somehow continued to keep me behind him in a way that prevented me from budging. But I could see, and what I did see was enough to turn my blood to ice.

The thugs wore old, ratty cargos, the khaki pants dirty and grimy, as if they'd never met a washing machine they liked. Their shirts had fared little better, both black T's and as torn and disgusting as the pants. Their arms were littered with tattoos, markings that made no sense to me. The one with the light on his head wore long, Rastafarian-style hair; the other was as bald as a cue ball. Both sported ragged headbands and an overall I-haven't-showered-this-year scent.

"Here's what we're going to do," Curly said to Moe in a voice that sounded as if he'd eaten glass shards for lunch. One of his front teeth sparkled like a diamond. "We'll take 'em up the river, and do 'em there."

"That's a stupid idea," Moe said.

Curly growled. I swore dust rose up from his dreadlocks. "Are you calling me stupid?"

"Something wrong with your hearing?"

Curly turned his gun from us to his partner in crime, and bared his teeth. "Take it back."

"Nope."

"Take. It. Back."

"Or you'll what?" Moe sneered.

"I'll tell Mom. Now say you're sorry you said I was stupid."

"Fine. I'm sorry you're stupid."

Steam came out of Curly's ears. "You're going to pay for that."

Moe didn't look too scared. He was too busy trying to catch a good glimpse of me behind Kellan. Finally he gestured with his extremely lethal-looking gun. "You," he said. "Hot stuff. Come out from behind there."

Kellan's hand tightened on me, but he needn't have worried. I was not anxious to come out from behind him.

"Now," Moe said.

"No," Kellan said.

Moe leveled his gun at Kellan's head. "How about now?"

Terror struck me right through the heart, and I backed out of Kellan's grip, not an easy feat, since he didn't want to let me go. "Kel, please," I whispered. "Don't give them an excuse to shoot you."

Jaw tense enough to shatter, Kellan turned his head and kept his eyes on me. "No closer," he commanded.

Not a problem. My feet had turned to concrete and weren't going anywhere.

"You." Moe gestured to Kellan. "Back up."

Kellan didn't move.

Moe did something to his gun that sounded like it was now cocked and ready to blast a hole through Kel's head.

Kellan backed up a few feet and put his hand behind him, where I knew he had the gun tucked in his waistband.

We couldn't have touched if we wanted to, which I realized was exactly the goal of our company.

"Pretty," Curly said as he looked me over, from my bare feet to my camisole, which was fairly inconsequential, as I'd not had the chance to put the sweatshirt back on.

"Leave her alone," Kellan said to Curly when he came close enough that I could smell his rank breath.

Yeah, leave me alone. Fear had given me a chill, and I crossed my arms over myself to cover my breasts, which had Moe letting out a low, appreciative laugh.

"Nice," he said, and nudged my arms with the blunt tip of his gun. "Drop 'em."

Kel pulled his gun and aimed it right at Moe. "Don't touch her."

Curly simply leveled his gun on Kel. "Drop it, or she dies."

Kel didn't move.

Curly stepped closer to me, and aimed right between my eyes.

Kel, looking tortured at the choice he had, which was no choice at all, dropped his gun.

I hugged myself harder. I could see Curly's heart thudding, which surprised me, since I would have sworn he didn't have a heart. I could also see other reactions going on in his body, which made my parts shrivel up and go *ewww*.

"Drop 'em," he said again, not nearly as nicely.

"Don't, Rach," Kel said, and Curly hit him in the face with the gun.

Kel fell. I cried out and lurched toward him, but Moe shifted his gun back to me, and I went still.

Moe gave me a slow smile that made me feel sick. "Now," he said, running his tongue over his disgusting teeth. "Where were we? Oh yeah, drop your arms."

Before I could, Kel pushed up to his knees and swiped his bleeding mouth with the back of his hand. "Touch her, and die," he said.

"How about we touch her, and you die?" Curly asked conversationally.

"You can't kill me; I've got what you want." Kel met the guy's gaze straight on, and a chill went through me at the look on his face.

He was prepared to die. For me.

Oh God. "We'll give you whatever you want," I said quickly. "Just don't hurt him again."

Curly's eyes lit with greed. "See, now that's what I'm talking about. Some cooperation." He eyed me up and down and then back up again, eyebrow raised in a dare. Should I go on and torture Kel, his silence said, or are you going to drop your arms?

Since I was fresh out of tricks, I dropped my arms. He spent a long moment leering at my hardened nipples, until Curly jabbed him in the back with his gun. "Move, you're hogging the view."

Kellan's jaw was tight enough to shatter, the cords in his neck standing up in bold relief, as the two of them looked their fill.

I didn't know what to do. My stomach felt funny, my legs incapable of holding me. For the first time, I understood true terror.

Kellan was looking at me, mouth still bleeding, his gaze filled with everything he was thinking. Fear for my safety. Frustration that he couldn't do anything about it. Anger that he'd allowed this to happen. His heart was speeding up, too. My biggest fear was that he'd do something stupid and get himself killed.

"Let's tie 'em up," Curly said.

"Wait." Moe held Curly back with his gun. "Which one of 'em has the strength?"

"Don't know." Curly looked at me, and for some reason, I nodded. "You?" he asked.

"That's right." Now *my* heart was going as fast as Kellan's, while Curly slowly circled around me, making sure to stay out of arm's reach.

I lifted my chin to nosebleed height. "You don't want to mess with me."

"Rach," Kel warned very softly.

I knew what he wanted. He wanted me to remain quiet. He wanted me safe and far away from here. Well, that made two of us.

"Whatcha going to do?" I asked, sounding far more brave than I was feeling. But if I could divert their attention from Kel, then maybe he could do something.

Moe growled, but a thunk from down below stopped them both cold.

"What was that?" Curly asked.

I looked down at the floor, and focused. Axel was just outside the back door of the kitchen, brushing his hands off. There was a fallen stack of chopped wood at his feet.

Had he just been out there chopping wood by coincidence, or had he actually thrown a piece of wood against the house as some sort of message?

Hard to tell.

But then, he did it again, picking up a log and tossing it hard against the siding.

On purpose.

"Shit," Moe said, unable to see any of this, of course. He jerked his head, indicating that Curly should go check it out.

"Why do I have to do it?"

"Because I always have to do the dangerous stuff," Moe answered.

"You," Curly said to us. "Stay. We'll be right back."

"Don't hurry on our account," Kellan said.

Oh perfect. Now he was baiting them.

"You'll pay for that when we take ya upriver," Moe promised.

Kellan, bleeding, bruised, just looked at them.

Moe leaned in and whispered, "And then after we have our fun with ya, you're gonna give me your ability."

"You think so?" I asked, desperate to get their attention off Kel.

Curly and Moe looked at me and then at each other, with raised brows, that said, Whoa, look at the brave broad.

Too bad I wasn't feeling so brave.

Another thunk from below had both Curly and Moe jumping. Curly jabbed the gun at us. "Stay put, you hear me? We'll be right back. Then . . ." He made the motion of slitting his throat, and my blood went cold.

"We can't just leave 'em," Moe said, pointing at me. "She can break out of just about anything, remember?"

"Right. Come on."

They both stalked toward me, making my stomach run cold. I stepped back. "Um, Kel?"

"Don't lay a finger on her," Kel warned them, holding himself very still, with his arms at his sides, looking poised and muscular and dangerous as hell.

"Oh, we won't lay a finger on her," Moe promised with a smirk as Curly moved behind me.

Moe smiled, but before I could figure out why, I saw stars and everything faded to black.

I woke up with a hell of a headache to find my hands tied and stretched taut, up over my head.

Kellan was across the room, sitting in a chair near the window, hands behind his back and tied. The cut on his mouth had stopped bleeding, but he had a hell of a shiner going.

The door behind me was just shutting, and I opened my mouth, but Kel shook his head, his eyes filled with warning.

He didn't want me to speak.

Not easy, but I nodded, and as soon as we were alone, he tore free of his bonds in a very Hulk-like move that was quite impressive actually, and came to me.

I'd never been happier to see anyone in my life. "Kel—"

He put a finger to my lips, then gently tunneled his hands through my hair, looking me over from head to toe to make sure I was okay, feeling for the lump on the back of my head, courtesy of whatever Moe had hit me with.

I winced, and his jaw tightened. He ran his hand up the rope that held my hands over my head, his expression going even more bleak, if that was possible.

It took me only a moment to see why. Curly and Moe thought I had the strength ability, so they'd looped my hands above my head, attaching the rope to the heavy chandelier. If I pulled and broke free, the heavy glass would fall right on me.

Ingenious, really, for a couple of stupid pirates from an alternate universe far, far away . . .

Kel felt the rope, and didn't look encouraged.

I knew why. It'd been pulled tight enough to be digging into my skin. There was no give, not an inch, or he could have broken through it. If he tried now, the entire glass fixture above would come down.

On my head.

He looked at me, then put his mouth to my ear. "We can do this. I can break it. But when I say go, I want you to shove backwards. Do it fast, Rach."

"No, I—"

"Listen to me. It's going to be loud, and we're going to bring attention to ourselves. Be ready to run. Can you do that?"

I nodded. Was he kidding? For our lives, I'd dance to the moon. "Where are Curly and Moe?"

"Curly and Moe?" A ghost of a smile touched his lips. "Good names." His hands covered mine, his body pressed against me in a way that put him, not me, in direct danger from the glass shards that would fall from above.

"Kel—"

"Go!"

I shoved back as promised, and hit my butt hard, my eyes glued to the heavy light fixture as it broke free of the beam and headed toward Kellan's head, ready to stab into him, spearing him into pieces right before my eyes. *"Kel!"*

Chapter 21

Kel also shoved back hard, and the resounding crash and glass splintering made the floor between us shudder.

Still on my butt, I covered my face with my arms, but before I could even draw a breath, Kel was there, hauling me to my feet, running his hands over my body. "You okay?" he demanded.

I didn't want to let go of him, *ever*, but he forced me to back up so he could continue to check me out. I looked up at the gaping hole in the ceiling where the heavy light fixture had once hung, and shuddered. "That was close."

His hands tipped up my chin. "You're okay."

"Define okay."

"You. Just the way you are."

How was it he always knew what to say? God, the things I felt for him . . .

"Come on." He pulled me to the window.

I looked down, and felt myself pale. "This way?"

"Yeah." Kel ran his fingers over the lock.

"Because that's four flights and at least forty feet down, you know. I mean, look how hard the ground seems."

Kel broke through the paint and the lock in one swift motion, and raised the window. "Out."

I looked at him, needing to get something said before I fell to my grisly death. "Kel? I think I'm falling for you."

His eyes went wide with shock for one moment, before he pulled it together again.

He didn't believe me.

"We have got to go," he said.

"Did you hear what I just said?"

"Yes." He gave me a smile, profound in its sadness. "Don't worry. I understand."

"You . . . understand."

"It's all the craziness, the fear. The Superman heroics. It's okay . . . but thank you."

"Thank you?" This was not quite the reaction I'd expected. *"Thank you?"*

"Yes, thank you. Sincerely."

I stared at him. *"Sincerely."*

"Yes, sincerely, damn it. Look, I'm aware that you have no idea how much my heart just stuttered to hear your feelings. But we're going to get out of here, damn it. So no fucking good-byes."

"No, you don't understand—"

"We *are* getting out of here," he repeated. "I promised you, remember?"

"I do. But I really could fall for you."

He looked at me, his eyes full of things that took my breath. "Fall for me."

"Yeah." *Give him the rest.* "Kel, I l—" But damn if that elusive word wouldn't slip off my tongue. "Like you." *Like?* What, was I in middle school? I felt like an idiot.

Kel just sighed. "Can we not do this now?"

"Damn it, I want a reaction."

"Okay. You like me. Great. I *like* you, too. Only here's my problem, Rach. When we get out of here, I'll go back to being just the reliable, stable guy next door. Your best friend's brother, who you once hooked up with on some crazy weekend in Alaska."

"Three times."

"What?"

"We hooked up three times."

"My point is," he said through his teeth, "I'm not ever going to be that adventurous badass guy you always go for, just my own blend of sure-and-steady Kel. The Kel you *like*."

"There's nothing wrong with sure and steady."

"No, but we both know that's not what floats your boat."

"Okay, so I've gone for some real winners before. We both know that. But people can change what they want, Kel."

He just looked at me. "You're changing?"

"Yes." Maybe the thought of going back to Los Angeles and my dating scene made my gut tighten. I didn't want my usual dating scene. I didn't want *any* dating scene.

I wanted Kel.

I knew he had no reason to believe that I could feel this way for him. And actually, that hurt more than the bolt of lightning had the other day, but it was my own fault. I couldn't even say the L-word.

"Out the window."

I looked down. "It's far."

"There's a drainpipe. We can shimmy down that."

There were so many things wrong with that statement, beginning with "drainpipe" and ending with "shimmy," and I gulped.

"It's not so bad when you consider the alternative." He guided my leg over the ledge. "How's your head?"

I clung to the ledge. "If I say bad—really, really, really bad—do we still have to do this?"

"Yes."

Oh God. There were a few bushes to break our fall.

And our necks.

Because I was staring at them with dread, I could see through them, to the hard, hard ground. To the bugs burrowing in that ground. "Kel—"

But my sensitive, laid-back, easygoing Kellan just shoved me the rest of the way out the window.

I clung to what felt like a very, very small window ledge with my toes, my fingers refusing to let go of Kellan.

He merely pried my fingers from his, reached through the window and guided my grip to the drainpipe. Then he looked into my eyes and softened slightly. "Hold on tight."

"You have any better advice than that?"

"Yes. Don't look at the ground."

Right. Not looking at the ground. I began to inch down, my gaze locked on the sky, which wasn't a bad view really as Kellan climbed out after me.

"Rach?"

"Yeah?"

"Faster."

"Oh. Right." Hand over hand, foot over foot. After a minute, I was level with the third-floor window, one of the staff bedrooms, which I really hoped was empty versus being filled with pirates holding guns. Then I realized my eyes were closed, and I forced them to open, so that I could peek inside—

"Hey," Axel said, sticking his head out the window, looking unusually tense, his shoulders blocking my view of the room behind him. He wore a big, nasty-looking gun strapped over his chest. "Where's Marilee?"

I nearly fell. "*Jesus.*"

"Nope, just me." He didn't flash his usual stoner smile. In fact, he looked intense, reminding me what I'd read about him in Gert's Blackberry.

He wasn't really a stoner. He'd only been acting like one.

"Have you seen her?" he demanded.

"Uh, no. But there's—"

"Pirates. I know. I distracted them away from you and Kellan by making noise."

"Is that what you were doing?"

"What did you think?"

Telling them in code to kill us.

"Look, I've got to go," he said, as if talking to me hanging off the drainpipe was the most natural thing in the world.

"Right. No, I'm good. Thanks for asking."

"I can see you're good, and you've got Kellan."

"Thanks," Kellan said from above. "But I'd feel better if she had someone at her side who actually knew what the fuck was going on."

"Just stay away from the guys with guns."

I looked at the gun Axel still had strapped across his chest, which, if I wasn't mistaken, had come from Gertrude's stock.

"That doesn't include me," he said.

"You going to help us?" Kel asked.

"Yes. Meet me in the woods. Where the swap occurred." He pulled back inside the window, but then hesitated. "Oh, and probably the best thing would be to hurry."

"How about you scoot back and let us inside?"

Axel grimaced regretfully, scratching his head. "I'd like to, but if they find you, it'll go worse for all of us."

"It can't get any worse."

"Sure it can. We could all be—" He mimed being hung by his neck, complete with tongue sticking out and eyes bugging.

It was an image that made me shudder.

"This is serious shit, dudes," Axel said.

"Yeah, thanks for that valuable info."

"Dudette, listen to me." I'd never seen Axel look so serious. "If you believe anything, you've got to believe this is bad. The worst. I'm going to go find Marilee and help her. Meet us in the woods. And hurry."

Hurry. No problem. But then I made the mistake of looking

down, which caused black spots to swim sickeningly in my vision. "Damn it."

"I told you not to look down," Kel said above me.

Yes. Yes, he had. Gritting my teeth, I began moving again, not quite quickly enough for Kellan, though, who urged me on with his size-thirteen feet, which kept threatening to clock me in the head.

"You should have gone first," I hissed up at him, concentrating on hand over hand, foot over foot, and on *not* falling to my certain death.

"If I'd gone first," he said with maddening calm, "you'd have never gotten out on the ledge."

True enough.

"Hurry, Rach."

If one more person told me to hurry, I was going to seriously lose it, and I swear, if I had it to do all over again, I'd have poked him in the ass instead of staring at it.

"Breathe, Rach. Are you breathing?"

"I am now." To prove it, I inhaled deeply, letting it out slowly. "I need cookies. And a Prozac."

"Keep moving."

Hand over hand.

Foot over foot.

Don't breathe too fast, but don't forget to breathe.

Oh, and don't look down.

And don't fall either.

Falling would be bad. Really, really bad. Finally I arrived at the second-floor window. It opened into one of the guest rooms, a particularly rustic, country-styled room with a queen-size four-poster bed and a golden pine dresser with a mirror, through which I could see the rest of the room reflected.

Axel wasn't in there, but I received an even bigger shock.

William and Serena were tied to a chair, gags in their mouths, staring at us.

No Axel or stinky pirates in sight. "*Kel.*"

Kel, just above me, squatted, too, looking in the glass. "*Shit.*" Then he opened the window.

"What are you *doing*?"

"Keep going. I'll be right behind you before you touch the ground." With lithe ease, he swung into the room.

William went white. Shook his head violently.

I caught the message. *Don't stop for us. Save your own damn necks.*

Not that Kel listened. He never listened. He moved quickly to Serena and untied her hands, then turned toward William.

But before I could drop into the room as Kel had, Serena yanked off her gag. "Kellan! No! Take Rach and get out!"

It terrified me, hearing her fear, but before I could climb inside, the bedroom door slammed open.

I jerked back and nearly fell off the damn ledge.

Moe leveled his gun at Kellan. "Tie them back up."

Kellan didn't move. Nor did he look at me. But I could feel him, desperate for me to get out of sight.

"Tie them up *now*," Moe said to Kel.

The voice was terrifying, the gun even more so, and I pressed back out of view, willing Kel not to do anything stupid, so he wouldn't die right here.

"You deaf?" Moe yelled at Kellan. "I said *tie them up*."

"No," Kellan said.

I think I stopped breathing as I clung to the drainpipe, trying like hell to vanish into thin air.

If I could somehow shimmy down, then find a way to rescue them all—

With what? My X-ray vision?

Oh God. I was panting for air, and it was so loud, I was shocked Moe hadn't stepped to the window to investigate. Any minute now I would hyperventilate and pass out.

And fall to my death.

No. Not going to fail Kellan. Omigod, Kellan, who was right this very second staring down the wrong end of a very long, very-powerful looking barrel.

What if they killed him?

I actually had to stop and hold still for a second at this thought: my life without Kellan in it. It was too dark, too overwhelming, too lonely, and I couldn't even contemplate it.

He wasn't going to die.

No one was.

Because I was going to get down.

That's right. I was going to get down, and then I'd find my own weapon and somehow save the day. Me, a muralist, a pacifist, a woman who hated conflict. I was going to do this one thing, and I was going to do it one step at a time and not think about it too hard.

First, down the drainpipe.

Easier said than done in a state of near-panic. Hand over hand . . . Finally I managed to get within five feet of the ground, and feeling triumphant, I glanced down.

And gasped in new terror.

Because Curly stood there, gun pointed directly at me.

"Hands up," he said, with a nasty smile revealing his distaste of daily hygiene.

I went from icy fear to furious anger. Gun or no gun, I was getting damn tired of the fear. In fact, I wasn't going to be afraid again. Unless I saw a spider. "I can't let go," I said, gripping the drainpipe.

"No problem." He took aim. "I can shoot you from right here."

Ah hell. "Okay," I said. "Maybe I can let go."

"Atta girl."

With nothing else up my sleeve, I had little choice. I began to slither down the pipe, heart pounding in my throat. "Shooting me would be a bad idea," I said, just in case he got trigger-happy.

"Why's that?"

"Because I've hidden the laptop."

He just looked at me.

"You need it to do the swap of the abilities," I reminded him.

"No problem." Curly smiled evilly. "Because you're going to tell me all about where you hid it." His fist closed at my nape, and squeezed. "Start talking."

"Um."

"Faster, hot stuff." His breath was rank enough to nearly knock me out. To add insult, he ran the gun up my ribs, over the side of my breast.

I'll never know where the move came from—probably from watching too many Jackie Chan movies—but I kicked back and nailed him in the knee.

"Fuck!" He bent, and somehow I managed to elbow him in the throat.

He let out a gargling sound and hit the ground.

Okay, so far so good. I whirled to run, but he recovered quickly, damn pirate, and wrapped his arms around my legs.

Then tugged.

Hard.

And down over the top of him I went. He smelled like week-old garbage, but his body was whipcord hard and sinewy, which did not bode well for me. While I was still in shock, he rolled me beneath him and grinned down at me.

I kneed him in the balls, hard enough to make him pale, but not hard enough to incapacitate him.

Bad idea, Rach.

We rolled around for a minute, me trying to get loose, him trying to cop a feel and control me at the same time, but neither of us getting much of what we wanted.

Finally I crawled free—

Only to feel his gun jam into my back.

"Now, I've gotcha," he said.

Chapter 22

Kellan's view of things

You know what would be nice? If I could just wake up from this nightmare. Only unfortunately, I'm not dreaming. I really am standing with my hands up, facing a thug who thinks he's a pirate from an alternate universe.

And oh yeah, he has a helluva gun.

All this, with Rach on the drainpipe outside the window. *Please let her still be safe on the drainpipe outside the window.*

"Down," the pirate that Rach had nicknamed Moe said to me.

I hoped like hell Rach was sliding down that drainpipe and running for her life, and not planning on doing something stupid, like rescuing me.

Moe pointed his gun to the floor impatiently. "I said down, asshole!"

Rachel, walk away. Do not take this as a challenge to come save my hide.

But I could think it all I wanted. I had no telepathy skills, and in any case, Rachel didn't have such great listening skills. She did what she wanted, when she wanted, which truthfully, was part of what made me love her so damn much.

"Are you deaf? Get *down*!"

I hesitated, thinking if he just came even a little bit closer, I could wring his neck, even if said neck was five times thicker than mine. See, getting superpowers had to be good for something.

Tired of me, he turned and fired off a round about a foot from William's head, reminding me that he was dead serious.

Serena screamed as down I went, first to my knees, then to my hands, thanks to a vicious jab in my ribs from Curly.

"Flat on your face, asshole."

Nice new nickname.

"Now!"

So with another bone-crunching jab to yet a different rib, I kissed the ground, thinking maybe I should just be thankful he was more fond of jabbing at me than actually shooting me. Bruises were a helluva lot easier to recover from than gaping holes in the flesh.

As my cheek pressed into the floor, dust tickled my nose. Seemed Marilee was an even worse maid than a cook, and that was saying something. I sneezed.

Moe leaned down and peered into my watering eyes. "Shut up."

In answer, I sneezed again.

"I mean it. *Shut up.*"

Pissed off, I lay there, inhaling dust, trying not to sneeze, and contemplated my choices.

And it occurred to me for not the first time that the extra strength wasn't nearly as convenient as Rach's new vision, or, say, the ability to read the minds of these jerks. Unable to hold it back, I sneezed again, and a new pain radiated through my head. As my vision faded to black, I had to sigh. Yeah. Definitely, I'd rather have had a mind-reading ability, as then I'd have been able to anticipate that blow to the head . . .

* * *

I woke up with a headache from hell and the taste of blood in my mouth. But I had all my teeth and appeared to have all of the rest of me as well, though every single inch hurt like a son-of-a-bitch.

I was sitting, my back to a beam in the center of the room.

Moe was tying me up, my hands behind me, my feet straight out in front of me. He yanked the ropes far tighter than he needed to, cutting into my skin. When I winced, he slid his eyes to mine and made sure to back up to a safe distance, holding his gun on me. "I did you a favor tying you up in front of the chick." He jerked his head toward Serena. "You can see right through her clothes, right?" He chortled. "Lucky dog. Enjoy it, because soon we're going to drag you out to the woods and do the swap, and then *I'll* get to look through her clothes all I want."

His thinking I had Rach's ability was probably the only thing that had kept him from seriously incapacitating me. If he'd known I had the strength, he'd have had to be much more thorough in hurting me so that I couldn't hurt him back.

I glanced at Serena, still tied to her chair. She'd been crying, and she had a bloody lip. But as she glanced at the rope they were using on me, her lips quirked with genuine wry humor. We both knew I could break the rope with one flex of a muscle.

William was tied at her back, facing away from me, and he murmured something to her, and she nodded.

Moe moved to a corner of the room, sitting on the bed to talk into a radio he held.

Serena met my gaze. "It's nearly sunrise," she said softly.

The dot on Gertrude's calendar weighed heavily on my mind, as did the gut-tightening fear over Rachel and where she was right at this moment. "What happens at sunrise?"

"The reverse swap. We need the laptop," she whispered. "It puts us in control. And—"

"Jesus. There's more?"

"It affords us a certain protection. Without it . . . things could go bad."

As opposed to how great things were now, I supposed. "Where is it?"

"I left it in the kitchen, which is where they nabbed us. It's in the pantry. I'm so sorry," she whispered, her eyes filling. "I'm so sorry this is happening to you and Rachel."

Moe glanced over at them, his gun at the ready, but went back to talking on his radio.

"Can Rachel get the laptop?" Serena whispered.

"I don't know." I tried not to think about all that could be happening to her right now.

"This shouldn't have gone down like this," William said over Serena's shoulder. "You and Rachel should have gone home tomorrow and never have known about any of this."

"That would have worked for me. Maybe you people should move your vacation spot to a different location. Say Siberia. Or better yet, stop vacationing all together."

"I know it seems strange to you," Serena said, "but our abilities get heavy. When we come here, we can drop them for the weekend, and rest."

"Not drop," I said. "*Swap.*"

Guilt flashed across her face. "Well yes. Swap."

"You gave them to unsuspectings. That's against the rules."

"Ah." Serena nodded. "You've read the rules."

"They were in the Blackberry."

"The blackberry!" Serena whispered, relief flashing over her face. "That'll work. Do you have that?"

Moe glanced over at us, and we went quiet. When the pirate went back to his conversation via radio, I looked at Serena. "Tell me what happens after the swap."

"Normally? We just go home."

"How?"

"It's a sort of molecular rearranging. You've heard the boom."

"The lightning."

"Not really lightning, but yes, that's the noise it makes. We do it here because no one hears it."

"Yeah, we used to do it in Nevada," William said. "But the noise eventually drew too much attention. People thought we were aliens from another planet. It got messy."

"So you came to Alaska."

"Right. But it's problematic here, too. It's butt-ass cold here for one, and also getting too well known. Like I mentioned, we're building a new place in the Bahamas. Warm *and* isolated. Do you have the Blackberry or not?"

Moe slipped his radio into his pocket and eyeballed us in a way that put my back up all over again. I certainly didn't answer William. I was thinking about how to get the pirate close enough so that I could break free of my bonds and get his gun.

Before *he* used it.

"Hey," I called out to him. "Did you hear that?"

Moe frowned. "What?"

I jerked my head toward the door. "Right out there." *Come on, asshole, walk right by me to get to the door.*

Instead, Moe aimed the gun at the door and blasted eight holes in it. The sound was deafening, and made him grin. "Hope that wasn't your hot stuff. Be a shame to hurt her before I get her ability. That strength, it's going to come in handy." He waved his gun, taunting me. "So big guy, how many bullets do I have left, hmm?" He aimed right between Serena's eyes.

She cringed back against William.

Moe laughed. "Do I have one left to nail her or not?"

"Leave her—"

The doors, filled with holes, burst open, and Curly stood there, a gun around his neck, another in one hand, and in his other . . . I couldn't see past the doorjamb. He looked right at me, smiled malevolently and tugged.

Rachel fell against him.

"Says she doesn't have the laptop," Curly announced.

"She doesn't!" Serena cried. "*I* do."

Rach was looking a little worse for wear, sporting an already blackening eye, a cut lip and a torn camisole. "I'm sorry," she gasped. "Oh, Kel. I'm sorry."

"No." An unholy fury went through me, but I forced myself to concentrate on the obvious. "Don't be sorry, Rach." She was alive, and alive was good.

Curly shoved Rachel, and she hit her knees hard. Then, with his really big gun in our faces, he gestured for Moe to untie Serena and William. He nudged them to the door. "We're going to get the laptop. Don't either of you two move," he said to me and Rach. "We'll just take care of this little matter first, then be back for you."

"You need them alive," I said. "Don't kill them."

Curly shook his head. "Nope, it's *you* two we need alive."

"Oh, please don't kill them!" Rach cried, hopping back up to her feet.

Curly came close to her. Then, because he was clearly just a little afraid, he jabbed at her with the tip of his gun for sport.

"Leave her alone," I said.

But Curly, miscreant that he was, had just discovered something. By running the gun down Rach's throat and tucking it beneath the material of her camisole, he could pull the top out and look inside.

Rachel slapped away his gun, and in return, he slapped her—hard.

Again she hit her knees. She lifted her head and glared at him. "I'm guessing you don't have a girlfriend."

"You're my new girlfriend, hot stuff."

I tried to keep breathing rather than dive at him, because all that would do was get me killed and leave Rachel alone to face this mess.

Curly jabbed his gun at Serena and Will, heading with them to the door, but Rach called out, "I'm warning you. Don't kill them. If you do, the crack between the alternate planes will close up, and you won't be able to get home."

Curly's mouth gaped open. "What?"

Moe scratched his head at that one, and dust rose from his dreadlocks.

Serena nodded so hard, her hair fell into her face. "It's true. Our deaths would upset the balance."

Curly shoved her out, and nodded to Moe, who turned back to us, cradling his gun. Our guard, apparently.

And then, from above us, came another mysterious thud.

"*Shit*," Moe muttered. "*Now* what?"

"Don't worry, it's probably just the other guests," Rach offered.

"There aren't any other—"

"You sure?" she asked him.

Moe growled. "*Damn it.*" He pointed his gun at her. "I swear to God, if you move while I'm gone, I'll kill you both. Got it?"

"Yes, sir."

He slammed out, leaving us alone. I had no idea how long that was going to last, so I ripped out of my bonds and hauled Rach up against me, never being so happy to hold her in my entire life. "Are you okay?" I demanded, at the same time that she caught my face in her hands and demanded the same thing.

We looked at each other, then bear-hugged again.

"God, Kel, I was so scared for you—"

"I was hoping you'd gotten away—"

"I heard the gunshots—"

I squeezed her tighter. "I'm okay."

"But Serena and William—"

"Can you see them?"

She looked down at the floor. Biting her lip, she narrowed her gaze, searching. "Oh!"

"What?"

"Curly has them." She frowned. "That's weird."

"What? Where are they?"

"In Gertrude's office." She shook her head in surprise. "Why—"

"She led them there for the laptop."

"Which is no longer there," she said slowly, "and she knows it. Oh God. She's stalling. For us!" Her eyes went wide and wild with panic. "Do you think he'll kill them?"

"Not until they get what they want. They're not that stupid. Look again, Rach," he instructed. "Where's Moe, and what is he doing?"

She focused. "He's upstairs, walking down the hallway. We have a minute." Gripping me, she looked right into my eyes. "Back there, on the drainpipe, when you went in for William and Serena, I thought I'd never see you again, that we'd die before—"

I put my finger over her lips. "Let's just get out of here."

"But—"

Click.

We both looked at the bullet-torn door—specifically, at the handle, which was slowly turning.

Chapter 23

Don't scream, Rachel, don't scream. This is what I repeated to myself over and over as I tried to focus.

Kel pulled me behind him, around the side of a tallboy, his hand on my hip, gently squeezing, whether to hold me in place or try to soothe me, I had no idea. Whatever the reason, it caused a lump the size of a regulation football to form in my throat. Of course, it might just have been due to old-fashioned fear, because any second now, we were going to die.

I'd never in my life been on edge so much for so long. If I ever got out of here and back to the real world—was there even a real world?—I was going to embrace my quiet, lovely life.

But the person who pushed open the door wasn't a pirate with a gun. It was Marilee. At the sight of us, she let out a cry of relief, and slipped inside. "Okay, listen. We can still get you out of here. All you have to do is—"

"Axel is looking for you," I said. "He's frantic—"

"I found her." Axel came in behind Marilee. He had smeared lipstick on his lips. Marilee followed my shocked look and let out a rough laugh as she reached up and gently swiped a thumb over his lips. "My bad."

Axel smiled down at her. "It's okay. I like wearing you."

"Oh, Axel." She put her head down on his shoulder, and the man pulled her in close, squeezing her tight, closing his eyes, as he sighed her name.

Marilee pulled back and looked into his face. "You meant it, right?"

"Meant what?" I asked.

Marilee smiled dreamily, something that softened her features and made her even more beautiful, if that were possible. "He said he loved me, that he would always love me. That even without my abilities, he wanted to be with me until the end of time."

I blinked. "Without your abilities?"

Marilee's glowing smile slowly faded. "Um, did I neglect to tell you about our abilities?"

"Yes," Kellan said. "You could say you forgot to tell us that. You could also say you forgot to tell us just about every damn thing."

Axel unstrapped one of the two guns around his chest and handed it to Kel. "This might ease some of the pain."

Kel took the gun, inspected the chamber, or whatever it was called. I had no idea how he knew to do such a thing, or why he looked so big, bad and tough as he then pulled the strap over his own shoulder. He lifted his head, his eyes sharp and focused, without an ounce of fun, easygoing guy in sight. "So you two are from . . ."

"An alternate plane, yes," Marilee admitted quietly, slipping her hand in Axel's. "Our abilities were stolen a few years back and never recovered. It happened in Gert's place." She paused, and brought shaky fingers up to her mouth.

"That's why she still gets uncomfortable in there," Axel said, and slipped an arm around her. "It was awful for her."

"What happened after your powers were gone?" I asked. "You went home?"

"Not without our abilities. Can't. So we stayed. Gertrude hired us."

"And the whole pretend-you're-not-a-couple thing? What's that about?" Kellan asked.

"Oh, that part was real." Axel's eyes locked on Marilee's. He brought their joined hands up to his mouth and kissed her fingers. "Until today."

"While this is touching," Kellan said. "We—"

"Have to go," Axel answered for him. He glanced at Marilee's watch. "Gotcha. Let's get to the woods for the Sunday return."

The thought of what lay ahead made me quiver. "We need the—"

Marilee held up the laptop. "Found it."

"What about Serena and William?" Kel asked. "Don't they have to be there to get their abilities back?"

Marilee and Axel looked at each other.

"Goddamnit," Kel gritted out. "No more secrets."

"Once the swap occurs, the pirates will leave you alone," Axel said. "You'll be safe."

"*We'll* be safe," I said. "But Serena and William—won't they be as good as dead?"

"Are they still in the house?" Kel asked me.

I looked through the floor beneath us. Blinked. "No."

"Let's get out of here," Marilee said. "*Please.*"

We raced quietly down the stairs, toward the front door, and as we did, I looked behind us. Focused. "Found Serena and William. Curly has them outside Gert's house."

Kel looked at me, and I knew what he was going to say. I felt the same way, so I put the words out there. "We can't leave them."

Axel and Marilee stopped, and stared at me in shock. "But it's you two they want. The abilities."

It was one thing to be armchair brave—that is, while watching a horror movie and willing the stupid people to get out of the stupid haunted house before they got killed.

It was another entirely to be brave for real. To have to consciously make the decision not to walk away from someone you knew, someone whose eyes you'd looked into and whom you'd had conversations with . . . because if you left, they would die.

I couldn't walk away.

And looking back at Kellan, looking into his eyes, I was grateful to see the same decision in his, that I wasn't alone, that he couldn't walk away either.

"We aren't leaving them," he said.

Axel sighed, and also stopped. "No. We're not."

"Let's just get outside," Marilee begged. "We'll figure it out from there." She reached for the front door, just as a bullet slammed into it, splintering the wood right over my head.

Moe.

Damn, almost forgot about him.

With my ears still ringing, Kellan shoved me out of the way, slamming me into the wall, covering my body with his own.

Given the cry I heard from Marilee, she'd gotten the same rough treatment from Axel. Axel, who knew Marilee loved him, and who, if things went bad today, would die knowing it.

I gripped Kel's shirt in my fists. He had his back pressed to me, and was holding the gun in a terrifyingly fierce way, willing to protect me to the death. God.

With Moe coming down the stairs, covering the front door with his big gun, Kel grabbed me, yanking me under the stairs, then into the large reception room, toward the sliding glass door. Axel and Marilee were right on our heels. We ran out into the dark without meeting any pirates or guns, stopping at the far corner of the inn for protection, looking back at the building.

If I'd learned anything, it was that life had a habit of going the unexpected route. Today was no exception, and I had no guarantee on the outcome, no control, except over myself and my own feelings.

Which meant it was now or never. I looked at Kel's profile,

proud and tense. He was determined to see me safe, and all that I felt for him burst inside of me. No way could my feelings be attributed just to what had happened to us here this weekend. The feelings and emotions were far too deep for that. I had to make him understand before it was too late, before even this last chance was gone. "Kel."

"Hang on," he said, staring at the inn, at the open front door, braced for a fight.

"*Kel.*"

His jaw bunched. "Please, Rach."

"About that whole me-falling-for-you thing."

He never took his eyes off the door, but he whispered my name again, just my name, in a low, soft voice filled with regret. "No good-byes, goddamnit. We're going to live to argue about this another day."

"I know you think it's crazy, me just realizing all these feelings for you. I know you think it's because of the abilities, and your new muscles—"

Marilee let out a sigh of agreement, and I glanced at her. "Sorry," she said. "Just agreeing with ya. He's got muscles."

"*Hey,*" Axel said.

"Oh, you do too, baby," she assured him.

I let out a sound of frustration, and looked at Kel. "It's not about how . . . how *hot* you are," I insisted. "It's about your insides."

"Yeah?" He didn't take his eyes or his gun off the inn's door. "Then why didn't you see it before?"

"Fair question," Axel said, and at my long look, he lifted a shoulder. "Just saying," he muttered. He went back to watching the inn with Kel.

"I didn't see it before because I was stupid and selfish, okay?" I said to all of them. *Sheesh*! "Because I was scared. *Kel*—"

"You can't even say the word, Rach. You can't even say 'I love you,' so—"

"I love you." Oh God. My throat closed up a little, but I didn't choke. My eyes burned though, and I felt like both laughing and crying as I beamed. "See? I said it. And I meant it."

"It's the healing powers of the mountain," Marilee whispered. "Don't ever doubt it."

Kel, stiff and still watching the inn, gave nothing away of his thoughts, the stingy bastard. "Yeah, let's see if you still feel this way in five minutes, after the swap."

He still didn't believe me. Hurt, I fell quiet.

"Kind of harsh, dude," Axel said to Kel.

"Jesus." Kellan risked a quick glance at me. "We are not doing this now. Not with lives in danger. Not with an *audience.*" He shot a meaningful glance back at Axel and Marilee. "I mean it."

He meant it. Kellan McInty putting his foot down. It gave me a thrill, which told me Moe must have hit me harder than I'd thought.

"Now can you all please shut up?" Kel said.

Whoa. He'd said to shut up. I had to be real hurt, because that got me, too.

"Hey!" shouted Curly from just inside the front door. "We know you're out there! The two of ya with the abilities, drop any weapons and walk slowly toward the front door!"

"Burn in hell!" Marilee yelled.

"Way to keep quiet," Kel said on a sigh, sighting the gun in his hands like he knew what he was doing.

"*Now,*" Curly yelled, and let off a shot that ricocheted far too close for comfort. I heard Kel let out a grunt of surprise, and Axel swore loudly and viciously as he got into a better position.

"Come on out!" Curly called, with what sounded like insane glee.

"Okay, change of plans," Kel said to us, sounding like he was talking with his teeth gnashed together.

I glanced at him, but he was still giving nothing away. Damn him.

"Hey, listen up!" he said loudly enough for everyone to hear, including the pirates. "You're going to send out your two hostages. Nice and easy. No more shooting."

"And why would we agree to that, mate?" Moe called.

"Because then you get to keep your pretty teeth."

I couldn't quite wrap my mind around the fact that this tough-talker was Kellan—sweet, kind, gentle, talk-to-dolphins Kellan. Riveted, I stood there and watched him take over, falling even harder for the guy, if that was humanly possible.

"I'll give you some time to think it over," he called out.

"How much time?"

"Until the count of three. *One!*" He lifted his gun and sighted on the front door.

My God. He was serious.

"*Two!*"

"Wait!" Moe called. "Jesus! Don't go off half-cocked now. We just want the abilities. Tell us where the laptop is, and we'll swap, and then you'll go free. Everyone will go free."

Sounded good to me.

"Deal?" Curly yelled.

I could feel everyone holding their breath.

"No," Kellan responded. "No deal." And he aimed for one of the windows closest to the front door.

"Uh, Kel?"

"Not now, Rach."

And then he pulled the trigger.

Chapter 24

In that split second that the bullet shot out the window and glass sprayed, time seemed to stop.

Kellan stood there, feet wide, holding the gun, looking fierce and determined and outrageously tough. But even with his new strength, he'd remained true to himself. The old Kel wouldn't have done anything differently than this Kel.

And now, because of me, we stood here in a no-win situation. Chances were, someone was going to get hurt.

Or killed.

Unless . . . unless I could face my fears once and for all, and commit, with my whole heart and soul. Commit to getting us out of here, commit to loving Kel for the rest of my life. I'd do *both*, I decided, and pushing past Kel, I ran out into the spot in front of the porch where everyone could see me.

"Jesus, Rach!" Kel started to run after me, but I whirled back and held up my hand.

"No, wait!" Craning my neck, I looked at the front door, knowing Curly and Moe were hanging on my every action. "This has to stop," I called out. "We're all armed. Someone's going to die."

Curly's face appeared in the shattered window, his gun trained right on me. "Hey, hot stuff. We just want the abilities."

"Then let's swap," I said. "Right now. We have the Blackberry. We can do the swap with that." Or so I hoped.

Moe's face appeared, and then Serena's, with Moe's gun in her face. "No funny stuff!"

"No funny stuff," I promised, hoping I would be able to keep that promise, because I knew I couldn't control the variables—meaning Kel, Axel and Marilee. I could only hope. I turned back to them, Moe's and Curly's guns making my shoulder blades itch. Axel held a gun in one hand and Marilee's hand in the other. They were both looking at me as if I were crazy.

And I probably was.

But it was Kellan I wanted to reach.

At the moment, he was further from the San Diego dolphin trainer I'd ever seen, without an ounce of the easygoing, laid-back, slightly self-conscious guy I knew so well visible. He stood there, his dark shirt ripped, the cut on his face bleeding again, his eye swollen, his jaw bruised, every part of him streaked with sweat and dirt from the attic and from the climb down the side of the house. He held that huge, scary-looking gun as if he might use it at any second, his eyes dark and focused, his body tensed and ready for battle.

And I loved him.

The knowledge and epiphany were no longer so shocking. I loved him. I knew it with every fiber of my being.

It wasn't this place or the "abilities," as he thought, but the situation that had led us here, the experiences we'd shared. It was watching him be the man he was in shocking and extreme circumstances, all of which had taught me more about myself than I'd learned in my entire lifetime.

He was everything to me, and though he didn't believe it yet, I knew now how to prove it to him. "Put down your guns. Everyone!"

"No," Kellan said.

"No," Curly and Moe said together.

"Fuck no," Axel said.

"If you don't," I said as calmly as I could with panic shrinking my voice, "we're going to stand here all night at an impasse."

"What does 'impasse' mean?" I heard Moe ask Curly.

"How the fuck should I know?" Curly answered.

"I mean," I called out, "that we'll get nowhere. We'll stand around looking stupidly at each other, and no swap will get made."

"Well, that's not exactly true," Marilee said.

Ah hell. More stuff I didn't know. I debated with myself, because how much worse could this get? Answer: a lot worse. I glanced at Marilee, and lifted a brow.

"Never mind." She lifted her hands, waved me on. "It probably won't matter. You just go ahead."

Ah hell. "Tell me."

"Well, when the abilities are taken without permission, it's dangerous for the person they're taken from. They can get really sick, even die."

I stared at her. "Did that happen to you?"

"No." She looked . . . guilty? "It didn't happen to me."

"Why not?"

"Because at the time," she said very quietly, "I, um . . ." She sighed. "I wanted my ability stolen."

"What?"

"I sold out, okay? I was in debt and having some trouble. When the pirates came, I made a deal. I took cold hard cash. I'd give anything to be able to take it back, but I can't. It's done. But the truth is, my ability wasn't stolen; I sold it."

I stared at Axel, who was not looking shocked by this revelation. "And you?"

"I gave it willingly to stay here with Marilee."

Marilee gasped. "You did? Oh, Axel, that's the most romantic thing anyone's ever done for me."

"And *dangerous,*" I said.

"So dangerous!" Marilee couldn't take her eyes off Axel. "My cousin's brother's best friend's fiancé went into a coma on her wedding day when their abilities were stolen! I can't believe you did that for me."

A coma. *God.* "Your cousin. Did she ever wake up?"

"Four years later, to find out that her best friend had married her fiancé. So you want to be real careful here, because believe me—" She squeezed Axel's hand. "A good fiancé is damn hard to find."

"I'm not paying anyone cold hard cash, even if your ability comes wrapped in pure gold," Curly yelled, lifting his gun again. "So don't even think about it. I don't care who ends up in a coma, as long as I walk away with the strength ability."

"Yeah, you're going to need that brawn," Kellan muttered, "to combat the lack of brains."

"Hey!" Curly leveled his gun at Kellan. "That wasn't nice!"

I leaped forward in my haste to get between the two. "No shooting, remember?"

"Too late," Curly sneered.

"What do you mean?" My heart kicked, but everyone was here and accounted for . . .

"Nothing," Kel said grimly.

"Let's do this," Curly said.

"You're going to take the ability and go, right?" I pressed him. "You'll leave all of us alone?"

"The moment the swap is made," he said, and showed those disgusting teeth. "Scout's honor."

Uh-huh. And his honor meant so much. "*No* shooting, right?"

"Tell him," Curly said, and gestured at Kellan.

I looked at Kellan, who shook his head. "Bad idea, Rach."

"It's the only idea we've got." I looked at Serena and Axel. "You willing?"

They nodded. I had no idea what would happen to them without their abilities, but being alive seemed far more important at the moment.

The faintest purple light tinged the edges of the night sky now.

Dawn.

I turned to Axel. "What exactly happens at dawn?"

He glanced at the pirates, then whispered, "Well, you might have noticed their increased desperation and violence."

"What happens at dawn, Axel?"

"They have to leave or risk getting stuck here."

"Then why aren't we stalling instead of bargaining?"

"Because they have guns," he reminded me. "Big ones."

Oh yeah.

"Lead the way!" Curly yelled. "To the clearing right now!"

Axel looked at Marilee, who as the new expedition leader lifted her chin regally and took the front.

We all followed, tromping through the woods in eerie silence. Even the birds were quiet today, and when I looked up, I had to execute a double take.

The crystal-clear night had shifted. The massive black, swirling cloud was back, building steam that made me gulp.

The wind had picked up, too, just like the last time, and as we finally stepped into the clearing, the first few drops of rain began to fall.

My heart kicked into gear.

With every fiber of my being, I felt . . . terrified. No other word described the feeling gripping me. There were so many variables and what-ifs that my brain couldn't even take it all in. It didn't help that the *first* lightning bolt was still far too fresh in my mind. It hadn't been a piece of cake. It had hurt like hell, and all that confusion afterward, the mind-numbing fear . . . I didn't want to go through it again.

Knowing how dangerous it all was didn't help, nor did the knowledge that doing this again could send me spiraling into a coma—

I looked over at Kel, who looked bleak, his expression closed, and my heart lurched even more.

Then he staggered in a rare misstep, and I reached for him.

"I'm fine," he said, shaking me off, not looking fine at all, but deathly pale.

Curly gestured for us to go ahead of him into the clearing, and when we both hesitated, he lifted his gun at me. "I'll shoot her this time."

"This time?" I looked at Kel, and I just *knew.* I searched him with my eyes—His dark shirt. *God.* I ran my hands over him and found the stickiness at his shoulder, down his side. "Oh my God! You were shot!"

"Just in the shoulder," he said, jaw clenched so tightly he had to fit the words through his teeth.

I thought I'd been terrified before, but now it raced like ice up my spine. "Kel—"

"Later." He moved into the clearing, but just as he did, a harsh gust of wind blew through, knocking us all into each other and down to our knees.

The clouds seemed to swell, then they lowered, surrounding us in an inky blackness that blocked out the growing dawn.

Someone gasped, and the rain began to fall in earnest, soaking into my clothing in a blink. It was going to happen any second now, I knew it.

Kellan was ahead of me. He'd pulled out the Blackberry and was crawling into the clearing, his face tight with the pain of the gunshot wound and, undoubtedly, fury with me.

Now, Rach. Now or never. Trying to be careful with his shoulder, I jumped on him, and with the element of surprise on my side, took him down to the ground and grabbed the Blackberry from him.

While he groaned and ate dirt, I sprinted up and into the clearing myself.

"Rach, no!" he yelled after me, and snagged my ankle so that I got only one foot inside before the huge *CRACK* sounded, and with it, screams.

Marilee?

Serena?

Actually, maybe it was me, because it hurt like hell, but only for a second, because as before, everything faded to black.

At least I *alone* got into the clearing, I thought with relief.

Kel was safe . . .

Chapter 25

I woke up to the feel of something wet dripping on my face, and every single inch of my body screaming with agony. I gasped with it, tensing.

"Jesus, Rach. Talk to me."

At the sound of Kel's voice, low and rough with urgency, I felt my heart tighten. I didn't have to look at him to remember everything about him: how his eyes could see through to my soul, how his skin smelled, how yummy he always tasted, how he sounded when he was buried inside me and so turned on—

"*Rach.*"

I opened my eyes. I was cradled against his chest. He was a little sweaty and a whole lot wild with worry.

And shot! God, let's not forget he was wearing a bullet, one he'd taken because *I'd* brought him here. "I'm fine. It's you—"

"Shh." He just shook his head, and held me. "Give me a minute."

I needed one, too. Already the pain was fading, and I ran my hands over him, wanting to cry when he sucked in a pained breath. "Oh, Kel."

"It's not bad."

A lie.

I was smoking again, which reminded me. The abilities.

The swap.

I stared up at the sky.

Just blue. Plain blue.

I focused on the tree above us. Just a trunk with branches and pine needles, still dripping from the deluge of rain I barely even remembered.

I couldn't see through the tree trunk, or into the individual water droplets. In fact, I could see through exactly nothing.

I was back to normal, though even the word "normal" seemed, well, abnormal.

I looked at Kel. It was just him, beautiful, passionate, wonderful Kel. I looked at his bloody shirt, but I couldn't see through it. Still, somehow I knew his heart was beating steady as a drum. "I'm not in a coma, right? Or . . . dead?"

His eyes flashed with emotion, and his arms tightened on me. "Neither, though I might kill you myself for that little stunt."

Stunt? *Stunt?*

"I mean, what the hell were you thinking, pushing me aside and leaping headfirst into that bolt of lightning?" he demanded.

"I was thinking of *you*."

He just kept staring at me as if he couldn't believe I was all in one piece and unhurt. "You might have gotten yourself killed."

"But she didn't," Serena pointed out, peeking over Kel's shoulder at me. William nodded with her. "No one did, except the bad guys."

"Right," Kel said, so much of his soul and gut and heart in his gaze, I could scarcely breathe. "And you're alive," he whispered. "Alive is damn good." He hauled me against him again, then sucked in harshly.

"The bullet exited," Marilee said, looking down at him. "Painful, I'm sure, but you're not still sporting steel, so that's a relief."

"Wait." I blinked, looked at all of us. Me, Kel, Axel, Marilee, Serena and William. "Where are Curly and Moe?"

Serena and William looked at Marilee.

Marilee looked at Kel.

Kel looked at Axel.

Axel spread his hands out in front of him. "They won't be bothering anyone anymore."

"Because . . . ?"

"Let's just say, I'm more handy with this thing than I let on." Axel lifted the Blackberry. "I sent them to another plane."

"It was very impressive," Serena said.

I looked at Kellan, who was . . . *squinting.* "Your eyes," I said very softly. "Why can't you see?"

"Because he threw himself in front of you," Marilee said.

"Marilee," Kel said in soft warning. "Don't."

"Don't what? Sing like a canary?" She shook her head. "And he took that lightning bolt right in the chest—"

"Damn it, Marilee."

"Shut up, Kellan. Rachel, I'm telling you, it's a miracle he's alive. It was the bravest thing I've ever seen anyone do."

I couldn't tear my eyes off Kellan as it all sank in. He'd been the one to take the direct hit, not me. Which meant . . . I looked at William and Serena, who looked . . . normal. Their odd glow hadn't returned. I looked at Axel, who'd been able to handle Moe and Curly. At Marilee, who'd taken one look at Kel's dark shirt and been able to tell the bullet had exited.

"You two!" *They had the glow!* "*You* got the abilities in the swap!"

Marilee smiled grimly. "Accidentally, I assure you. When we saw Kellan leap forward, we went after him and got in the way."

"So you got your abilities back!"

"Well, not ours." Axel looked at Serena and William, who smiled serenely, still happy without their abilities.

Axel hugged Marilee. "And we'll owe all of you for this forever."

Marilee sniffed, and buried her face in Axel's chest. "God, it's good to be back, to be going back."

"You're going back?" I asked.

Looking thrilled, they both nodded. "But no worries about Hideaway." Axel said. "William and Serena want to run it, and trust me when I say this; You'll be better off with them doing so."

Serena and William stood arm in arm, looking ecstatic.

"You do?" I asked. "You *really* want to stay here?"

"So much," William said.

I was happy for them, but . . . I turned to Kellan, who was clearly hurting like hell and looking worse for wear. "*I* wanted to step in front of *you*, damn it." I fisted his shirt in my hands and hauled him nose-to-nose with me. "I wanted to prove how much I love you." I let out a huff of air. "Damn it."

"You already said that." He was staring at me, his gorgeous eyes blinking as slowly as an owl's, trying helplessly to focus in.

I sighed, and reached into his breast pocket for his glasses. Opening them, I stuck them on his nose. "There."

He pushed them up higher. "Thanks. But back to that other thing."

"Which? Where you stole my thunder?"

"No, the other part. The I-love-you part."

"Oh, Kel, I do. I love you so much. But for once, *I* wanted to put my heart on the line. *I* wanted to be the one to risk something."

"But you did," he said, sounding a little awed. "You risked a hell of a something. You risked everything."

"It doesn't count when you beat me to the punch."

"Oh, it counts," he said very softly, and hauled me back onto his lap, burying his head in my hair, breathing me in, then pulling back again to look into my eyes. "So it's true then?"

"All of it," I promised, cupping his face, never more sure of anything in my life. "I love you. You. Just as you are right now."

"Without the strength."

"Yes, without the strength. Look," I said with a choked-up smile, "I couldn't have afforded replacing all those doors you'd have kept breaking anyway."

"I'm blind as a bat," he warned.

"I love your squint." I gently pushed his glasses farther up his nose. "And they have this newfangled contraption called contact lenses."

He let out a half-laugh, half-groan. "I'm serious, Rach."

"So am I. Look, I've loved having you as a good friend, loved knowing you were in my life. But I held back because I was afraid. After all, good things never last, right? But you know what? Good things never need to last. It's the *great* things that need to." I drew a deep breath. "And we're pretty great, Kel."

He looked staggered. "Rach."

"We've been through so much. And now I know what real fear is. Fear is knowing we could die and I'd held back. Maybe I needed to go through everything we did here because I needed to be led to this minute, to you."

He smiled, his eyes shiny. "I'm growing quite fond of this minute."

"Believe me, Kel, I won't ever hold back again, that I can promise you."

Looking touched beyond belief, Kel lowered his forehead to mine. "God, I love you. So damn much. I would have died a little inside if, when we got back home, things went back to the way they were."

I tightened my arms around him. "The way we were was nice. But this is nicer."

"Nicer." He made a face. "Let's throw that word out along with 'fine.'"

I laughed. I don't know how he did it, but he always could make me laugh. "How about amazing?"

"Better, I guess."

"Fantastic?"

He eyed me, a smile lurking around his mouth. "Keep going."

"Incredible. Extraordinary."

"Extraordinary, huh?" He surged to his feet, then bent to lift me up as well, a feat that just yesterday he'd managed with such ease, he'd nearly sent me to the moon, but that now made him groan, stagger with my weight, then nearly drop me.

"Kel, careful of your shoulder—"

He leaned back against the tree, and gave me a weak smile. "I'm really going to have to work at this superhero thing."

"No," I murmured, my lips to his as I stood on my own two feet. "I like it best when we each carry our own weight."

Cupping my face, he whispered my name like I was everything to him.

And in that moment, I felt as if I had the superstrength. Because with him at my side, I could do anything.

Epilogue

We watched Jack's plane come in for a landing. He opened the door, and grinned. "How was your weekend?"

"Eye-opening," Kel said, and took my hand.

We'd already said good-bye to Marilee, Axel, William and Serena, but we stood on the shore of the river hugging each of them again. Well, I was hugging them. Kel had his shoulder bandaged up, thanks to Serena's healing skills, and wasn't hugging anyone.

"We'll be back," I promised William and Serena. "You have the laptop," I said to Axel. "Use it."

Marilee hugged me hard. "Take good care of him," she said. "And don't be strangers. We'll meet you here. *Oh!* You should come back for Halloween. You won't believe how some of the guests enjoy that holiday."

I could only imagine.

We got into the plane, trying not to be nervous about the flight back. I took in the sights of the towering mountains all around us, the gently swaying trees, the gorgeous day. "I never imagined that I'd actually say this," I said, "but coming here was the best thing I've ever done. Let's fly up once a season."

Kel paled. "That seems a little frequent."

"Once a year then."

"With no swapping, right?"

I grinned impishly. "I don't know . . . think of all the possibilities . . ."

"Rach."

"Well, okay. Maybe once we're married with little ones running around, swapping might get out of control."

He went very still. "Married? Little ones?"

I stared at him, feeling my cheeks go red. "I didn't mean to say that. It just came out."

His eyes, misty and gorgeous, shimmered brilliantly, no longer filled with wild worry, but back to calm and deep and sure. "A plan, Rach? From you?"

"Yeah." My throat was so tight, I could scarcely breathe. "Go figure, but I've developed a fondness for plans. Especially plans that involve you."

He smiled, and tugged lightly on my ponytail, tipping my face up for a kiss. "I like being in your plans. It's convenient and all, considering you're in mine."

"I am?"

"Oh yes." He kissed his way to my ear, and once there, whispered the sort of plans he had, and all my nerves about flying, about anything, vanished, because in his arms, there was room for nothing but him. *Us.*

Together, with or without the abilities, in or out of this world . . .

Take a look at Diane Whiteside's
THE SOUTHERN DEVIL
available now from Brava!

The mantel clock began to chime.

Jessamyn's head flashed around to stare at it before she looked back at Morgan.

She forced back her body's awareness of him. "I needed him as my husband, you fool! For two hours, starting now."

"Husband?" Jealousy swept over his face.

"In a lawyer's office," she snarled back. "I have to be there with a husband in fifteen minutes, or all is lost. Damn you, let me go!"

The clock chimed again.

His eyes narrowed for a moment then he pulled her up to him. His grip was less painful but just as inescapable as before. "A bargain then, Jessamyn. I'll play your husband for a few hours—if you'll join me in a private parlor for the same span of time afterward."

She gasped. A devil's bargain, indeed.

"Nine years ago, before you married Cyrus, I promised you revenge for what you did—and you agreed my claim was just. Two hours won't see that accomplished but it's a start," he purred, his drawl knife-edged and laced with carnal promise.

Her flight or fight instincts stirred, honed by seven years as an Army wife on the bloody Kansas prairies. She reined them in sternly: No matter how angry he'd been, surely Morgan would never harm a woman, no matter what preposterous demands he'd hurled nine years ago when she'd held him captive.

Her fingers bit into his arms, as she tried to think of another option. But if she didn't appear with a husband, she'd lose her only chance of regaining Somerset Hall, her family's old home . . .

The mantel clock sounded the third, and last, note.

She agreed to his bargain, the words like ashes in her throat. "Very well, Morgan. Now will you take me across the street to the lawyer's?"

Morgan escorted Jessamyn across the street with all the haughtiness his father would have shown escorting his mother aboard a riverboat. It was a bit of manners ingrained in him so early that he didn't need to think about it, something he'd first practiced with Jessaymn when she was five and their parents first openly hoped for a wedding between them. Such an ingrained habit was very useful when his brain seemed to have dived somewhere south of his belt buckle as soon as she'd agreed she owed him revenge.

What was he going to do first? There were so many activities he'd learned in Consortium houses: How to drive a woman insane with desire. How to leave her sated and panting, willing to do anything to repeat the experience. More than anything else, he needed to see Jessamyn aching to be touched by him again and again.

A black curl stroked her cheek in just the way he planned to later. He smiled, planning, and reached for the office door.

Ebenezer Abercrombie & Sons, Attys. At Law announced the sturdy letters on its surface.

Morgan stiffened. Her lawyer was that Abercrombie? Halpern's friend and Millicent's godfather, whom Morgan had dined with last night? Who'd beamed approval as Halpern and his wife had shoved Morgan at their daughter and he'd made no mention of a wife?

Damn, damn, damn.

Jessamyn, who'd never been a fool, caught his momentary hesitation and glanced up at him.

He shook his head slightly at her and put his hand on the door knob. Suddenly it turned under his fingers and swung open to frame Abercrombie's well-fed bulk. The man's eyes widened briefly as he took in both of his visitors.

Jessamyn leaned closer to Morgan and squeezed his arm, with all the assurance of a long-married woman. God knows he'd seen her do it with Cyrus before.

Morgan shifted himself so she could fit comfortably, as he'd seen his cousin do. She settled easily within a hand's-breadth of him and tilted her head at Abercrombie expectantly. The entire byplay took only a few seconds.

The lawyer's eyes narrowed and his mouth tightened, before a polite professional mask covered his face. "Good afternoon, Evans. What an unexpected pleasure to see you here today."

Morgan smiled with all the smooth charm he polished as one of Bedford Forrest's spies. "The pleasure is entirely mine, Abercrombie. I've the honor of escorting my wife. Jessamyn, my dear, have you met Mr. Abercrombie?" He could have kicked himself. His Mississippi drawl was slightly heavier than usual, a telltale sign of nervousness.

Jessamyn took Abercrombie's hand, with all the charm of her aristocratic Memphis upbringing. "Yes, Mr. Abercrombie was my uncle's lawyer for years. I've known him since I was a child. Hello, sir."

Abercrombie kissed her cheek. "My dear lady, I'm so glad you were able to bring your husband." His eyes flickered to Morgan but his countenance was impassive. "Your cousin Charles and his wife are seated in my office, waiting for the reading of the will to begin. Please come with me."

And now Rosemary Laurey's
"In Bad With Someone"
in the sexy anthology
TEXAS BAD BOYS
available now from Brava . . .

Anger, shock and a touch of fury propelled Rod across the road with just a quick "Gotta go!" to his buddies. He pushed open the door and looked around *his* bar. What the hell was Mary-Beth playing at? The two suits were getting ready to leave. Maude Wilson and her cronies were playing rummy as they did most afternoons, practicing character assassination as they bet for nickel points. The only other occupant was the sharp-looking redhead he'd noticed earlier walking up Center Street.

Her perky little butt was poised on one of the counter stools while she ate . . . he walked closer . . . a burger and onion rings. A bacon burger with Swiss.

Cold rage at Pete's double-dealing clenched Rod's gut. Still not quite believing. Suspecting some twisted joke, Rod met Mary-Beth's eyes. She shifted them sideways to the redhead.

Shit!

Okay, deep breath here. He could hardly yank her lovely butt off the stool and slug her one. His mama had taught him better than that, but dammit, what did she think she was doing claiming his bar as her own? Might as well find out.

Giving Mary-Beth a warning glance to stay cool, he took the stool nearest Madame Bar Snatcher. "Hey there, Mary-Beth. How about pulling me a nice cold beer."

"I'm sorry. Excuse me," the redhead said and moved her pocket book, giving him a glimpse of deep, green eyes before she turned back to her onion rings, cut one in four, stabbed it with the fork and chewed carefully.

Snob and prissy wasn't in it! Nice boobs though. Not that it was likely to do him any good. Her hair was something else though: the color of new pennies, and cut short in a mass of curls. He itched to reach out and let a strand of hair curl over his fingers. Pity it came with a bar snatcher attached.

"Here you are, Rod." Mary-Beth set his glass down with a thud . . . and a smirk. "Anything else I can get you?"

"I'm fine thanks. This is just what I need."

She rolled her eyes and proceeded to refill Miss Prissy's ice water. What exactly Mary-Beth had done to earn that wide, smile he'd like to know, but it did enable him to catch Miss Prissy's eye.

"Howdy!"

"Good afternoon," she replied, with a little nod.

"Enjoying Silver Gulch?" he asked before she had a chance to chop up another onion ring.

She paused as if weighing up whether to snub him or not. "It's interesting. Smaller than I imagined but . . ." She gave him the oddest look as her mouth twitched at the corner. "Definitely fascinating."

"Here on a visit or just passing through town?" He asked, nicely casual, as he lifted his glass and took a drink

She smiled, almost chuckled, her green eyes crinkling at the corners as she looked him in the eye. "I'll be staying, Mr Carter."

Rod almost spluttered his Hefeweizen all over himself and the counter. He grabbed his handkerchief and wiped his mouth, thanking heaven he didn't have beer running out of his nose. Damn her! Damn the smug little smirk on her pretty face! And double damn Mary-Beth for setting him up like this!

"It wasn't Mary-Beth, so don't give her the evil eye like that."

Reads minds does she? “How did you know who I was?”

“An educated guess, Mr Carter. Gabe Rankin told me your name. Minutes after I identify myself to Mary-Beth you appear off the street where you were chatting. How many Rods are there in a town this size?” While he digested that, she held out a slim, long-fingered hand. “I’m Juliet French. My grandfather left me this building and the business.”

“We’ll see about that!”

He felt her green eyes watching him as he stormed out. Gabe Rankin had some explaining to do.

After twenty minutes cooling his heels to see Gabe and an acrimonious ten minutes face-to-face, Rod learned old man Maddock had done him dirty and given away the Rooster from under his feet.

“We had a deal!” Rod protested.

“I know you did,” Gabe replied, shaking his head. “He knew it too. Said he had only three parcels of property and they had to go to his granddaughters. Said he’d make it right with you.”

But the old codger had upended his fishing boat before he could. “So what now? I get kicked out after building up the business?”

“Now, calm down, Rod,” Gabe went on. “It’s not too bad. Part of the agreement was Mizz French keep on all the employees.” So he was an employee now, was he? “If you ask me, she’ll not hang around long, whatever she’s saying right now. You mark my words, give it a couple of months and she’ll be back in London and you’ll be running the Rooster just like always.”

Not quite like always. He’d no longer be working for himself but prissy Mizz French. “What if I just quit?” There was an idea!

Gabe waved his hands palms outermost and shook his head. “Now don’t you start making hasty decisions, Rod. Why not bide your time and see how things go? The Rooster wouldn't be the same without you." It wouldn't be anything without him and Gabe damn well knew it. "You just hold on a week or two. See how things work out between you and Miss French."

Fat lot of help Gabe was.

Rod was even more steamed when he walked back into the Rooster, ready to hash out a few details with the new owner.

Who wasn't there.

Neither was Mary-Beth. Lucas, the cook, was standing in at the bar. Where the hell were they? Off doing each other's hair? And he'd been stupid enough to think Mary-Beth was on his side.

"Don't look so sour, boss," Lucas said.

"Where the hell is Mary-Beth? She's got two more hours of her shift."

"She took the new owner on the tour. Say, is she really old man Maddock's granddaughter?"

"Yes, Rod, we were wondering that." Old Maude and her cronies swooped on him like the furies. "Is it true? And Pete left her the Rooster. How nice!"

It wasn't nice and it got worse. Two days later, Juliet French had settled in. There was no stopping her.

She could have stayed in the comparative comfort of Sally Jones's B&B, or even the Hunting Lodge just outside town, but Miss French insisted on moving in. Since the other apartments were boarded up and uninhabitable, she moved into his. After a night on the lumpy sofa, she drove into Pebble Creek and the next morning, carpets and furniture were delivered and she spent the afternoon hanging drapes and unpacking as she staked her claim on one of the empty rooms. His final objection that there was only one functioning bathroom was met with a bland smile and the unblinking assurance not to worry, she promised not to use his razor to shave her legs.

A weaker man would have given up.

Rod Carter braced for survival. He'd outlast Juliet French and be a gentleman about it.

Don't miss this sneak peek at
Shannon McKenna's
HOT NIGHT
coming in October 2006 from Brava . . .

Abby was floating. The sensual heft of Zan's black leather jacket felt wonderful over her shoulders, even though it hung halfway down her thighs.

They'd reached the end of the boardwalk, where the lights began to fade. Beyond the boardwalk, the warehouse district began. They'd walked the whole boardwalk, talking and laughing, and at some point, their hands had swung together and sort of just . . . stuck. Warmth seeking warmth. Her hand tingled joyfully in his grip.

The worst had happened. Aside from his sex appeal, she simply liked him. She liked the way he laughed, his turn of phrase, his ironic sense of humor. He was smart, honest, earthy, funny. Maybe, just maybe, she could trust herself this time.

Their strolling slowed to a stop at the end of the boardwalk.

"Should we, ah, walk back to your van?" she ventured.

"This is where I live," he told her.

She looked around. "Here? But this isn't a residential district."

"Not yet," he said. "It will be soon. See that building over there? It used to be a factory of some kind, in the twenties, I think. The top floor, with the big arched windows, that's my place."

There was just enough light to make out the silent question in his eyes. She exhaled slowly. "Are you going to invite me up, or what?"

"You know damn well that you're invited," he said. "More than invited. I'll get down on my knees and beg, if you want me to."

The full moon appeared in a window of scudding clouds, then disappeared again. "It wouldn't be smart," she said. "I don't know you."

"I'll teach you," he offered. "Crash course in Zan Duncan. What do you want to know? Hobbies, pet peeves, favorite leisure activities?"

She would put it to the test of her preliminary checklist, and make her decision based on that. "Don't tell me," she said. "Let me guess. You're a martial arts expert, right?"

"Uh, yeah. Aikido is my favorite discipline. I like kung fu, too."

She nodded, stomach clenching. There it was, the first black mark on the no-no's checklist. Though it was hardly fair to disqualify him for that, since he'd saved her butt with those skills the night before.

So that one didn't count. On to the next no-no. "Do you have a motorcycle?"

He looked puzzled. "Several of them. Why? Want to go for a ride?"

Abby's heart sank. "No. One last question. Do you own guns?"

Zan's face stiffened. "Wait. Are these trick questions?"

"You do, don't you?" she persisted.

"My late father was a cop." His voice had gone hard. "I have his service Beretta. And I have a hunting rifle. Why? Are you going to talk yourself out of being with me because of superficial shit like that?"

Abby's laugh felt brittle. "Superficial. That's Abby Maitland."

"No, it is not," he said. "That's not Abby Maitland at all."

"You don't know the first thing about me, Zan."

"Yes, I do." His dimple quivered. "I know first things, second things, third things. You've got piss-poor taste in boyfriends, to start."

Abby was stung. "Those guys were not my boyfriends! I didn't even know them! I've just had a run of bad luck lately!"

"Your luck is about to change, Abby." His voice was low and velvety. "I know a lot about you. I know how to get into your apartment. How to turn your cat into a noodle. The magnets on your fridge, the view from your window. Your perfume. I could find you blindfolded in a room full of strangers." His fingers penetrated the veil of her hair, his forefinger stroking the back of her neck with controlled gentleness. "And I learn fast. Give me ten minutes, and I'll know lots more."

"Oh," she breathed. His hand slid through her hair, settled on her shoulder. The delicious heat burned her, right through his jacket.

"I know you've got at least two of those expensive dresses that drive guys nuts. And I bet you've got more than two. You've got a whole closet full of hot little outfits like that. Right?" He cupped her jaw, turning her head until she was looking into his fathomless eyes.

Her heart hammered. "I've got a . . . a pretty nice wardrobe, yes."

"I'd like to see them." His voice was sensual. "Someday maybe you can model them all for me. In the privacy of your bedroom."

"Zan—"

"I love it when you say my name," he said. "I love your voice. Your accent. Based on your taste in dresses, I'm willing to bet that you like fancy, expensive lingerie, too. Am I right? Tell me I'm right."

"Time out," she said, breathless. "Let's not go there."

"Oh, but we've already arrived." His breath was warm against her throat. "Locksmiths are detail maniacs. Look at the palm of your hand, for instance. Here, let me see." He lifted her hand into the light from the nearest of the streetlamps. "Behold, your destiny."

It was silly and irrational, but it made her self-conscious to have him look at the lines on her hand. As if he actually could look right into her mind. Past, future, fears, mistakes, desires, all laid out for anyone smart and sensitive enough to decode it.

"Zan. Give me my hand back."

"Not yet. Oh . . . wow. Check this out," he whispered.

"What?" she demanded.

He shook his head, with mock gravity and pressed a kiss to her knuckles. "It's too soon to say what I see. I don't want to scare you off."

"Oh, please," she said unsteadily. "You are so full of it."

"And you're so scared. Why? I'm a righteous dude. Good as gold." He stroked her wrist. "Ever try cracking a safe without drilling it? It's a string of numbers that never ends. Hour after hour, detail after detail. That's concentration." He pressed his lips against her knuckles.

"What does concentration have to do with anything?"

"It has everything to do with everything. That's what I want to do to you, Abby. Concentrate, intensely, minutely. Hour after hour, detail after detail. Until I crack all the codes, find all the keys to your secret places. Until I'm so deep inside ya . . ." His lips kissed their way up her wrist ". . . . that we're a single being."

She leaned against him, and let him cradle her in his strong arms. His warm lips coaxed her into opening to the gentle, sensual exploration of his tongue. "Come up with me," he whispered. "Please."

She nodded. Zan's arm circled her waist, fitting her body against his. It felt so right. No awkwardness, no stumbling, all smooth. Perfect.